VALENSHEK

RESTORATION

TATE JAMES

Tate James

Restoration: Valenshek Legacy #3

Cover design: Tamara Kokic
Photographer: Lanefotograf
Models: David and Isabelle
Editing: Heather Long (content) and Dolly Jackson (line).

For Heather. Are you happy now? Please can you unlock the cell door, I need to pee and it's cold in here

PREVIOUSLY IN
THE VALENSHEK LEGACY...

ILLUSTRATIONS BY JOANNA HADZHIEVA

The Slippery Lips

BUT I'M HORNY, DAD

DON'T TOUCH TRISTIAN AGAIN!

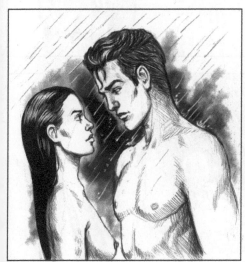

RESTORATION

VALENSHEK LEGACY #3

TATE JAMES

John

one

An animal-like scream of pure hatred laced with agony tore from her as she dove for my discarded, bloody knife on the floor of her ruined home. My heart shredded for her, for the intense pain and loss she'd experienced as Nelson's life ebbed away, but she wasn't thinking straight. Who the fuck could? I sure as fuck wasn't.

Right now, she wanted vengeance.

She wanted to inflict the pain she experienced on *me*. I got it. I understood. Fuck, I wanted to rain that agony down on someone for her too. I wanted to extract the pound of flesh she was so righteously owed.

But I didn't do this.

I didn't kill Nelson.

"Tris, stop!" I barked, trying—and failing—to reach

1

the knife before her. Those long, delicate fingers of hers wrapped around the handle with a sure grip, and she slashed out at me. The blade sliced through my forearm with a sting of pain, but I'd rather it be my arm than my face.

She wasn't going to stop, though. She'd just lost someone closer to her than her own parents, her mentor and father-figure. There would be no getting through to her until I was just as dead as he was. Fuck, I wished I was as dispassionate as those thoughts seemed. Understanding and assessment flashed through me. I could see it all play out.

Still, I had to try. "Tris—Venus, I didn't do this!" I grunted, scrambling backward to avoid her wild slashes. She had no precision or skill, but that didn't seem to matter. What did she have to lose? Nelson was dying—no, he was dead. Beyond all of that, I didn't want to hurt her—not anymore and not again. I'd done so much to her already, and she was already in so much pain. I couldn't just forcefully disarm her, because what if I accidentally broke her wrist or something?

Better I bleed than her.

Anything would be better than the tormented hell shimmering in her eyes.

A feral snarl rent the air as she rushed me, the blood-coated knife aimed for my torso. I twisted, then tripped on Nelson's body, and the blade glanced over my ribs as she stumbled with momentum. I swallowed my reservations and grabbed her wrist, holding her firm as she came at me again. Blood slicked us both.

"Tristian," I implored, "*listen* to me. This was *not me*, and right now you're wasting time while Nelson's killer gets away." Probably not the kindest thing to say. But I needed to get through to her.

"Fuck you, John," she spat, desperately trying to free her wrist from my grip. "You killed him. You kill—" Her words hitched with a sob, her face twisted in grief.

Sympathy flooded through me. Agony wrapped my Venus up in chains. I loosened my grip and she wrenched free with an enraged cry. It was a dumb fucking move, but I simply couldn't bring myself to hurt her... even if it meant I suffered in the long run.

Tris immediately stabbed out at me again, but right before the sharp tip penetrated my flesh she crumpled like a puppet with cut strings. Shock held me captive as I barely caught my collapsed angel.

"You're fucking *welcome*," Tink snapped, jerking my focus up to where she stood just a foot behind where Tris had been a moment ago. In her hand she held a frying pan, which she must have just smacked over Tris's head.

"Jesus, Tink!" I barked, sinking to my knees and

3

cradling Tris. "Was that really necessary? You could have killed her!"

My partner in crime just rolled her eyes. "As opposed to what she would have done to you with that knife? What the hell *happened* here, John? Is that Nelson?" Her horrified gaze took in the dead body on the floor, then swept to the blown out false wall. "Oh fuck. This is—"

"Bad," I agreed. "We need to get out of here."

"The painting?" Tink asked as she glanced over at the destroyed wall again. In the room beyond, I had already identified multiple famous works of art of similar black market value as *Poppy Flowers*, but that was the only one taken. The only one that had been listed as a *goddamn* Game piece.

Gritting my teeth, I curled Tris's unconscious form up into my arms. "Gone," I muttered. "So we should be, too."

Tink knelt down beside Nelson's body and closed her eyes for a moment. Praying? She didn't strike me as the faithful type. "This changes things," she said softly, shaking her head with sadness. "Did you...?"

"The fact you're even asking that question tells me how little you really know me, Katinka," I snapped, shifting my grip on Tris so she was easier to hold. "Let's get Tris back to the safe house. Maybe when she wakes up she will give me a chance to explain."

Tink nodded, snagging my bloody knife from where Tris had dropped it and then following me out of the trashed apartment. What a fucking mess. Tris was never going to forgive me this time. Not when the Game had caused Nelson's death. Hell, I doubted I could even forgive myself at this point.

"Why's she still out?" Tink asked once we were safely inside my car and driving away from Tris's building. "I didn't hit her *that* hard, did I?"

"I fucking hope not," I growled, glancing in the rearview mirror at the sleeping woman. Dark circles underscored her eyes, even deeper than her lashes covered. Her skin seemed paler than usual, and her collarbone jutted out sharper than it should. "I think... I *hope*... she's just exhausted. In shock. This hasn't been the easiest few weeks."

Tink wrinkled her nose dubiously. "Maybe I misjudged how strong my frying pan arm is and accidentally cracked her skull... she could be bleeding out right now." She leaned over into the back seat to check Tris's pulse and then ran her hands through my girl's raven dark hair. "Nope, we're good. All intact."

She waggled her blood-free fingers to support her conclusion, and I just glared back at her. My fucking blood pressure was high enough right now without her adding to the situation.

"I hate you," I muttered, shaking my head.

Tink snickered. "Sure you do. So... are you going to tell me what the *fuck* happened back there? How did Nelson get killed? And the painting? Who has it now? I'm straight up fucking speechless that Tris had it the whole damn time. And did I see a *Degas* in her hidden gallery?"

I shot her a sidelong look. "For someone supposedly speechless, you sure have a lot to say."

"It's a coping mechanism, dickhead," she fired back. "Something you're going to need when Tris wakes up. Fucking hell, John, this is..." She trailed off, blowing out a long breath of disbelief.

I didn't reply, because what the fuck could I even say? My head was spinning with everything that had just happened, and the implications for the Game. And for us... Tris and me. She needed to hear me out, to let me explain. If she really thought I'd killed Nelson, there could be no resolution. As it was, the Game got him killed, and that was bad enough.

We drove in silence the rest of the way back to our rented Hestia safe house, then I carried Tris's sleeping form inside while Tink unlocked doors and deactivated alarms and cameras. The last thing we needed was a recording of how messy we were.

"What do we do now?" Tink asked, after I gently laid Tris down on my bed.

"I have no fucking idea," I admitted, scrubbing a blood-stained hand over my face.

A moment of silence passed as we stood there staring at Tris, then Tink made a noise of disgust. "You're dripping," she informed me, pointing to my arm. "These safe houses charge a fuck load for blood stains on the cleaning bill. I'll grab the first aid kit."

I nodded vaguely, still trying to work out what the *fuck* to do with Tris. Eventually, though, I decided it was too dangerous—for all of us—if she woke up in that same violent rage. So I reached into the bedside drawer for a pair of handcuffs.

"Sorry about this, Venus," I whispered with reluctance, lifting her wrists to the headboard and looping the cuffs through the bars. I tried to be careful. I didn't want to hurt her. She'd be *furious* when she woke, but at least this way I stood a slight chance of her hearing me out. If nothing else, no one would get stabbed.

I needed the chance to tell her the truth. To make this right.

She deserved so much damn more than me.

Tris

two

Pain throbbed in my skull, and my stomach churned like I was on a boat. But I wasn't... I was in bed? In a bed that I didn't recognize with my wrists handcuffed to the headboard.

"Help!" I squeaked in panic, yanking uselessly on the cuffs. Where was I? What the hell happened? Did I have clothes on? Yes. Okay, I was still dressed.

The confirmation that I was fully clothed eased some measure of fear, but the dull persistent ache in my head screamed at me that I'd been taken by force. From where? The last thing I remembered was being in the trunk of Bram's car as I escaped Grimaldi manor. Had we been caught?

Oh God, was it Sin? I didn't think he'd handcuff me. But I hadn't thought he'd lock me in a room either.

"Hello?" I called out again, my breathing shallow. "Is anyone there?"

Heavy footsteps sounded outside the room, and terror flooded through me. Was it Dex? Was he finally making good on his threats?

The door opened and I gasped. "John? What...?" I trailed off with a moan as a wave of intense anger, hatred, and *grief* slammed through me. My vision went blurry. All of a sudden, the loss struck. It was right there. Bram delivered me to my apartment building. I rushed upstairs... pushed open my apartment door. The horrific scene...

Nelson.

And John... crouched over my dying friend, his hands soaked in blood.

"No," I moaned, desperately trying to scrub the memory of Nelson's death from my mind. "No, no, no, it was a dream. It never happened. He's not dead... John, please tell me it was all a nightmare." I pleaded with him to tell me what I wanted to hear, what I *needed* to hear.

He couldn't give it to me though. His brow creased, he sank down to sit on the edge of the bed as he shook his head. "Tris, I'm so sorry..."

"No!" I shouted, my back arching with the agony tearing through me. "No, he's not dead. He can't be! This is all just... It's just a really, really bad dream."

"Tris..." John started, his gaze full of *pity*.

All that blazing anger returned with a vengeance, powering through my system like the grief was gasoline and it was fire. My eyes narrowed.

"*You*," I hissed, my skin prickling with fury. "You *killed* him. How could you? Was this all part of your stupid fucking game?"

John's brow furrowed, and he shook his head. "I didn't," he replied. "I know it looked bad when you arrived, but I swear to you, Tris, I didn't kill Nelson."

Just him saying Nelson's name made bile rise in my throat. This man... he'd played me so fucking hard from day one. He'd used me, betrayed me, fooled me, and I'd been the idiot who'd fallen in love. But this? No, there would be no coming back from this.

"You're lying," I gritted out, my cheeks wet from the tears streaming down my face. They dropped into my ears, a hot reminder of the lies he spouted. Salted my lips, spoiling like the kisses he gave me. Drowning me. Just. Like. John. "All you ever do is *lie to me*."

John's expression saddened, but he nodded slowly. "You're right. I've lied to you *a lot*, but this...? I wouldn't lie about this, Venus. I couldn't. Nelson was—"

"Don't you fucking dare tell me who Nelson *was*," I

10

screamed, tears choking my voice, "You didn't know him. He was a hundred times the man you are, John Smith, and he had *nothing* to do with your stupid fucking *game*."

John swiped a hand over his face, nodding again. "I agree." He paused, his gaze on the floor. "Nothing I say to you right now will make it hurt less, Tris, but please, *please* believe me when I tell you I didn't kill him. Nelson's death was not at my hands, no matter what it looked like."

His phrasing was so careful, so rehearsed, I didn't believe a fucking word he was saying. "Bullshit," I spat. "I saw the bloody knife. I saw the" —my voice cracked and my breathing hitched— "the wounds in his chest. I *saw it all*."

"And it looked bad, I agree," he confirmed. "But I *didn't* kill him. I was trying to *save* him when you arrived but he was too far gone already and then—"

"Why am I here, John?" I growled, unable to stomach any more of his lies. "Why am I handcuffed to your bed?" I assumed that was where we were. I hadn't even made it as far as his bedroom the last time I'd visited. When he told me he loved me. When I made up my mind to break off the fake engagement with Sin and negotiate a new contract with Mr. Grimaldi. Those happy memories were now soured and tainted black.

11

His lips tightened, his jaw tensing as he glanced at my restraints. "For safety," he muttered, though at least he had the grace to wince at his own bullshit.

I scoffed. "Whose? Mine or yours?" I gave a pointed look at the bandage on his arm. "Did I do that?"

He nodded, then raised his shirt to show me another wide dressing on his side. "And this. You were... understandably irrational. We thought it safer to cuff you until you can get the whole story and then, maybe—"

"We?" I cut him off, frowning my confusion. My throbbing skull took that opportunity to remind me how much it was hurting. "Tink. She knocked me out?"

The betrayals just kept coming. Was anyone in my world *not* lying and deceiving me? Probably just Nelson and Hank, and now...

"Where's Hank?" I asked, sniffing in a futile attempt to stop crying. "Does he know? How long has it been? Why am I *here*, John? You ran from the scene, I get it, but why drag me along with you?"

John made a frustrated sound, pushing up to his feet and pacing a few steps away. "This is fucked up," he muttered, looking over at the door like he was seriously considering just leaving and running away. Like trying to explain his actions was all too hard.

Why was I even bothering asking him questions in

the first place, when I already knew he wouldn't tell the truth? "You lied to me, John," I choked out, my throat tight with the betrayals. "You said *Poppy Flowers* wasn't part of the game. You said I was safe."

"You lied to me, too!" he exploded, throwing his hands in the air as he spun to face me. "You could have told me you *still* had it all along! You could have mentioned the hidden gallery inside your apartment and maybe Nelson wouldn't be dead right now."

His words smacked me in the face hard enough to hurt, and I recoiled as much as I could with cuffed wrists.

"Fuck," John groaned, scrubbing his hand over his hair. "I didn't mean that, Tris, I just—"

"It's true, though," I said in a small voice I barely recognized. Had I gotten Nelson killed? I'd stayed with Grimaldi, let him think the painting was gone. I'd done that to protect Nelson too. I didn't want anyone to know Nelson was involved. John was right—this was my fault. "If I had just given the painting back, Nelson would still be alive. This is as much my fault as it is yours."

John shook his head. "No, it's not. I'm sorry, I shouldn't have said that. Fuck, this whole mess is so..." He gave a frustrated growl, pacing the small patch of carpet beside the bed. "I need to explain, Tris. I *need* you to hear the truth, even if you don't believe me."

I swallowed, trying so fucking hard to sound strong while inside I was just a pile of broken pieces. "Honestly, John, I'm finding it really hard to give a fuck what *you* need right now. Uncuff me, let me leave. I won't try and stab you again, if that's what you're scared of." Not today, anyway. I didn't have a knife.

"It's not that simple!" he barked, glaring down at me. "I wish it was, Tris, believe me I wish more than anything I could just let you walk away and never look back, but it's just *not that simple*. Not now."

I said nothing. I was *done*. Talking to him was pointless, so I just looked to the side and locked my eyes on a patch of the wallpaper. Sooner or later, he'd get bored of spewing his fiction to a stone wall and leave. Then maybe I could work out how to escape.

"Tris. Please listen to me. You're hurting, I get it. You feel betrayed and rightly so. But you're not thinking rationally. I *didn't kill Nelson*, and deep down I know you believe me. I tried to save him. I swear I did. This thing between us is stronger than the lies, isn't it? It's deeper than the deceptions. Your heart knows mine, and it knows I could never hurt you like you're hurting. Tris... I didn't kill him."

God damn the way my heart fluttered in response to the earnest, sincere tone of his gruff voice. Why did he have to make it all so much worse than it already was?

My soul was being torn to ribbons, my heart beaten useless, and he just kept going. When would enough be enough?

Against my better judgment, my gaze shifted back to him. He was on his knees now, his clasped hands on the side of the bed like he was praying for my understanding.

I had to ask the one question that'd been bouncing around my head this whole time. I had to know what he would say.

"You didn't?" I whispered hoarsely. He shook his head, imploring me to believe him. I licked my lips, my glare hard as I met his pleading gaze. I wanted so badly to believe him. Too badly. I wanted his lies—what the hell did that say about me? "Then *who did*? Because all I saw was *you*. Your hands covered in his blood, your knife on the floor, your—"

"Does it matter?" he cut me off, his expression tight and pained. He *knew*, there was no doubt in my mind. "It wasn't me, Tris. Please believe me that I'll find the person responsible and make him pay."

I hated that I wanted to believe him. "Of course it matters. You want me to believe you didn't do it? Then tell me who did!"

He wet his lips, and I could practically smell the lie

as he replied, "I didn't see them. It all happened so fast and my focus was on Nelson."

"You're lying again," I moaned, shaking my head and yanking violently on my cuffed wrists. The way I wanted to hit him was all consuming. "You're lying! Why are you protecting a murderer, John? If it wasn't *you*, then *who killed Nelson?*"

"Christ," he muttered, dropping his head onto his hands. "I'm not protecting *him*, Tris. I'm trying to protect *you*. It's all I want right now, even if you never forgive me. I just want to *protect you*. Won't you let me do that? Venus, please."

A feral growl of fury rolled out of me. "I don't want or need your protection, John. Ever since you stepped foot in my life, we have been on a collision course with a fucking meteor. Stop pretending you care, when you clearly don't. Tell me the truth for once in your fucking life, John. Who killed Nelson?"

John inhaled deeply, raising his head up to meet my eyes again. His eyes tight and his jaw tense, he gave a pained sound. "Hank. It was Hank."

My jaw dropped and a high pitched ringing sound filled my ears. "Wow," I coughed, my own voice echoing through my head. "*Wow*. I knew you were committed to the lie, but accusing *Hank* of killing Nelson? Are you delusional? In what world did you seriously think I

16

would swallow that shit? Hank fucking *worships* Nelson, they're so in love. He can't even kill spiders let alone—"

"I saw it happen," John gritted out, his eyes dropping away from my face again. "Tris, I'm so sorry. He's not who he seems."

"No," I whispered, squeezing my eyes shut. "No. No, no, no, stop *lying!* Just get out. *Get the fuck out!*"

"Tris—"

"*Get out!*" I screamed so hard the words burned my throat raw. I kept my eyes screwed up, hot tears pooling behind my lids, and I prayed for the nightmare to end. I just needed to wake up and this could all fade into the murky depths of my subconscious.

The door creaked as it closed, leaving me alone with my pain.

Sobs wracked through me and I curled onto my side as best I could with my wrists bound. It was all too much. There was no way it was real. Sooner or later, I'd wake up. I had to.

Please let it all be a nightmare.

Please let Nelson be okay.

Please.

John

three

"She's asleep," Tink informed me, returning to the living room after checking on Tris. "Do you want to tell me what happened when you talked? I notice you haven't released her cuffs so I have to assume it didn't go well?"

She'd missed the whole messy scene, returning with coffees just minutes after Tris screamed at me to get out of the room. Out of her life.

"It went about as badly as expected," I admitted, sinking my ass down onto the couch with a groan. "Probably didn't help that she likely had a blazing headache." I shot her a glare and she raised her hands defensively.

"Don't go trying to shift the blame onto me, champ. I only knocked her out to save your ass, so I think what you meant to say was *thank you, Tink, I owe you.*" She crossed to the kitchen, picking up the huge cup of coffee she'd just come home with. "So, she was still in a homicidal rage then?"

"Something like that," I muttered. The depth of her grief and anger was entirely understandable, but I'd handled it all *badly*. I had no experience to draw from for how best to empathize *or...* apologize. Ultimately, though, words only went so far. And I *was* responsible for this whole mess. If I hadn't targeted her as my mark for *Poppy Flowers* in the first place, then maybe she'd be safe and happy right now.

Tink left me to my glum thoughts, sipping her coffee as she scrolled through her phone for a while, then sighed and put the device down. "Want me to talk to her?"

I wrinkled my nose. "Probably not a great idea right now." Not while Tris was still mad as hell *and* hurting. The fact it was Tink who knocked her out wasn't going to land well on a good day.

"How much did you explain?" Tink asked, glancing at the bedroom door. "Did you make sure she knew you didn't kill Nelson?"

"I tried," I growled, rubbing my eyes. "She wasn't very inclined to believe me." Why should she? I had lied and lied and lied.

Tink scoffed. "Are you shocked? You haven't exactly built your relationship on honesty and trust. I probably wouldn't believe you either, in her shoes."

"So helpful, Tink. Thank you. I love when you point out the fucking obvious for me to feel worse than I already do." I glared daggers and she didn't even flinch. Infuriating woman. No wonder she and Tris had become such fast friends.

"I'm just saying..." she muttered, then took another sip of her coffee. "Okay so whether she believed you or not, you still told her the truth. Right? You told her everything, so she can take her time thinking it all over and drawing her own conclusions?"

I shifted my eyes away from her penetrating gaze, spreading my hands in helplessness. "I mean... sort of?"

A tense silence sat between us. "John," she eventually said in a pained voice. "I mean this in the nicest way possible. Fuck you're an idiot, sometimes. What do you mean by *sort of*? Did you or didn't you?"

"I... *tried*. But she wasn't exactly ready to hear all the nitty gritty details, okay? I told her it wasn't me. I told her that I was trying to *save* Nelson and that's why my hands were all bloody. But when I said it was Hank, she lost it." I winced, recalling the raw anguish in her voice as she screamed at me to stop lying. "I couldn't get her the rest. She didn't need to hear how Hank held a gun to

Nelson's head and forced him to open her hidden gallery. She definitely didn't need to know how Nelson deliberately triggered the booby trap and took the full blast when the wall exploded... or how Hank literally stepped over his husband's dying body to take *Poppy Flowers* off the wall."

Cold son of a bitch.

"Goddamn, John," Tink murmured, shaking her head. "Anyone ever tell you that your social skills fucking blow?"

"It's been mentioned. Thanks." I glared at her and she just shrugged. "Besides, I *didn't* tell her that, so surely that earns me some points?"

Tink wrinkled her nose. "I guess... but now she probably thinks you're not just a liar but also a heartless bastard who is trying to shift the murderous blame onto literally her only remaining family member, which in turn makes you seem like an emotionally abusive control freak who is trying to isolate her from any sort of support network." She paused, sipping her coffee. "None of which is helped by the fact that you probably threw *me* under the bus with you, so now she not only lost her family but she also lost her only friend in the process."

"You are just full of positivity and support today, Tink," I told her with dripping sarcasm. Not that she was wrong. I'd done that. I'd detonated every foundation I'd been trying to build.

The twin beeps of our phones interrupted our depressing discussion, and I leaned forward to scoop up mine from the table.

"Oh good," Tink groaned, checking her own messages. "No prizes for guessing who the new front-runner is on the scorecard. *Faroeice*... must be dickish for Hank the betrayer."

Faroeice. It seemed like a made up alias but there was something niggling at me about the name. Like it had a hint of familiarity and I couldn't put my finger on *why*. Maybe he'd competed against me in previous Games?

"He's taken the top place?" I peered at the list in disbelief. "How many fucking points was that painting worth?"

"Too many," Tink grumbled. "I wonder what the next piece is going to be."

I shook my head, my mood sour as I tallied the collateral damage of today's Game piece. "Whatever it is, I don't think I care. Not now." I gestured to my closed bedroom door as if Tink had any confusion what I meant.

She let out a frustrated sigh, ruffling her fingers through her short blond hair. "What are you going to do about Tris? You can't just keep her handcuffed to your bed forever."

"I know." I sulked. Of all the ways I'd pictured handcuffing Tris to my bed, *this* wasn't one of them.

"And she has every right to feel how she's feeling right now. She just lost not one but two parental figures, her mentors, and her only family. All because of *you*." Tink gave me a hard look. "Not being a dick, just stating facts. And before you go sinking any deeper into self-pity, she was already forging paintings long before the Game came to town. If it wasn't you, it would have been someone else... I'm just pointing out how *she* would see it right now."

She was right, but knowing that didn't soften the blow. I tossed my phone back on the table and slouched back in my seat. "It doesn't look good."

"Well... maybe she will be less cynical? Let's see. You took a job as her teacher to gain her trust, made her fall in love with you, then stole a priceless painting from her place of work where she would undoubtedly be the prime suspect... oh and her boss is well known for killing people who steal from him. But then you *did* come back for her, except that all seems a bit self-serving when ultimately her home is destroyed and her loved ones lost, and there *you* are at the center of it all with blood on your hands... and then she gets knocked out and wakes up handcuffed to your bed." Tink grimaced. "Yeah... I don't see you talking your way out of this one."

I glared death at her. "And I'm the one with shitty social skills? You have the bedside manner of a mortician."

"All I'm saying is that I don't think you'll make any progress with her handcuffed and literally held captive. Come up with another plan because this one isn't it." Her expression turned guilty and she rubbed the back of her neck. "But in the meantime, we should probably get back to Tris's place before the council sweeps in with their cleanup crew."

I squinted my suspicion. "Why?" The Game council had been very efficient with cleanups, making sure the rest of Whispering Willows had no idea of the bloody Game being played under their noses. Less than twenty-four hours after each *mess* was created, it was like it'd never happened.

Tink cleared her throat, shifting in her seat. "It just occurred to me that Tris had all those priceless *stolen* works of art hidden in her secret gallery and she probably wouldn't appreciate anyone taking them."

I scratched my chin. "Who would take them? *Poppy Flowers* has already been turned in, no one other than the council has any reason for stepping foot in her apartment, and they wouldn't take anything unless they thought they had a claim to it..." I trailed off, my jaw dropping as the guilty expression on her made sense. "Oh no. You didn't..."

Tink winced. "I didn't *know* she had all that there! If I had, I would never have listed her apartment as Game collateral but now—"

"Fuck's sake, Tink!" I exclaimed, rising to my feet. "We need to get over there and hide them. Otherwise, the council *can and will* claim every last piece."

"That's sort of my point," she muttered, getting to her feet and grabbing her coat. "What are we doing about Tris, though? We can't just leave her here like that. What if a fire starts?"

Great, now my anxiety was at a level ten and I couldn't erase the mental image of Tris burning in a fire. "I hate you," I snapped, tossing her the car keys. "Go get the car out of the garage, I'll be a minute."

"You're doing the right thing!" Tink called after me as I stomped toward my bedroom.

I hesitated with my hand on the knob, still trying to formulate *some* kind of plan in my mind. Nothing seemed like a safe option. None of the scenarios in my head worked out the right way... or the way I wanted them to, anyway. Logically, I knew the answer. Someone had to lose here, and that someone needed to be me. But was I really willing to risk Tris's safety in the process?

Whether she knew it or not, she was in this now. There would be no running from it.

She needed more information, so she could make smart decisions. I just... had to get her to listen. Somehow.

I silently opened the door and my chest tightened at the sight of my Venus. She was never going to forgive me, but was I really ready to let her leave?

Not a chance in hell. I doubted I'd ever be ready. She *owned* me now.

Tris

four

Grief and anger lulled me into sleep, and when I started to surface into consciousness again those same sour emotions were right there waiting for me, welcoming me back into their cold embrace. I didn't *want* to deal with it, though. I wanted to slide back into my memories and live there where my world was still whole. Where everything was as it used to be.

Before Nelson died in my arms.

Before *John*.

But if I was honest with myself, deep down I knew it'd all started before John Smith targeted me. It all started with me and Nelson... and a priceless painting of *Poppy Flowers*.

Eight months ago

"It's perfect, Ivy," Nelson praised, inspecting my latest completed painting. "You just keep astounding me with that talent of yours."

I tilted my head to the side, my eyes scanning every inch of the painting and searching for flaws. "I can safely say, pop art is definitely not my favorite style. I don't see the appeal in Warhol's work, but who am I to judge?"

Nelson chuckled, lifting my forgery of Andy Warhol's *Liz* from the easel and placing it carefully in the transport case we had prepared. "Well, your part is done. I'll make the switch tonight, and Hank can transport the original to our locker in Cloudcroft tomorrow."

I shrugged, grabbing out a fresh canvas to set up on my easel, ready for a new project. "Be safe, okay? Mr. Grimaldi doesn't fuck around if he catches anyone trying to screw him."

Nelson grinned and patted me on the shoulder. "It's sweet that you care, Ives. Hank and I have been doing this a *long* time, remember? We know what we're doing."

I rolled my eyes. They *had* been doing it a long time, much longer than I'd been alive, but that didn't mean they were ever *safe*. "Yeah, well, don't blame me for worrying. You aren't exactly—"

"Don't you dare finish that sentence, Tristian Ives," he grouched, shaking his head. "I am not *old,* and if Hank ever heard you imply he was anything but youthful he'd skin you alive."

I grinned but held up my hands in surrender. "Sorry, sorry, how dare I? You don't look a day over thirty-five." Then under my breath I added, "...times two."

"I heard that," Nelson warned. "Impertinent child. Now, I wanted to talk to you about another passion project."

My brows rose and I gave him a sly smile. "What happened to not taking too many from the same collection?" We had rules. I'd taken the job with the Grimaldi family specifically for the *Warhol* since we already had a buyer lined up, but after gaining access to the gallery both Nelson and I had been like naughty kids in a candy shop.

Nelson's answering grin was pure mischief. "Just one more. While you finish the academic year out at Boles."

"Didn't you say *only* one more, before?"

He grinned. "This time I mean it." Then he winked.

He knew I was an easy sell. "Which one?"

"*Poppy Flowers.* And then at the end of the year you

can transfer your degree to any university you want and we can set up a new home base. New projects. New clients. Sound good?" His eyes twinkled with mischief, and I couldn't fight my smile.

"I *do* love Van Gogh..."

"I know you do," he agreed, "and it would be such a pretty addition to the collection."

I groaned. "Okay you got me. What do we tell Hank, though? He knows *Liz* is finished, so how do we justify why I'm still working for Grimaldi?" Because Hank did *not* know about our passion projects. Those were just between Nelson and me, since we did them for the love of art not to sell on the black market. If Hank knew, he would be horrified at all the missed opportunities hanging on the wall in our secret gallery.

"Leave Hank to me, Ivy. I can easily explain that you enjoy the work you're doing for Luther and that it's providing us excellent intel into the underground art auctions. He won't suspect a thing." He shot me a cheeky wink. "As always, it's our little secret."

"Our little secret," I agreed, nodding. "Let's do it."

Present

"Our little secret," I mumbled, the sound of my own

voice shaking me out of sleep once more. I blinked a couple of times, my head hazy and my thoughts a tangled mess. Where was I? What day was it?

Disoriented, I sat up and ran a hand over my face. Then I jolted with confusion, because my wrists were no longer handcuffed to the headboard. Fuck, now it all came back to me. *John.*

My wrists were banded with a red ring where I'd been tugging on the restraints, but now the cuffs lay innocently on the bedside table on top of a scrawled note. In that fucking serial killer handwriting I now recognized as John's.

Tris, you're free to leave if that's what you choose. I hope you won't, though. There is so much you don't know, and I need to explain. Please, give me a chance.

It was signed with a scrawled J and my fingers closed instinctively around the paper, strangling it like I would like to do to John. How *dare* he?

"Give you a chance?" I spat out loud, swinging my legs off the bed and wincing at the throbbing in my skull. "I'll give you a chance... to take my foot so far up your ass you can suck on my toes. Bastard."

On the upside, at least I was still fully dressed in the clothing I'd worn from Grimaldi manor. That upside very quickly shifted to a downside when, after peeing in John's bathroom, I saw myself in the mirror. Dark splotches stained my gray sweatshirt, and bile rose in my throat as I realized what they were.

Frantic and horrified, I tore the sweatshirt over my head just seconds before the contents of my stomach emptied into the toilet. My abdomen convulsed, heaving even after there was nothing left to eject, and I gave a pathetic moan.

Bracing my hands on the vanity I forced myself to take some calming breaths, willing my stomach to unclench. Only after I stopped dry heaving did I turn the tap on to splash some water on my face. Except, I paused halfway through the motion, staring in anguish at my hands.

Someone—probably John—had clearly tried to clean the worst of the blood from them, but dark stains around my nails and in the creases of my knuckles remained. Blood. Nelson's blood.

His dying moments flooded back into my head, and my knees went weak. I crumpled onto the floor, a low moan rolling out of my chest as I hugged myself in a desperate grip. Grief and loss rattled through me, my whole skeleton *aching* with the stark reality of what had happened.

I lost track of time as I lay there on the bathroom floor, sobbing quietly. My whole world had crashed down around me. Eventually, though, I forced myself to climb back to my feet simply so I could scrub my hands properly clean. I couldn't stand having Nelson's blood on my skin for a single moment longer, so I soaped my hands frantically and rubbed them raw under the running tap. Then I grabbed John's toothbrush to get the last of the stains from around my fingernails.

When I finished, my hands throbbed and glowed red, but they were clean. They didn't *feel* clean, though, but I doubted that would change any time soon. Some stains couldn't be removed with soap.

"Fuck," I gasped, dragging my tangled hair back from my face. My scalp ached at the back, and I took a wild guess that I'd been hit with something heavy. A cautious exploration with my fingers found a swollen lump but no cuts, so hopefully I wasn't suffering any lasting damage.

Sniffing back my tears, I washed my face with cold water in an attempt to control my own emotions. Then I tied my hair up in a ponytail with the elastic on my wrist and headed back into John's bedroom.

I picked up his infuriating note and carried it through to the kitchen with me as I tried to work out what the *fuck* to do next. As much as I wanted to throttle John with my bare hands, I couldn't deny the truth of his note. There was *so much* I didn't know, but the trouble was I didn't know who to trust to tell me the truth. Not him, that was for sure.

Tink? She was in on the Game with him.

Hank... *shit*. John had told me Hank was the one who killed Nelson, but there was *no way*. He'd adored Nelson, nothing on this earth could have made him even hurt his soulmate let alone murder him in cold blood.

What did John hope to achieve by making that accusation, though? Surely he had to know how insane it would sound? How utterly unbelievable? So why even try to spin that story unless...

Unless he believed it.

Hank had no clue that I was keeping a secret gallery, let alone that Nelson and I had recently added *Poppy Flowers*. Even if he had known, why would he care? Sure, he'd be pissed that we kept him out of the loop—that could have netted us an easy hundred million if we'd sold it—but that wasn't worth killing anyone over. Not worth murdering the man he'd loved for some forty odd years, that was for sure.

Hank wasn't in the Game... was he?

Suddenly, I was questioning everything I'd ever known. Every*one*. Nothing felt certain or true, and I was just the dumb twit who'd played into everyone's hands.

I needed answers, but not from John. I needed to go back to my apartment and see the scene with my own eyes. Would Nelson's body still be there? Would it be a crime scene? Or would whoever was pulling the strings for the Game have already scrubbed everything clean to erase any evidence of their mess? Would they make Nelson disappear?

That thought gutted me all over again.

Going back to my place was a terrible idea. An empty one. There was only pain waiting for me there.

Whatever. That was where I needed to start my search for answers, so I grabbed a marker pen from the kitchen counter and scrawled a response on John's note. I found a light coat tossed over the back of the sofa and grabbed it. Then I left the apartment, not bothering to lock anything after me. If he got burgled then that'd just be karma at work.

Fuck you, John Smith. I'll figure this out on my own.

And yet, I couldn't seem to stop the hot tears from rolling down my face as I walked away. My stupid heart was such a traitor.

John

five

Everything seemed very *normal* when we returned to Tris's apartment building. Calm. Too fucking calm. Tink and I exchanged a worried frown as we rode the elevator up to the seventh floor in silence. The doors slid open with a cheerful ding, and we stepped out into the shared corridor.

"Shouldn't the cleanup crew be here already?" Tink murmured as we passed Nelson and Hank's door. "It's been like two hours..."

"Be glad they're not," I replied, scowling at her. "I imagine they're in no hurry since no one else lives on this floor. Probably waiting for the cover of darkness." Which was imminent since the sun was sinking below the horizon already.

The only reason the blast in Tris's apartment had

gone unnoticed was that it'd happened during the day while no one was around to hear it. Bram lived in the unit directly below, and he'd been at work. No one else would have likely paid it any mind if they'd even been home.

Tris's front door stood ajar, and I pushed it further open with a gloved hand to let us enter.

"Fucking hell," Tink muttered, "what a mess."

She wasn't wrong. Furniture lay tipped over and broken, bits of debris scattered everywhere and smears of blood coating far too many surfaces. Most notably the bloody handprints on the white sofa and the wall beside the window... and the smeared stains on the window itself.

"I wounded him," I commented, my gaze locked on Hank's escape route. "I stabbed him at least twice before he got away. That has to count for something, doesn't it?"

Tink gave a grunt. "If Tris is giving out points for critically injuring her one and only remaining loved one, sure."

She was incredibly not fucking helpful. I glowered at her. "He murdered Nelson."

Nelson, whose lifeless body still lay there on the floor surrounded by a pool of blood. Guilt and regret filled my chest and I forced myself to look away from his corpse. There was nothing I could do now. He was long gone.

Tink shrugged. "I know that, but I just don't think Tris will accept it so easily. In the meantime... we have a bigger problem." She pointed toward the destroyed false wall and at the hidden room beyond. The *empty* room.

"Fuck," I breathed. "We're too late."

The faint ding of the elevator arriving on the seventh floor sent a jolt of urgency through me, and I grabbed Tink by the arm, dragging her out the door and farther down the hallway to the fire stairs. We slipped inside *just* as the elevator opened and I grabbed the door handle to prevent it slamming and betraying our position.

"John, what—?" Tink whispered but I shushed her with a sharp look.

Holding the door just an inch open, I tipped my head to listen. The footsteps were a woman's with a faint scuff of high heel on the carpet.

"...out of time," a familiar voice said and Tink clapped a hand over her mouth to stifle a gasp. "I have collected all the artwork to be held as collateral, per the rules. I'm picking up the last one now but I've just heard an anonymous tip called into Whispering Willows PD so I need the clean up crew here *yesterday*. Am I clear?" She paused and I realized she was speaking on the phone.

Her next words were quieter, and I slipped back out into the hallway to continue listening. Carol was inside Tris's apartment now, but clearly so confident that she was alone she hadn't closed the door. Tink was right on my ass, and we both pasted ourselves to the wall beside the door.

"...couldn't have predicted this..." she was saying, and I noted the distinctive snaps of an art carry case being locked. She'd cleaned out Tris's gallery, and now I would have to steal them all back for my girl. "Just tell them to hurry up. We don't need to draw extra attention when we're this close to the end."

I desperately did *not* want Carol to see us lurking, so I pushed Tink back into our fire escape hiding spot before Carol exited the apartment once more. The elevator was still sitting there on our floor, so it was only a moment before she was gone.

"Who was that?" Tink whispered, despite the fact we were alone once more. "Did you know her?"

I raised a brow at her with interest. "You don't? How interesting."

Tink narrowed her eyes at me in irritation. "I'm not quite at your level of fame, Hermes. Was she one of the Game Council?"

"Apparently," I agreed, bypassing Tris's door and heading for Nelson's. I pulled out my lock picks and

39

made quick work of our access. "*That* was Carol Atwood." I glanced over my shoulder to see if the name registered any recognition for Tink.

"Is she a big deal?" My little accomplice just blinked innocently.

I sighed. "She's Guild. Circle."

Tink's jaw dropped. "Excuse the fuck out of me? Aren't they a *myth*? Like Bigfoot or the Tooth Fairy?"

I snorted a laugh picturing Carol flapping around in a pair of sparkly wings. "No, they're real."

"But the stories are grossly over-exaggerated, right? Like... aren't they all meant to be serial killers?"

I cast a long look at her, then gave a simple, "Yep," in response. I didn't specify which question I was referring to though. "Let's look around quickly and get the fuck out before the cleanup crew arrives."

We worked quietly, not having anything *specific* that we were searching for. I did find a collection of stones that were the most flawless fakes I'd seen in a *long* time, as well as a ring that I could have sworn I'd seen before. Somewhere. Apparently forgeries weren't *just* Tris's hobby after all.

I pocketed the ring, not wanting cops to find it and blame Nelson's death on his extracurricular activities. Regardless of the Game, I wanted to ensure Hank was the prime suspect and punished accordingly, so I spent a few precious minutes checking the scene over with that in mind.

"We have company," Tink called out to me, peering out the window.

"Game council?" I asked, crossing over to her and looking for myself. "Ah, cops. Let's go."

We re-locked Nelson's apartment—since it would undoubtedly be searched by the local police—and took the fire stairs to exit the building. Cops weren't coming in hot; it was just one squad car and two uniformed officers. Responding to the "anonymous tip" but not expecting to walk in on a murder scene. It wouldn't be long before the building was crawling with authority and we'd end up trapped. As much as I wanted to hang around and lurk, I reluctantly led the way out into the street.

Our car was parked across the road, so we slid inside and waited. Watching.

"Who do you think the anonymous tip was from?" Tink asked after a minute of silence.

I'd been wondering the same thing since hearing Carol mention it. "No clue. Maybe one of the other Game players if they arrived on the scene after we left?"

Tink shook her head. "That's a rule break. No one would risk it with stakes as high as they are. Could have been someone in the building, maybe?"

"Maybe," I agreed, my eyes locked on Tris's window high above us. "Or maybe it was Hank."

"Guilty conscience?" Tink mused. "Possible. He must have spent a *long* time lying to Nelson about who he was. That has to have taken a toll. Maybe he has regrets?"

I scoffed. "Doubtful. I bet there's something he wants... something he had to leave behind when I interrupted. If it goes into police evidence then he stands a much better chance of getting it back, rather than if Game cleanup scrubs the scene."

Tink made a disgusted sound and folded her arms across her chest. I agreed with her response. Hank was a dirty piece of shit, but I clearly didn't know the whole story. How had he become involved in the Game in the first place? And why was winning this more important than his partner of forty years? What kind of psychopath could switch off their emotions that easily?

When I'd arrived at Tris's apartment after the *Poppy Flowers* text clue had come out, it was to look for *clues*. I'd never in a million years suspected the painting itself was still inside her home, but Hank had already worked it out. When I walked in, he had a gun pressed to Nelson's head and such a cold look in his eyes that I nearly didn't recognize him.

Nelson triggering the booby trap had been a

deliberate act of desperation. When the blast hit him, dozens of shards of the broken wall perforating his body like a shotgun spray, I'd been frozen with shock.

"Here comes the cavalry," Tink commented as the evening lit up red and blue and the air filled with the urgent sound of sirens. The first cops had called for backup quickly, thanks to Tris's door being wide open and Nelson's corpse still on display.

I still couldn't shake the memory of Hank stepping *over* his husband's dying body to retrieve the painting from the hidden room. Or the sneer on Hank's face as he spat his parting remark at Nelson.

"Selfish fucking prick, I hope it takes you a long time to die so you can suffer. You deserve it for how you've betrayed me."

It was that comment that made me launch at him, desperate to get *vengeance* for Nelson's murder rather than save the cursed painting. I didn't give a rat's ass who won that Game piece; I just wanted him to pay for what he'd done. For deceiving Tris so thoroughly and for breaking Nelson's heart before ending his life.

Ultimately though, I'd let him escape when Nelson had croaked my name.

"He told me to keep her safe," I murmured, staring at the cops pouring out of their cars with unfocused eyes. "Nelson... before Tris arrived. He called out to me, then asked me to look after her, keep her safe. Leave town, leave our lives, leave the Game... He wanted her to know he was sorry for ever dragging her into his criminal world."

Tink stared at me for a long, tense moment, her gaze boring into the side of my face. "That's intense."

I inhaled deeply, releasing the breath with a sigh. "Yep."

"But... he clearly asked you because he knows how much you love her."

That observation gave me pause. Had that been the reason? Or only because I was *there*? I couldn't help thinking that if there were any other circumstances, Nelson would have told Tris to dump my ass and run the fuck away. He knew I was bad for her, just as much as I did.

"Oh, wow," Tink chuckled, nodding at a van rolling slowly past our parked position. "Bit fucking late for the cleanup crew to arrive."

I didn't ask how she knew the unmarked van was the Game cleanup crew, but they continued cruising past then sped up and took off again around the corner. I sighed again, feeling *heavy* with everything that'd happened.

"At least Nelson's body has been found," I murmured. "At least there will be an investigation into

44

his murder, rather than have him simply disappear without a trace. That's something."

"Yep," Tink agreed with a sad smile. "It's not *much*, but it's something. You know the spouse is always the first one they look into. That's something too? Right?"

"Yeah," I said. Maybe I was as desperate as she was to grasp at whatever scraps life would offer us.

What else could we do? I turned on the car ignition, shifting into drive. We needed to get home before Tris woke up. Hopefully she would hear me out. Hopefully we could explain and, if nothing else, caution her to stay safe.

The dread twisting my stomach told me I was a fool, but I had to hope.

The second I stepped out into the street, I had to admit to myself that I had not thought my plan through. I had no phone, no money, no car... at least I had clothes—after stealing one of John's shirts to replace mine—and shoes, and I'd grabbed one of Tink's coats on the way out so I was warm enough. I just wished I'd been thinking clearly enough to also grab some *money* to pay for a taxi.

As it was, every time a car passed I had my shoulders bunched up with tension and fear. There was no way in hell my paranoia would let me hitchhike, so I resigned myself to walking the three miles back to my building.

The whole way, I kept myself company with an endless soliloquy about what an asshole John was, and how stupid I was forever trusting him. Twice. That made the whole damn thing so much worse, for the fact I'd fallen for his lies *twice*.

"Idiot," I muttered to myself for the hundredth time. "You stupid, naive, tunnel-vision idiot. You know better, Tris. No man is worth overlooking so many bare-faced lies. *No man*. Like you don't have enough toys to take care of business alone."

Ugh, that thought only made me ten times madder as I remembered how many vibrators John had stolen from me. Or, that's what I suspected had happened to all the toys mysteriously missing from my bedroom.

Anger fueled me as I stomped through the streets of Whispering Willows, but an hour later when I entered my neighborhood, all I felt was empty. Heartbroken and empty, with the weight of a million bad decisions sitting on my shoulders.

My shoes scuffed the pavement as I rounded the corner of my block, then I stumbled when I saw the scene ahead. Probably a dozen cop cars surrounded my building, their lights reflecting on all the windows and filling the street with red and blue. What else did I *expect* though? It was a crime scene; of course there were police investigating.

I approached at a slower pace, my eyes locked on my own window above. Part of me had thought that whoever was running this stupid thieving Game would just... make it all disappear. Like they'd done with the explosion at Boles only so recently. Within twenty-four hours the story was that it'd been a gas-leak and no mention of the fatality.

This was better, though. This was a *relief*, wasn't it? The Whispering Willows police couldn't all be corrupt and covering for whatever billionaire psychopath was running John and Tink's Game... They'd investigate it properly and, hopefully, find Nelson's killer.

Right?

They'd get justice.

I drifted closer, approaching the small crowd of spectators and journalists gathered behind a line of police tape, desperate to *know more*. Had they found John's bloody knife? Were they looking for him as Nelson's murderer already? Maybe I could assist and tell them where John was staying?

Fuck. Would I really do that? Point the cops right in his direction?

It was easy to say *yes*, if he had indeed murdered my friend. If I truly believed that he'd been the one to stab Nelson dozens of times then kneel there over his dying body, waiting for him to expire.

Except I didn't. Even just in those few words we'd exchanged while he'd held me captive, he'd got under my skin and created *doubt*. Fucking hell, what a mess.

Obviously I didn't believe him that *Hank* killed Nelson, there was no fucking way that was the truth. But maybe if the real killer had looked like Hank at a glance, John could have been mistaken?

"Hey, do you know what's going on in there?" a woman beside me asked, glancing in my direction. "Was it a burglary or something?"

A man on my other side snorted. "With this level of police presence? No way. I'm putting my money on murder. Maybe even a serial killer."

The woman gasped, pressing her hand to her mouth. "In Whispering Willows? No way, that sort of thing doesn't happen here. This is a good neighborhood." Her hand shifted to her throat and a small voice in my head wondered if she was trying to clutch some pearls under her sweater.

The man made a noise, and I glanced back his way to see the puzzled look on his face. "Lady, I don't know which Whispering Willows *you* live in, but that sort of shit is hardly uncommon around here. My guess? This was a Grimaldi hit. Sending a message to someone who hasn't paid protection."

I swallowed hard. How had I so blindly waded into crocodile-infested waters? And now I was so deep I couldn't see the shoreline.

The woman was replying, but I had stopped

listening. All I could hear was the frantic thumping of my heartbeat and the white noise static filling my head as I edged closer to a mental breakdown. I was horrified to admit that both these nosey strangers were right. It was a burglary *and* a murder.

As I watched, several uniformed officers exited the front door of my building, closely followed by a medic guiding a gurney. A gurney transporting an unmistakable black body bag.

Nelson.

"See?" the man crowed. "Knew it."

My head swirled as I took a step forward, only to be blocked by the police tape barrier. Frustrated and grief stricken, I just ducked underneath, not letting a strip of plastic tape stop me from...

From what? What the fuck was I even doing?

Someone grabbed me, a strong hand gripping my arm and causing me to stumble as they dragged me away.

"What—?" I started to protest but the man hissed at me to *shut up* and continued hauling me in the *opposite* direction to where the coroner was now loading Nelson's body into his van. I needed to go with him, didn't I? I needed to tell them who he was, how he died, and who was to blame.

Frantic, I tried to jerk my arm free, but it was a futile effort at best.

"Tris, cut it out," the man yanking me away from the crime scene snapped. "I'm trying to save you."

"Bram?" I asked, my head fuzzy with confusion. "What are you doing here? I need to—"

"I'm here to stop you from doing something dumb, obviously," he replied, giving me a hard glare and using my confusion to pull me even further down the street.

I frowned, shaking my head. "No, you don't understand. That was *Nelson* in the—"

"I know," he snapped, not pausing even a moment.

"Bram!" I shouted, digging my heels into the pavement. "Nelson's *dead*!"

"I know," he barked back at me, giving my arm a little shake as though he was hoping that would shake sense into me. "They think *you* killed him."

That stopped me. My jaw dropped. "What?"

"Your neighbor, your apartment, your prints all over the scene, it's not exactly a shock that you might be the prime suspect, Tris. So don't be a fucking idiot and go hand yourself in to those incompetent fools. Get in the car." He let go of my arm to pop open the passenger door of his car.

I hadn't even noticed that was where he'd been

51

dragging me. How long had he been out here, watching out for me?

Wetting my lips, I glanced back to the crime scene. I couldn't see much from where we were, just the lights and the backs of all the nosey neighbors. An ice cold trickle of dread ran down my spine, though, and I shivered.

"I was framed?" I asked, sounding utterly pathetic.

Bram shook his head. "Wrong place, wrong time. Please let me take you somewhere safe? If they grab their first suspect, they'll just stop looking any further. Is that what you want? For the real killer to walk free while you take the punishment for something you didn't do?"

That statement didn't ring entirely true, and I stood frozen. I *should* take punishment for Nelson's death. It was all my fault, wasn't it? If I'd just given *Poppy Flowers* back to Mr. Grimaldi in the first place, then there would have been no one breaking into my apartment. No reason for the old man to get caught in the cross-fire of this insane, fucking Game John was playing.

"Tris," Bram prompted. "I can see you're processing, and you're in shock. But can you please process inside the car? Thank you." He gave me a less than gentle push, and I automatically climbed into the passenger seat.

He gave a short sigh of relief as I pulled my feet

inside, then he firmly closed the door before circling around to the driver's seat.

"They think I murdered Nelson?" I asked again, the skin of my arms all raised up in goosebumps even underneath Tink's coat. I was starting to shiver, and logically I knew it was shock. Logic didn't make me any less cold, though.

Bram gave me a sympathetic look, firing up the ignition and guiding his car out of the parking space. "Sorry. It does look bad, though."

A lump formed in my throat and my eyes heated with building tears. "I loved him like family, I would never..."

"I know," he replied softly. "But they don't, and it's sort of their job to think the worst of anyone."

Unable to form words, I just nodded and turned my face to look out the window. Maybe if I held my breath, Bram wouldn't realize I was crying.

I stared at the familiar scenery passing us by, barely taking any notice, until we turned down a road I knew all too well, and I stiffened. "Where are you taking me?"

He glanced over, quirking a brow in confusion. Then he must have realized why I was poised to jump out of his moving vehicle. "Ohhhhhh, no. Don't worry, I'm not taking you back to Grimaldi's house. Chill, Tris, I wouldn't do that to you."

I frowned, still not totally sure if he was telling the truth. "Why not? You don't really know me, so why *wouldn't* you take me back there? Especially if Mr. Grimaldi was offering some kind of reward or threatening someone you love."

He laughed, which seemed like an odd reaction. "Um, okay well I guess you don't really know me that well either so telling you to *trust me* doesn't mean much. So, how about this? I'm already wealthy, there is no monetary value that could make me hand over a scared, defenseless woman to a man known for his ruthless and violent outbursts. And as for threatening the people I love?" Bram laughed again, this time with even more amusement.

"That's... funny to you?" I was failing to see the humor.

He nodded between chuckles. "Yeah. It is. Uh, I guess it's only funny if you know my family, but yeah, it's not a concern for me. So as hard as it seems and as dumb as it sounds, can you please just trust me, Tris? Your safety is my number one priority and returning you to Grimaldi goes in direct violation of that."

When no response sprang into my mind, I just kept my mouth shut and nodded. What other choice did I have? Shitty ones, really. Trusting Bram right now was the least shitty option.

"Also," he added after a minute of silence. "I went to all that effort sneaking you *out* of Grimaldi's house and probably losing my job in the process. Why would I bother doing that if I was going to flip flop on you just hours later?"

Hours? That was all it'd been since Bram had dropped me off at my home? Mere hours. It felt like days.

Sick with guilt, grief, and worry, I just nodded again and slouched back in my seat. Wherever Bram was taking me, it surely wouldn't be even deeper into those croc infested waters. Surely.

My fingers tightened around the sheet of notepaper, crumpling it into a ball, and my teeth ground so hard it hurt my jaw. Of course I'd known it was a possibility when I unlocked the handcuffs, leaving Tris unguarded while Tink and I returned to the crime scene, but...

"Damn it, Tink!" I roared, "I knew this would happen!"

She lifted a brow in my direction. "Don't fucking blame me, John. This is your mess."

I loved how she liked to throw the blame on me—repeatedly. Like I didn't fucking know. "You told me to release her, and now she's out there with no protection, no information, and likely—"

"Ah, excuse the fuck out of me, *Hermes*, I told you

that it wasn't safe to leave her handcuffed to the bed while no one was here. You didn't have to leave with me, you could have stayed. You could have just locked the front door, or asked someone to keep an eye on her while we were gone. You had options *other* than simply writing a note." She snatched up the ball of paper from where I'd just tossed it across the room, smoothing it out to read. "Okay well, there's your first fucking mistake. Is that *seriously* your handwriting? Looks like something out of a slasher flick."

Frustration and guilt nearly choked me, and I threw my hands in the air. "That's irrelevant, Tink!"

She just rolled her eyes, flipping the note over to read Tris's response. "*Go fuck yourself, asshole.* Ah yeah, that probably doesn't mean she just popped out for a pizza."

"Tink!" I implored her. "Where do we start looking for her? She could be hurt or—"

"Calm down, John, you're getting emotional, and that doesn't really help the situation." Tink discarded the note and looked around our shared living room. "She took my coat, so that's something. At least she'll be warm. Are you missing any money or credit cards or anything?"

I blinked at her, dumbstruck for a moment. Had she just called me *emotional* like I was a Victorian-era woman on the verge of swooning? The insult was enough to redirect my energy and I went to check my lockbox hidden in my bedside table.

"No, nothing missing. I don't think she even opened it." But fuck, what did I know? Tristian Ives was a woman of many secrets, so maybe she could pick a lock without leaving any trace.

"Okay so she's likely on foot," Tink concluded. "She isn't the type of girl to hitchhike, so I'm guessing she walked. We've been gone for roughly two hours... depending how long ago she left, she could be... hmm..."

"Basically anywhere in a ten mile radius. Super helpful." I leveled a sarcastic glare in her direction and she responded with an extended middle finger.

"If you're just going to give me attitude, I'll leave you alone to spiral into paranoid hypotheticals," she informed me, heading back through to the living room. "But let's give Tris the benefit of the doubt here, John. She's not a fucking idiot. Nor does she have a death wish. Don't forget she is still dealing with her own mess with the Grimaldis? I hardly think she will be taking unnecessary risks right now."

I folded my arms over my chest, desperately trying to reign in my urge to spiral like Tink said. "What are you suggesting we do, then?"

"Sleep." She punctuated her response by slamming

her bedroom door and the following silence nearly crushed me under its weight.

I waited, thinking she was just messing around, but after five minutes or so I had to accept the fact she was serious. Tink was sleeping, and I... had no idea what the fuck to do.

Tris was out there alone and totally in the dark about how treacherous her hometown had become, and that was *entirely* my fault. But I'd given her the choice to stay or go, and she'd chosen to go. Feeling sick, I retrieved the crinkled note again, staring at her response. The pen strokes were hard and angry, I could almost picture the furious look on her beautiful face as she'd written it.

Go fuck yourself, asshole.

A small smile touched my lips, appreciating the fact she'd used a comma even in her rage. Then a deep wave of guilt and shame washed over me as I remembered how deeply I'd impacted her education. I'd given no thought or care to how disruptive my *Game* was in her life, and now I was practically sick with the realization.

With a groan, I collapsed onto the couch and stared up at the ceiling. As much as I hated to admit it, Tink was right in everything she'd said. And everything she'd carefully *not* said. Tris didn't leave our safe house because she wanted to put herself in danger... she left to get away from *me*.

Did she still think I'd murdered Nelson? Surely if she thought about it, she'd realize it didn't make sense. Wouldn't she?

Then again, if I hadn't seen Hank holding that gun with my own eyes, I wouldn't have believed it either. He'd fooled me, so I could only imagine how hard it was for Tris to swallow.

Not to mention Nelson's reaction. Fucking hell, I'd never be able to forget that look of utter devastation and betrayal on the old man's face when Hank had put his gun to Nelson's head. To be with someone for that long, to love them *that* deeply, only to find out it was all fake? I couldn't fathom.

The similarity, though, in how I'd started my relationship with Tris... it made me uncomfortable. Was I really so much better than Hank?

If it came down to Tris or my grandfather's legacy... could I *really* say I'd choose her?

The questions plaguing my mind were making my pulse race and my palms sweat. I didn't like the revelations this was bringing. I didn't like the little voice in my head saying how much better off she would be if I never went after her.

Unable to sit still, I got up and found where I'd left

my phone. Maybe I couldn't go driving the streets of Whispering Willows in the hope of finding her, but someone else might know where she'd gone. Was she back at Grimaldi's house maybe?

I dialed Bram, but the call went straight to voicemail.

"Of course you don't answer your phone, you useless fuck," I muttered aloud. "God forbid you do the job I'm paying you to do."

I wet my lips, my thumb hovering over my phone as I tried to weigh the pros and cons of my next idea. Then, I huffed a short sigh and dialed Sin Grimaldi.

"I wondered when you might call," he said on answering, not even bothering with a *hello*.

I paused, second guessing whether this was a good idea. Then I tossed caution to the wind. "Can I speak with Tris?"

Sin gave a vexed sound, like he might be grinding his teeth together. "No, you can't."

"Damn it, Grimaldi, let me speak to her." My fingers tightened around my phone so hard I wondered if it might break.

He hissed a curse. "I *can't*, you insufferable fuck. I don't know where she is."

She hadn't gone back to him? I wasn't sure if that was a relief or a concern. As much as I hated his friendship with Tris, I didn't think he ever wished her harm. So I'd have felt better if she was with him. "You don't?"

"Do you seriously think I'd have taken your call if I did? Her apartment building is crawling with police right now. And I know she's not with you anymore, so I'm wondering *what the hell happened*, John?" Sin's words were terse, clipped, and tainted with an edge of guilt. What'd happened between him and Tris today? Why had she been alone when she arrived at her apartment?

"Call me if you find her," I ordered, ignoring his question. "It's important."

"Wait, what?" he barked back. "John, I don't owe you *shit*, if I find her—"

"You'll call me," I repeated. "Or that pretty blonde you've been scouring the planet for will disappear for good." I ended the call before he responded and dropped my head into my hands.

Threatening Sin Grimaldi was probably a bad idea, and I felt like dirt for implying I'd ever hurt an innocent woman. I wouldn't—I'd just let her know he was looking and help her relocate—but he didn't need to know that.

The weight of all my mistakes crushed me, and I slouched further down the couch, closing my eyes. The one thing Tink said that I was clinging to was that Tris was *smart*. Maybe she just needed to clear her head. Maybe she would come back.

I needed Bram to take my calls. If anyone could find her, it was him... even if he was the worst fucking Guild merc I'd ever encountered.

Unfortunately, the power of positive thinking didn't bring me the information I wanted. Nor did it make Tris walk her sassy ass back through the front door, and at some stage I must have fallen asleep where I sat because the next thing I knew, Tink was waking me with a cheery *good morning, John*.

Confused and foggy, I rubbed my eyes, stretching the kink out of my neck while pushing upright on the sofa.

"What time is it?" I mumbled, looking around for my phone. I found it down the side of the sofa where I must have dropped it in my sleep.

"Seven," she replied, her mouth full of berry muffin. Had she already left to get us coffee and breakfast? Why didn't she wake me? "Here, caffeinate yourself. We have to discuss what the hell is going on with the Game Council and what it means for Tris to have cops investigating Nelson's death. And then we need—"

Our phones beeping in unison cut off what she was saying, and our eyes locked. It wasn't time for another Game stage to be released yet; they were all done at eight. And they'd already updated the leaderboard... was someone being disqualified for a rule break?

I crossed my fingers, silently praying it would be Hank. He didn't deserve the win after what he'd done, and the idea of hurting him myself made my stomach churn. I'd do it, for Tris... and for Nelson... but it wouldn't be easy.

"You gonna read it?" Tink prompted, waiting for me to check my phone while she sipped her coffee and leaned against the counter.

I sighed and pulled my phone from my back pocket. Sure enough, it was an update from the Game Council, but sadly it wasn't announcing Hank's disqualification.

"They're changing the rules," I said aloud. "Again."

Tink's brows shot up and she grabbed her phone to read the info. "Oh, that's interesting. Harder Game pieces, so they're giving us more time on each one." She rolled her eyes and put her phone down again. "Is it just me, or is the council just making this shit up as they go along?"

Laughter bubbled out of me before I could stop it. "Seriously?" I chuckled when she frowned at me. "Tink, that's exactly what they're doing. I'm going to take a shower then go..." *looking for Tris at Grimaldi's house* "... get some air."

Tink gave me a skeptical look. "You're not going to

wait until we find out today's Game piece? We need to strategize and—"

"Nope," I cut her off. "I don't fucking care. Literally the only thing I want right now is to find Tris and apologize. That's it. Nothing more. The Game is dead to me."

I made it halfway to the bathroom before Tink's response stopped me dead in my tracks. "You want her to forgive you? Same. The best way to do that is to find that two-faced motherfucker *Hank* and hold him accountable for what he's done. And the best way to find him now? Is to play the fucking Game, John. Whatever today's Game piece is? That's where he'll be."

Shit. She was right, as per usual. Maybe I was done with the Game, but the Game wasn't done with me.

B ram had proven his sincerity when we bypassed the turnoff to Grimaldi Manor and continued out of town for some way. He'd then turned down a dirt road and spent the next thirty minutes taking twists and turns through unmarked trails deeper and deeper into the woods.

Eventually—right as I started questioning if he was going to kill me and dump the body—we arrived at a log cabin with a cheery *Home Sweet Home* doormat and figurines of ducks everywhere.

I'd been too numb and shell-shocked to chat, so Bram had shown me to the bedroom and given me a pair of men's sweats and a t-shirt from the closet to sleep in. Unsurprisingly, my dreams were plagued with more memories of Nelson, which left me feeling hollow and hurting when I woke the next morning.

Tears had soaked my pillow in my sleep, and my whole face ached. I lay there on the lumpy mattress, staring up at the ceiling, for a long time. Birds chirped and sang outside the window, and I tried to distract myself from reality by listening to them instead. Getting in touch with nature and all that shit. But the sound of Bram's voice somewhere outside tugged at my curiosity.

More specifically, the sound of Bram speaking with a woman. Who was out there with him? A girlfriend maybe? This cabin belonged to someone, surely. Then again, the floral bedspread and ducks everywhere didn't scream *young* woman. Unless Bram was into older ladies?

Intrigued, and more than a little bit worried, I climbed out of bed and let myself out into the living room. A quick glance around told me he must be outside the cabin, so I tiptoed over to the front door to get a look at who he was talking to. The fact that it was a woman reassured me it wasn't likely someone from Mr. Grimaldi's household... unless it was Naomi. Shit, now I didn't feel at all reassured. Was he negotiating a ransom?

A sleek silver Maserati sat behind Bram's Ford in the driveway, which was my first clue that this woman didn't own the cabin. Unless she was rocking some duck-printed seat covers in her luxury vehicle?

"...need to stop asking questions, Bram," the woman was saying. "The Game has been running for longer than you've been alive, and it's way out of your clearance level. Just... do the job you've been contracted for."

"That's what I'm doing," he snapped back, the frustration clear in his voice. "I was contracted to keep Tristian Ives *alive*, which is becoming increasingly difficult when I find she's somehow tangled up in the Game and people are getting murdered in her apartment. So, I think—"

Whatever else he said was lost as I burst out of the cabin in shock and disgust.

"Tris," Bram exclaimed, looking all kinds of guilty when he saw me. "I thought you were asleep."

"I thought you weren't lying to me," I shot back, parking my hands on my hips. "I guess we're all missing the mark today."

The blonde woman he'd been talking to turned to face me, and I quietly noted how beautiful she was, even if she was old enough to be Bram's mom. "Tristian, I apologize. I didn't realize we weren't *alone*." She turned a hard glare at Bram, who actually looked embarrassed.

"What did you expect?" he muttered. "She's the

prime suspect in a murder and was about to foolishly turn herself in. I had to take her *somewhere*."

"So you brought her here?" The woman gave an exasperated sigh, shaking her head. "Okay, well, what's done is done. Tristian, dear, we haven't officially met. I'm Carol." She approached with her high heels crunching on the gravel and extended a hand to me when she reached the bottom of the veranda steps.

I gave her hand a suspicious look but didn't shake it. Instead, I frowned at Bram and then turned my back to the woman. Carol.

"Bram, what the fuck have you dragged me into?" I asked, rudely ignoring Carol.

"Nothing you weren't already neck deep in," he replied, shooting me a suspicious glance as he strode up the steps to pass me. "I'll make coffee."

"Don't mind him," Carol told me with a smile. "He's cranky in the morning. How about we head inside and I'll explain a few things? I promise I'm not here to hurt you."

I cautiously nodded, but as she moved closer I noticed a gun holstered underneath her well-tailored blazer. What did a woman like this need a gun for while out in the woods? Still, she was offering me answers, and that was the best offer I'd had in a long time, so I only hesitated a moment before following her into the cabin.

Carol gestured for me to take a seat, elegantly perching on the edge of an ugly armchair like it was her throne.

"How do you take your coffee, Tris?" Bram called from the little kitchen as I lowered myself to the sofa.

"Um, I don't care," I replied, not holding out hope for an espresso machine or even fresh milk. So I'd settle for whatever he gave me, and shut the fuck up about it so long as it wasn't decaf. "Carol, was it? I don't mean to sound rude, but who the hell are you and why are you here? Actually, why am *I* here?"

The woman gave me another kind smile. "I believe you're here because Bram thought this to be the safest place given the current situation at your own home. He wasn't wrong about that, either. I understand things have become less than hospitable at the Grimaldi house?"

I frowned. "If you call being forced to kill a man, then blackmailed into an engagement *less than hospitable* then, sure." I blurted it out before really thinking about what I was saying, and instantly clapped a hand over my mouth, panic making my skin tingle. "I mean, um, metaphorically. Not literally. I'm not a murderer." *Except for that one time.*

"Of course," Carol agreed. "I don't think you're a murderer, Tristian, don't worry. But I was of the understanding that you had been managing your position with Luther quite well. Did something change recently?"

My frown deepened. "How do you know all this?"

"It's my job," she replied cryptically. "Did something change?"

I gave a hesitant nod. "Yes. I, um, I wanted to renegotiate things, and it wasn't received well. Bram helped me sneak out and dropped me to my place and then..." I trailed off, wincing. Then I shook my head. "Why am I telling you this? Who even *are* you?"

"Carol, dear, I already said that. Please keep up. Now then, you had quite the shock, so I'll try to stick with the important points and leave the superfluous details for another day." She paused as Bram handed her a mug of coffee then waited as he handed me one as well. As anticipated, it was instant coffee, bitter and weak, but it gave me something to *do*. Something to help me stay sane.

I bit my lip as Bram sat down on another floral armchair. "You said something outside about being hired to keep me alive. Who hired you?"

Sure, he'd been lying to me about who he was, but that seemed to be the norm in my life right now. At least

Bram was lying for the purpose of *protecting* me. Which now made his position in Mr. Grimaldi's house make *so much sense.*

"Confidential information," he muttered, not seeming quite as forthcoming with the information, so I shifted my attention back to Carol.

She took a sip of her bitter coffee and didn't even flinch as she swallowed it. "Let's start with the Game, hmm? What do you know about it all, Tristian?"

Understanding washed through me and I gave a small groan. "You're involved in *that*? I guess that makes sense since literally every bad thing in my life right now is linked back to this fucking *Game* in some way."

"Answer the question, Tristian," Carol ordered, making me blink. She hadn't raised her voice, nor had her expression shifted from the serene if somewhat cold look of interest. And yet, somehow the undertone of those words left me with no room to disobey.

"I don't know much," I admitted, my voice cracking with the shiver of intimidation chasing down my spine. "Just that it's about stealing things and that I was used to gain access to the Grimaldi gallery."

Carol inclined her head slightly. "To steal *Poppy Flowers*, yes. But imagine everyone's surprise to find it'd already been stolen by someone with no stakes in the Game." She chuckled, and I felt genuine amusement from her at this. Was my mistake somehow entertaining? Before I could ask, she continued speaking. "It's my understanding that you became aware of the Game through your friend Katinka, just a few days ago. I'm going to take a guess that she didn't give you much information or we wouldn't be in this position. Did she at least explain the collateral?"

I rubbed the bridge of my nose, feeling *stupid*. "She's not my friend." Not anymore. "And I don't understand. What collateral? She wouldn't tell me anything that I didn't guess for myself because of some rules or... something?"

Carol shot Bram a look, and he shrugged in response. Like he was saying that he was just as in the dark as I was on all of this, yet somehow I doubted *that* was true.

"Everyone involved in the Game must provide collateral. It's what protects the secrecy of the Game and ensures rules are followed. Due to the nature of participants, the collateral required is almost always a treasured possession or irreplaceable item." Carol placed her mug down and crossed her legs, clasping her hands at her knee. "It... mostly... keeps the players under control."

I nodded my understanding. "Okay... so why is this relevant? I'm not involved."

Carol's smile was full of pity. "Yes, dear, you are. After she tried to inform you with the use of loopholes, Katinka had to choose between losing her own collateral —and seeing you silenced—or listing you as a collaborator. She chose the latter."

This was a lot to digest, and my head swirled with the information. Then I looked to Bram with distrust fresh in my chest. "You're in the Game too?"

He shook his head. "Nope, I'm not."

Carol shot him an exasperated look. "He's not. But that doesn't mean he knows *nothing*. Hazards of my position, unfortunately; my children are all too nosey for their own good."

That took a moment to click together in my head, then I looked between the two of them again, this time with more understanding. They didn't look alike at all, but then they were familiar with each other. "She's your mom?" I directed the question to Bram, who nodded. "Okay, that's... irrelevant, I suppose." Nothing made sense anymore. I shifted my attention back to Carol. "What were you saying about Tink and her collateral?"

Carol pursed her lips, then gave a small sigh. "Not hers, yours. Unfortunately, I believe she did so without consulting you on the matter. After all, I don't think you'd have ever risked your home for the Game, given a choice."

I blinked. "Excuse me?"

"Your home was listed as your collateral, Tristian, along with everything within it. In light of what happened yesterday, and the subsequent police presence, the Game Council has removed some of your more valuable items for safekeeping." Carol delivered the news matter of fact, like she dealt with this all the time. Maybe she did? Fuck if I knew.

"Safekeeping?" I repeated, my tongue feeling heavy with shock.

Carol inclined her head. "Yes. Until the Game is over. If you don't break any rules, you'll get them all back."

All the air rushed out of me, and my head spun. She wasn't talking about my jewelry or the Tiffany lamp in my bedroom. She was talking about my gallery. Until now, I'd blocked that part out of my mind, somehow forgotten about the destroyed false wall exposing all my priceless stolen art.

And now they were gone. All of them. Taken by what sounded like a committee of thieves.

"Remember how I said I wasn't a murderer?" I murmured, staring at the floor to keep from fainting. "I just changed my mind."

Tink was fucking *dead* when I got my hands on her. John, too.

Dead.

John

nine

My first idea where to search for Tris was Boles University, since she'd spent so much time there prior to my arrival. Maybe she would think of it as a safe place. Of course, I quickly dismissed that idea when I spotted the charred remains of the art building and remembered the bomb blast that'd given Tris a different concussion.

So my next thought was to check Grimaldi's house. Sin may not have known where she was when we spoke last night, but that didn't mean he hadn't found her since then and decided not to call me. So I went into full stealth mode and broke into the manor itself, searching for her.

Frustratingly, she wasn't there. I even checked her painting studio that Tink told me about, and it was empty. Though, I was surprised to see the painting Grimaldi had her working on... *Le pigeon aux petits pois* by Picasso. Was he really expecting her to create a forgery without the ability to study the original? That was a tall order, even for an artist as talented as Tris was.

It took me some time to get back out again unnoticed, since it was broad daylight and the house was far from empty, but eventually I made it back to my car and stripped off my gloves. This wasn't *like* me. I prided myself on being able to find *anything*. Maybe that was my problem, though? Tris wasn't a thing to find; she was a force of nature.

"Shit," I breathed, smacking the heel of my hand against the steering wheel. Now what did I do?

As much as she was pissing me off right now, Tink probably had some bright ideas, so I grabbed my phone from where I'd stashed it in the inner zipper of my jacket. To my surprise, I had half a dozen missed calls.

"Finally," I muttered, seeing who they were all from. My phone had been on silent while I was sneaking around Grimaldi's house—because I wasn't stupid—but now I regretted it. I hit redial and anxiously waited for the call to connect. "Bram," I snapped when he eventually picked up. "Where is she?"

"I'm sending you some GPS coordinates," he replied,

"because I'm still under contract. But I would *advise* you to give it some time. She's safe here for now, but I can't guarantee the same for you if you ignore my warning."

I grinned. "Noted." I ended the call, and checked my messages. Sure enough, Bram had just sent a message containing a string of coordinates. I placed a quick call to Tink, telling her to be ready in five, and keyed the location into my car's navigation.

The fifteen-minute drive from Grimaldi's house to pick up Tink only took seven, and I reached over to shove the passenger door open before the car even stopped fully.

"Get in!" I snapped.

She arched a haughty brow, and took her sweet ass time taking her seat, so I stepped on the gas and made her yelp as she grabbed for the door.

"Dickhead," she growled. "What's the rush?"

"Bram found Tris," I replied, speeding out of the street.

She very pointedly buckled her seatbelt and gripped the handle on her door. "Okay, so I repeat, what's the rush?"

My response was an incredulous stare for longer than was really safe given my current speed. "I'm going to assume you're just trying to annoy me, Tink."

She gave a short sigh. "It's always an added bonus,

sure. But I'm serious, why are we in such a rush? Did Bram say she was hurt or in danger or something? Or are we just blustering in there with no plan and no respect for the fact Tris *made her choice* by leaving?"

I hated when she had valid points. But still, I wasn't going to just sit around and cross my fingers that Tris would change her mind and return to me, was I? The fact Bram and Tink both seemed to think that was even remotely an option was insanity.

"He didn't say," I muttered, not wanting to give her the satisfaction of being *right* but also quietly admitting she had a point. In fact, Bram had specifically said *not* to go rushing out there, and I was doing the plain opposite. I could handle Tris's anger, though.

Tink gave a mocking laugh, shaking her head. "For a smart guy, you're pretty fucking stupid. You know that?"

I scowled. "I'm aware."

But, in my defense this was all unknown territory for me. I didn't have *relationships;* I had useful alliances or marks. Feelings, real feelings that had the ability to make me stupid, were never a factor. Until now. Until her. Tristian Ives, my kryptonite.

"Shall we talk about the newest Game stage?" Tink offered, changing the subject. "We have two days this time, due to *increased degree of difficulty*."

I inhaled deeply, my stomach churning. "I don't care."

"Yes, you do," Tink argued. "Because I can bet anything that *Faroeice* the fuckhead will be turning up for it, and if you want to make things up to Tris..."

Somehow, I didn't think it would be that simple. Hank had been playing the long game for fuck only knew how long. There was no way he'd be easy to take down. Not now that his whole cover identity was blown out of the water.

Beside that fact, I hardly thought capturing—or killing—Hank would make up for Nelson's death. None of it would have happened without the Game in the first place. There was no putting that toothpaste back in the tube.

When I didn't respond, Tink muttered something under her breath about my pig-headedness and turned her attention out the window. I followed the navigation in silence, my foot heavy on the gas as we took endless dirt roads up into the woods outside Whispering Willows. As far as safe houses went, this was pretty safe.

There was a black Ford parked out the front of the little log cabin when we finally reached the GPS destination. I slowed to a stop, then hesitated in a moment of indecision. Had I made a huge mistake by ignoring Bram's warning? If she wanted to see me, she wouldn't have left.

"We came all this way," Tink grumbled, opening her door, "don't bitch out now. She already knows you're here."

I glared at her but she was already out of the car. I sighed and followed, walking somewhat slower across the gravel to the log cabin.

Bram stepped out onto the veranda, shaking his head. "I told you not to come," he snapped, looking tired and pissed off. "She doesn't want to see you."

Tink smirked, tossing me a smug look. "Told you. Maybe wait out here, Casanova."

"I wouldn't, if I were you," Bram warned her, but Tink paid him no mind as she sashayed past him and let herself into the cabin. A moment later, a feral sort of scream came from inside and something broke, making Bram wince. "I tried to warn her."

Panicked, I rushed up the front steps and into the cabin a step behind Bram, just in time to witness Tris hurling another plate at Tink's head.

"What the *fuck*, Tris?" Tink shrieked, ducking just in time to avoid the plate smashing against her face.

"You *bitch*!" Tris screamed, grabbing another plate from the stack she'd just been washing. She threw it without hesitation, and this time when it shattered on the wall beside Tink, some of the ceramic shrapnel bounced back to hit my little blonde accomplice.

Tink touched a hand to her neck where the plate shard had cut her, then gave a growl of fury when she saw blood.

"Okay, that's enough," Bram interjected, grabbing Tink around the waist as the spitfire launched herself in Tris's direction. "Let's get some air, shall we?" With a grunt, he tossed Tink over his shoulder and strode back outside, giving me a warning look.

Message received, asshole. Disarm the Valkyrie.

"*You,*" Tris spat, leveling her fury in my direction now that Tink and Bram were gone. "How *dare* you show up here after everything you've done? Was my note not clear enough?"

"Oh, it was pretty clear," I replied, holding my hands up in surrender as I crossed the little living room to where she stood in the kitchen. "But surely you knew I had to make sure you were okay, right? I couldn't just trust that you were safe all alone... especially when I knew you weren't with Grimaldi anymore."

Her face twisted up with anger and I reached out to slide the remaining plates away. "As if I'd go back there," she snarled. "That old fuck has no leverage on me anymore. What's he going to do, hurt the people I love? Oh wait. You already did that."

My jaw tightened as I rounded the counter, stepping closer to her. "Tris... you know that's not what happened." Or, I really fucking hoped she knew. She must, or she'd have sent the cops to my place the minute she left last night.

"Do I?" she asked in a gut-wrenchingly broken voice. "Because last I checked, you're the cause of all of it."

I blew out a breath, nodding as I stepped closer still. "You're right. I have a lot of blame in this, and believe me when I say I regret most of what's happened. But I would *never* have hurt Nelson. I had nothing to gain by doing so, and even if I had... it wouldn't be worth it. The idea of putting such pain in your eyes makes me want to die."

A flicker of uncertainty crossed her angry expression, and I took a risk by gently touching her cheek. She stiffened, jerking away, and I bit back my disappointment.

"What I *know* is that everything has turned to shit since the moment you came to town. This fucking *Game* must have one hell of a prize because everything and everyone is expendable to ensure you win. That's right, isn't it? You didn't come back after discovering my forgery because you *felt bad*. You came back because the Game wasn't over, and now it seems that destroying *my whole life* is just collateral damage. You are the *worst* thing to ever happen to me, John Smith. I hate you more than words can ever express."

She didn't yell those cutting statements, but they hurt that much more for the quiet calm behind them. The cold resignation underlining her truth made my chest tight and my pulse race with anxiety.

I wasn't at risk of losing... I'd already lost her.

She waited, staring, while I drew a slow inhale and bit my tongue. She didn't need my quick-tempered reactions right now, so I resisted the urge to argue. "Maybe you do," I said softly instead, "and you have every right to feel that way. I deserve it. But unfortunately, you're stuck with me, Venus."

Her eyes narrowed in suspicion. "Why?"

"Because I made a promise to Nelson, to keep you safe. I intend to see it through, whether you like it or not."

Shock made her inhale sharply, then her eyes darted to one of the knives just out of reach on the bench. Was she about to try and stab me again? It wouldn't shock me if she did. But then her gaze dropped to the floor and her shoulders trembled. Was she... crying?

"Tris—"

"No!" she shouted, looking up at me with eyes overflowing with grief. "You don't get to pull that card, John. How dare you use Nelson to *guilt* me when you're the reason he's dead? He's *dead*. He isn't here anymore to see you break that promise, so just fucking *leave me alone!*" Her voice broke and a sob hitched in her chest, tears pouring down her cheeks in twin streams of agony and loss. "Leave, John. Go play your game and forget we ever met."

I shook my head, unable to help myself. I cupped her face in my hand, my thumb swiping through the tears on her cheek. "Tris... you can hate me, you can hurt me, I deserve it all. But I will never leave, and I couldn't forget you if I tried."

What little control she was clinging to snapped and she fell to pieces. I wrapped my arms around her small frame, holding her close as she sobbed with soul-shredding agony. When her knees buckled, I gently sank to the kitchen floor with her, pulling her into my lap.

Whispering my apologies over and over, I stroked her hair and hugged her close. Held her safe in my arms. Hate me all she liked, I'd never let her go.

Tris

ten

Once again, I woke up in a strange bed with no recollection of how I got there. Once again, I was fully dressed, groggy, and my head hurt. One small mercy, this time, was that I hadn't been handcuffed to anything, and when my head cleared a little more, I realized where I was. Bram's cabin in the woods.

"Holy fuck," I whispered, running my hands over my face in an attempt to clear the haze. My sinuses ached and my eyes were hot and gritty, the result of my breakdown in John's arms.

For a moment I just lay there staring up at the ceiling, trying desperately to put all the broken parts of myself back together. Everything still hurt—the wounds were all so raw and fresh—but beneath it all my heart felt ever so slightly lighter. Like I'd somehow started healing, simply by crying.

The quiet hum of voices in the living room reached my ears, and a spark of anger rekindled in my chest. Tink was out there, talking to John and Bram. My shit aim with those plates had me all kinds of irritated as I lay there listening to the muffled voices. Listening to her laughing at something Bram said.

I wish I'd hit her square in the face with one of those plates.

We had a whole lot of unresolved *shit* that needed dealing with, but no matter how much I tried to talk myself into it, I didn't move. My whole body ached with exhaustion, and even lifting my hand felt like I was fighting against a lead weight. Maybe if I closed my eyes for a little longer...

"...she's still asleep," someone whispered a moment before the bedroom door clicked shut and footsteps faded away. Was that John? He hadn't been in here before; he'd been out with Tink and Bram.

Confused, I blinked my gritty eyes open to find the room bathed in a warm red-orange sunset. What the fuck? How long had I just napped for?

The pillow beneath my cheek was damp, and I grimaced as I wiped my mouth. Drooling. So sexy.

Groggy and disoriented, I forced myself to sit up so I

couldn't be tempted to slide back into sleep. The fuzziness told me I'd been asleep *way* too long, and I desperately needed a shower. And to pee. Man I needed to pee. Groaning, I wrapped the blanket around my shoulders and shuffled to the door.

John's voice murmured somewhere nearby, but it sounded like they were maybe in the kitchen so I could probably get into the bathroom without being seen. Thank fuck for small mercies, because my temper was even shorter than usual when I needed to pee.

The door slammed a little harder than necessary behind me as I shut myself in the bathroom, and I flipped the lock to prevent any unwanted visitors. The conversation in the kitchen paused, but I pushed John from my mind as I took care of business.

"Tris?" he called through the door a moment later. "You okay?"

"Define *okay*," I muttered, finishing up and flushing. He wouldn't have heard me, though, so I sighed and raised my voice. "Fine."

There was a slight pause before he replied, and I could picture his frustrated scowl as clear as day. "Do you need anything?"

"A time machine would be great," I snapped back, my filter officially not working. This time he must have heard me because his low, sexy laugh trickled through the door.

"I'll start searching the internet for one. In the meantime, clean clothes might help?" His question held such a potent taste of hope, it made my throat tighten. He was offering more than just clean *clothes*.

I leaned my hands on the edge of the basin, staring at my bedraggled reflection. "Sure." Then winced at my own bitchy tone. "Thanks, that'd be good."

John didn't respond for a moment, and I tipped my head to listen. "I'll leave them out here," he finally said. "Take your time. Bram is cooking dinner now, but he said it'll be half an hour at least."

I didn't reply, because all the emotions of our argument were welling up inside me once more, and all I could do to keep it at bay was hold my breath. His footsteps moved away from the bathroom door a moment later, and still I continued holding my breath, just staring at my pained, panicked eyes in the mirror. Fuck I looked terrible.

My lungs burned and my fingers tingled, and I released my breath in a gust. The tears were no longer threatening, though, and I was notably calmer.

Shower. I needed a shower.

I cranked the water on and shed my borrowed clothes while waiting for the hot water to kick in. Now that John had mentioned dinner, my stomach was gurgling and twisting, so I found myself hurrying as I scrubbed my tired body with the lemongrass soap and a rough loofah.

When I was surgically clean, I stepped out and wrapped myself up in one of the old lady pink towels. I'd washed my hair, so I wrapped that up in another of the pink towels before unlocking the door to find the promised clothes.

A small stack sat right there outside the door, and I scooped them up quickly, shutting the door once more to keep the steam inside. To my surprise, it wasn't another set of men's sweatpants and a t-shirt. These were brand new women's clothes in my own size. John must have gone into town while I slept?

As mad as I was, I had to admit it was a thoughtful gesture. With fresh, well-fitted underwear and bra I instantly felt more human. Less broken. With each item of clothing I put on, I rebuilt my walls and strengthened my mind. Buttery soft leggings hugged my legs like a security blanket, and the thin tank top in royal blue made my eyes seem brighter than usual. He'd included a cozy knitted cardigan in a charcoal gray, and a pair of warm socks, which I also put on.

I did the best I could to dry my long hair with a towel, then tossed it over my shoulder with a sigh. There wasn't much I could do for the tangles, but at least it was clean. It was incredible how much clean hair could do for one's mental health.

With nothing left to do, I sucked in a breath of courage and stepped out of the bathroom. A half dozen more cautious steps carried me out into the living room, and I folded my arms protectively around myself as John met my eyes.

Damn him for making my heart flutter. The thing between us was *dead*. He'd seen to that himself. Dead and decayed. Or, it should be.

"Tris, good timing," Bram called from the kitchen with a smile on his face. "I was just about to call you for dinner." He held up his oven-mitted hands like that was proof he'd been cooking.

I sent a small smile back to Bram, scuffing my warm, socked feet across to where John was setting the dining table. "It smells good. I can't believe I slept so long."

Tink cleared her throat dramatically, glaring at me from the kitchen. She'd been helping Bram with dinner but now she looked like she was considering attacking me. Hypocrite.

"Tris, I hope you're feeling better after your sleep," she commented with heavy sarcasm. "Do you have anything to say to me?"

I nearly choked on her audacity. "I really don't. Do

you?" I tilted my head to the side, my eyes narrowed as I glared back. "Anything you need to *confess*, maybe?"

Tink's eyes widened and her brows dipped with a slight frown. "Um, no?" She glanced at Bram with confusion and he wisely dodged eye contact as he carried a dish of parmesan roasted chicken breasts to the dining table. "Is this about the frying pan thing?"

"What frying pan thing?" I asked, looking to John for an explanation. Why I thought he would give me more honesty than Tink, I couldn't explain. No one told me the truth these days.

He just gave a small shake of his head. "Doesn't matter. That's not it, Tink."

"Does anyone want some wine?" Bram offered, pulling a bottle out of the fridge. "It's a Canadian *Gewürztraminer,* which should pair well with the chicken. Tris?" He poured a healthy-sized glass and held it out to me, which I accepted eagerly. Thank fuck Bram bought wine. At least a little buzz could take the rough edges off the awkward situation I'd landed in.

I took a small sip to taste the vintage first and was pleasantly met with florals and lychee undertones. "Yum," I commented, taking a bigger sip.

Bram smiled. "Thanks, it's one of my favorites out of Okanagan Valley."

"Hello? Can we focus? Tris tried to kill me with

crockery yesterday and I think I deserve an explanation," Tink snapped, folding her arms over her chest with a sullen scowl.

"No, you *deserved* to catch more than just a scratch from a broken plate, you backstabbing bitch," I shot back, licking my lips. Just two sips had calmed me already. "Were you ever planning to tell me how you signed over my home and all its contents to whoever is running this stupid game of yours? Or did it totally slip your mind that you handed a bunch of *literal thieves* some of the most valuable paintings on Earth when they weren't *yours* to hand over?"

Okay. I was a *little* calmer, but it was still just wine. It wasn't fucking magic.

Tink's mouth fell open and her cheeks flushed pink. Then she scowled. "Obviously I had no idea what you were hiding inside your freaking apartment, Tris, or I would have thought of something else! But as it was, they had me on the spot, and I needed to give them *something*."

"So you gave them my home? What the fuck, Katinka? I thought we were friends!"

Her expression was pained. "We are. Tris... I'm sorry. I had *no* idea... I just thought it was a nice apartment, and you don't own a car, so I couldn't think what else would be accepted as reasonable collateral by the

93

Council. And it was that or risk them silencing you for the remainder of the Game."

That was something Carol had mentioned, but I hadn't delved deeper into it at the time. Unease tightened my belly. "How do they do that, exactly?"

Tink shrugged helplessly. "I have no idea! But we've all heard rumors, and I didn't want to risk it. Tris, I am *so sorry*. If I'd known..."

"We did go back to try and recover the art before the police arrived," John said softly, gesturing for me to take a seat at the table. I hesitated a moment, but the low growl in my stomach pushed me forward. "Unfortunately, the Game Council beat us to it."

This wasn't totally new information for me, since Carol had already assured me she was keeping my *assets* safe. I sighed heavily, running a hand over my wet, tangled hair. Tink hadn't known what was lurking behind the false wall of my apartment. She didn't know how badly she'd fucked up. But the damage was done now.

"If your Game Council had never accessed my apartment, they would never have found *Poppy Flowers*. They would never have been able to set their trap. Nelson wouldn't be dead. That whole chain of events is on you, Tink." I kept my eyes on the table as I made my accusation, a hollow feeling gnawing at my insides. I wanted it to be all her fault, but in reality it was mine. I should have given that fucking painting back weeks ago.

Tink took a seat at the table across from me and nodded. "I know. I'm sorry, Tris. I fucked up. But we will make sure every single painting gets returned when the Game is over, even if we have to steal them back. Right, John?"

He murmured his agreement, and I yawned. How was I seriously still tired after sleeping through a whole day? Maybe more wine would help. The logic was flimsy but good enough, so I took another long sip.

"So. How do we finish the Game, then? How do I get my life back to the way it was?" As much as that was even possible now. Without Nelson... *and Hank*... Hank's life was even more destroyed than mine. He'd blame me. It was my fault. *Where even is he right now?* Were they questioning him? Was he mourning—alone? I couldn't think about this. I couldn't think about him. I couldn't think about any of it.

There was a pause so silent I could hear the wine swirling in my glass as I rolled the stem between my fingers, then John gave a confused hum. "We?" he repeated. "You want to play the Game?"

I shrugged. "Want to? No. But I already am, right? My collateral has been taken and I'm in the know... whatever I can do to end this shit and move on, I'll do.

Besides, I want to know who *actually* killed Nelson—because I don't believe you that it was Hank. So it seems like I don't have much of a choice."

I met John's worried gaze with my own calm, decided eyes. He stared back at me for a long moment, like he was trying to assess whether I was serious or not, but when I gave nothing back he broke eye contact to scrub his hand over his face. "Bram, I think we need something stronger than wine."

As much as I hated to agree with anything he—or Tink—said right now, I agreed with *that*.

Working together was going to need a lot of alcohol.

John

eleven

The more Tris drank, the more the ice between us melted. I saw it, and so did Tink apparently, because she kept refilling Tris's glass even after I tried to *gently* suggest she'd had enough. I wasn't dick enough—or brave enough—to say it to Tris herself, though, so had to bite my tongue and let it play out.

By midnight, Tink and Tris were equally drunk and had seemingly let bygones be bygones. I watched them as I sipped my tea, trying not to smile as Tris told Tink how pretty she was while petting her hair.

"Help me with this, would you?" Bram prompted, tossing the sofa cushions off to reveal the folded bed beneath.

Nodding, I placed my teacup down on the table and

moved to grab the other side of the heavy frame. It was an old one, with stiff hinges, but after some muttered curses we managed to get it set up, and Bram pointed me in the direction of the linen closet to grab sheets.

By the time we had the sofa bed fully set up, Tink was snoring loudly from her curled up position on the floral armchair. Tris was nowhere to be seen, but a moment later I winced as the sound of explosive vomit echoed from the bathroom.

"Yikes," Bram commented, shaking his head. "Better out than in, I always think." He scooped Tink up from her chair and laid her down on the sofa bed. Ever so gently, he unzipped her hoodie and stripped it off her before tucking blankets up to her chin.

"Do you have any aspirin?" I asked, while pouring two huge glasses of water. Bram pointed me toward the medical kit, and I set up a couple of aspirin and a water beside Tink's snoring form. Then I carried the same through to the bathroom where I found Tris curled up on the tile floor beside the toilet.

I couldn't help smiling, and she cracked an eye right at that moment, catching me.

"It's not fucking funny," she muttered, snapping her eye shut again as she held her stomach. "Why aren't you drunk?"

Crouching down, I brushed her hair off her face.

"Because I switched to tea about two hours ago when Tink started pouring tequila shots."

Tris moaned, her face gray. "Don't say that word."

I chuckled. "Are you done in here?"

She cracked an eye again, probably thinking about whether her stomach was sufficiently empty. Then she nodded. "I think so. I feel a little better already."

"Come on, let's get you into bed to sleep it off." I gently, slowly, lifted her to her feet then scooped her up into my arms with my hand grasping her ass. Her legs wound around me, and she gave a moan as her head rested against my neck. I wished the circumstances were different, but I wasn't complaining.

Gritting my teeth against the desire to kiss her shoulder, I carried her into the bedroom and tugged the blankets back with my foot to lay her down. She rolled her head against the pillows and glared up at me.

"There's water," I told her, gesturing to the nightstand. "And aspirin."

"So?" Just the barest hint of belligerence scraped over that single syllable.

"You might need it in the morning. Could help if you took it now."

"No." Then she rolled over and gave me her back.

That syllable was less belligerent and far more sulky.

I had to suppress a smile as I moved across the hall to shut off the light in the bathroom.

"John..."

I flicked off the light. There was still a small light on the nightstand, but it was dim. While I preferred the dark, I didn't want her to bump into anything if she needed to get back to the bathroom. "I'm still here."

"Why?"

The whole host of topics she could be asking about paraded through my head, but I wasn't going to play dumb. "Because this is where I want to be." I closed the bedroom door, shutting out Tink's snores.

"No," she protested and tried to flop on her back as I circled the bed to the far side. "Why me? Why did it have to be me? Why couldn't you have fucked Naomi? Or maybe Helen? Or—whoever? Why did it have to be me to get to *Poppy Flowers*?"

"Because you're beautiful and stubborn and willful and absolutely captivating." Rolling onto my side on the bed, I faced her, and she scowled at me. The scrunch of her nose and the tense lines of her forehead were adorable. "Because you made me chase you, Venus."

"Bullshit," she mumbled. "You just wanted some ass and some art, and I'm the gullible bitch who bought your crap. Then you kept stealing all my vibes. You suck."

"Yeah." I could admit that. "I did steal them. But sex with you wasn't part of the plan, Venus. It was just— fuck, it's an addiction. You've broken me for anyone else." Maybe I shouldn't admit that. "And I don't care how long it takes me, but I'm going to win you back."

"I'm not a prize. Not a damn game." Then she flailed out with a hand and smacked my arm. The blow lacked any kind of force. "You took everything..."

Capturing her hand, I pressed a kiss to her palm, and she scowled at me again, her expression trapped somewhere between scowl and pout.

"That's my hand."

"I know. You threw it at me so I'm keeping it." The fact her expression faltered and she blinked had me biting back laughter. It confused her, and I didn't want to confuse her. I also refused to take advantage of her inebriated state.

"I want it back."

"You can have it back in the morning, I promise."

"What do you promise me?" That question drew some blood. Welts across my soul because what did it mean to her?

"I promise you," I said against her fingertips, pressing a kiss to each of them as I spoke, "that I will give you your hand back in the morning. That I will be here. That I will keep you in the loop on the Game. That I will be at your side every step of the way. That I will get you justice for Nelson and your art back."

Tears welled into her eyes. "Why should I believe you?"

"You don't have to right now." As much as it killed me to admit it. "You don't. I'll prove it to you by keeping those promises."

Suspicion crept into her eyes. "I don't trust you."

"That's understandable," I agreed, tracing the outline of her fingernail with my thumb. "But it just means I have to try harder to earn that trust back."

She snorted, her eyes closing. "Back? You never had it. I never trusted you. There was always something sneaky about you, and now I get it."

As entitled as she was to her anger and resentment, the accusation of *sneakiness* kind of stung. "That's fair, I guess," I admitted despite my bruised ego. "I was never telling you the whole truth before. I am now."

She didn't reply for long enough that I figured she'd fallen asleep. But then her dark lashes fluttered open once more and her pale blue gaze seared into my eyes. "I don't like you."

Ouch. I licked my lips to refrain from arguing with her. This wasn't the time. "You don't?" I asked instead. She shook her head. "What don't you like about me, Venus?"

She dragged her lower lip between her teeth as she drunkenly considered my question, and I tried desperately not to stare at her mouth. Tris had the most perfect pout of any woman I'd ever met. She was a perfect artist's muse, so it was unsurprising she'd painted herself in her award winning piece.

"I don't like that you keep stealing my good vibes," she said after a moment. Then her lush lips curled into a smile and she giggled. "Literally *and* metaphorically. You know how embarrassing it is to be buying a new vibrator every second day in a town like Whispering Willows? There is *one* toy shop, John. One."

I had to grin at that. It really had become a favorite pastime to steal her toys, especially knowing how determined she was to replace them. Which meant she used them *a lot*. Crap, now I was picturing that and getting hard.

"Is that the only reason you don't like me?" I asked, instead of apologizing. Because I promised not to lie to her anymore, and I was *not* sorry.

Tris mumbled a sleepy *no*, and closed her eyes once more. "You have shitty taste in art," she informed me with a yawn.

That one confused me only a moment before I remembered our very first meeting, when I'd so boldly insulted her *Literary Woman* painting. "Ah, Tris my love, we both know I didn't mean what I said back then. Your work is breathtaking, even more so for the subtle middle finger to the dean."

She huffed, her brow creased. "I have more things I don't like about you. At least ten. I just can't remember them all right now."

"At *least* ten?" I mused, studying her face. The scowl had relaxed even if her nose was still scrunched up. I should probably let her go to sleep, but she was *talking* to me. "Well, the vibes would be one," I offered. "The painting is two..."

"You gaslit me," she mumbled, her eyes opening and that one wasn't as funny. The sadness in her eyes was pure reproach. "You kept breaking into my apartment and you pretended like I didn't lock the door."

"Yeah," I said softly. "I did do that."

She sighed.

"I'm sorry if that made you feel bad." She didn't need to prompt me for that one. "It was a shitty thing to do and I was pretending to not be who I was, but there were nights where sometimes I just wanted to see you."

That earned me a thoughtful look. "Your penmanship is shitty."

I laughed. I couldn't help it. "Serial killer scrawl, that's what you called it."

"Yes," she confirmed and the corners of her lips twitched. "S'not funny."

"It's a little funny."

"You could at least *agree* with me," she scolded and she sounded so genuinely scandalized and put out that I had to bite back another laugh.

"Sorry, Venus, I promised you no more lies. If I agreed that it wasn't funny, that would be a lie."

"Pffft," she dismissed my logic, but that hint of a smile was back.

"So that's four. What's five?"

A yawn cracked her jaw and she curled her fingers around mine as I continued to stroke them gently. It was the first time she'd actively tried to make contact that didn't involve hitting me.

"Um...I thought you were my teacher."

"I was your teacher," I said.

"But you lied about your credentials."

"Actually," I corrected. "I didn't. I do teach."

Surprise danced through her eyes as they rounded. "But I thought you were a thief."

"I can't be both?" I challenged. "You're an incredible student, TA, *and* master forger. How are you all three?"

Her mouth opened then snapped closed again after a moment. I pressed a kiss to her fingers and she sighed.

"So what's six?" If I had to pull them all out, I would.

I couldn't fight what I didn't know, and I needed to know.

"I don't remember," she mumbled and then used her free hand to rub against her face. "I'm tired."

"Then I'll let you go to sleep, Venus."

"You should go," she told me.

"I can't." That got her eyes wider and she stared at me again.

"Why not? This is my bed—well, not my bed, but the bed I'm using. You can sleep on the floor."

I gave her hand a gentle squeeze. "I have your hand. If I have to sleep on the floor, then so do you. I don't want you to sleep on the floor." The logic would not have worked on a sober, furious Tris, but wine-drunk, soft Tris?

"Oh," she said with a sigh. "Fine. You can sleep there. But no funny stuff."

"Yes ma'am." But I wasn't promising. Not making a liar out of me.

"And I hate you." The declaration didn't carry that much heat or sting. If anything it was a mumbled afterthought and a soft snore escaped her.

"I know," I whispered, stroking a hand over her hair as she curled into the pillow. "I know."

Tris

twelve

S omething had died inside my mouth. It was the only logical explanation for why my tongue tasted of decomposition and my breath could kill sixteen clowns. Clowns—I imagined—were otherwise indestructible. I barely even opened my eyes as I clambered out of bed and stumbled toward the hallway and the bathroom, smacking my elbow on the doorframe as I went.

"Ow," I moaned, supporting my weight with a hand on the edge of the vanity. Water would help the crime scene in my mouth, surely. And then toothpaste and—"*Fuck*." I didn't have a damn toothbrush in this cursed cabin, did I?

Dropping heavily to my knees, I yanked the cabinet open to search for a spare.

"Are you okay?" John asked, making me startle hard enough to bump my head.

"Fine," I growled back, my mood as foul as my breath.

He hummed a thoughtful sound then tugged open one of the drawers. "Looking for one of these?" He offered me a brand new toothbrush and toothpaste tube. "I picked them up for you yesterday with the clothes."

I snatched them and heaved my aching body back up to standing. "Thanks," I grunted, avoiding eye contact as I ripped the packet open. He was shirtless, wearing just his jeans, and even those weren't done up. How was that playing fair? I was one brain fart away from throwing myself at him simply because I was horny. Because I was. Really fucking horny. I really should have thought that through before drinking so much because it'd been *way* too long since I'd last orgasmed.

Orgasms—self-made or assisted—did wonders for a hangover.

"Why were you muttering about killing clowns when you woke up?" he asked, leaning one of those tree trunk thick biceps against the doorframe while I brushed my teeth.

Hell, I wasn't even brushing, I was scrubbing.

108

Attempting to exorcize the demon shit stuck to my tongue. Had I vomited last night? Yep. Yeah, I definitely had. The memory surfaced hard enough to make my stomach contract.

"Because," I mumbled eventually, spitting out a mouthful of toothpaste foam and rinsing my mouth with water. "They're tough motherfuckers. Everyone knows that."

John's brow quirked, and my heart raced as he met my gaze in the mirror. Fuck him for being so handsome. I frowned back at him, trying to remember what we'd talked about after he'd put me into bed. I knew we'd talked, and I recalled feeling... *warm*. Calm and content. Not a feeling I ever expected to experience with John again.

"Did you think of the other four?" he asked when I spent way too damn long staring at his reflection. I blinked, confused, and his lips curled in a smile. "Reasons why you don't like me," he reminded me, and it unearthed some hazy recollection of our conversation. How I'd been listing reasons why I disliked him. Oh, good. At least I wasn't swooning and begging for dick while drunk.

I flicked my gaze away from him, focusing on rinsing my brush and wetting a washcloth to clean my face. "Maybe," I muttered rather than answer while I sorted through the vague memories of what I'd listed off the night before. Fuck, my head hurt. Lowering the washcloth, I found him still there, hanging out. "Are you waiting on something?"

"Hmm-hmm," he said.

At my raised eyebrows, he nodded to the toilet and then tracked his gaze back to me.

"But I can wait, Venus. I'm fine just being right there."

He was fine. Too damn fine. He also smelled good. How the fuck did he manage to *smell* good? Masculine. Heat. Warmth.

Right, the reasons I hated him. "You stole my vibes, asshole."

"We covered that. It was right up at the top." The ease of his admission and the grin on his face should have infuriated me. It did—right? I considered my reaction. He wasn't denying it, but he also looked pleased with himself.

Dragging my gaze off of him, because clearly, staring at him was *not* helping me think, I eyed my own reflection. With some care, I tried to finger comb the absolute bird's nest my hair had become. There were tangles on my tangles. Shit, I'd showered, washed my hair and then—nothing. No brush and then sleeping on it.

Way to go, Tris, I complimented myself. Now I'd probably have to saw through it. I checked the drawers, but there was only a comb. Yeah, that wouldn't work. There was a package of scrunchies, so I dragged the hair back and tied it up. It would still look like a thicket, but hopefully less of a horrible one.

"You're enjoying yourself," I said before flicking a look to John, and he frowned. "This Game you're playing. Chasing me. Even this in the bathroom right now—you're enjoying it." Some resentment crept into my voice. His gaze lasered onto mine and I didn't try to look anywhere else. "You snuck into my apartment that last night—*after* you stole the painting, to what? Have one last bang for the road?"

Was I retreading old ground? Yes. Did I care? No.

"You have made this all about you. But you—*hurt* me. Maybe I took the painting. Maybe I did that. Maybe it was in my loft because Nelson and I were keeping it." Nelson loved that damn painting. I was starting to wish I'd never seen it. "But you hurt me, John. All of this...and the damn thing is, I want to trust you, I want to believe you. I shouldn't and I'm insane because your dick is amazing but dick doesn't fix everything."

There was no smile on his face now, but there was a measure of *something* moving in his eyes that told me to continue.

"So, yes, I hate you. I hate how you make me feel. I hate that I still want you. Most of all—I hate that I don't know how to make it stop."

He held my gaze, but didn't say a single word. Not a word to defend himself, to point out my own share of blame in the whole mess—which wasn't a small share, I could quietly admit to myself—or even to offer further apology. He just listened to what I was saying and took it in.

Part of me wanted him to react like an asshole, just to make it easier to shut him out. I wanted him to act like every walking red-flag ex-boyfriend would, so I could cut him off and tell myself I'd made the right choice.

But he didn't. He reacted... like a man in love. A man willing to *wait*, no matter how long it took, and a man prepared to put in the work to earn his forgiveness. That realization was tearing me up inside, because it was forcing me to acknowledge the sincerity of his *feelings* despite the insincerity of his words to date.

Swallowing hard, I turned away from the mirror and faced him. "Bathroom is yours," I said softly, like a peace offering. "I'm going to find some aspirin for my hangover."

He gave a slow nod, moving out of the doorframe to

let me pass. "Bedside table," he told me as I moved into the hallway, then closed the bathroom door between us.

For a moment I stood there, staring at the peeling paint of the door because the magnetic pull between us felt stronger than ever with a physical barrier in place. Like I wanted him to drag me back in there and bend me over the sink, convincing me to forgive him with every thrust of that perfectly thick cock.

But that was silly. Our problems couldn't be solved with sex, no matter how hot it'd be. That was like slapping a Band-Aid over an amputation and calling it good.

Still, try and tell my heated pussy that. Traitor.

With a groan of frustration, I went in search of the aspirin. It was where he said, sitting on the bedside table with a glass of water, so I gulped the pills down then went in search of coffee and breakfast.

As I padded into the kitchen, a loud snore from the couch made me hesitate. Then Bram appeared from around the corner and grinned. "You don't need to be quiet," he told me as I started to tiptoe. "You could *probably* drop a meteor on the cars out front and she wouldn't stir. Seriously, I've never seen a woman sleep so... uh..."

"Deeply?" I offered, fighting back a grin of my own. I

shouldn't make fun of Tink, but shit, she was making it easy.

"Yeah. Deeply. That's what I was going to say." Bram arched his brow and I chuckled in response. "How are *you* feeling this morning, Tris? Can I make you a coffee?"

Nodding enthusiastically, I followed him into the kitchen. "Yes, please. I don't feel *amazing*, if we're being honest this morning. We probably didn't need the tequila shots last night, huh?"

He laughed as he poured me a mug of freshly brewed coffee, then handed it over. It was black and bitter, but I wasn't in any position to judge. In fact, it was perfect for chasing away the phantom taste of tequila that'd just made my saliva glands freak out.

The rumble of Tink's snore almost made me laugh. She sounded like some old man. John came out of the bedroom—wearing a shirt thank fuck, because my traitorous body had been enjoying that view too much —and headed right for the coffee. Bram had the fridge open.

"Hungry?"

"I could eat," John said, then eyed me.

"Whatever you have that's greasy." Because that sounded good and between the coffee and imagining greasy food, my stomach actually gurgled with hunger rather than contract with illness.

"I can do some bacon butties," John said. He didn't even pretend to be quiet. "If you have any bacon."

"I got bacon, and bread," Bram told him, and the two of them started hustling around the kitchen like they knew what they were doing. John took a drink of his coffee before firing up the heat on the pans.

It wasn't long before the sizzling smell of bacon perfumed the air and I let out a happy sigh. Well, okay, maybe not happy, but my mouth was watering.

"I do not get how such a little body produces that much sound," Bram said, moving to stand next to me and drink his own coffee.

"No idea," I admitted, though John laughed.

"She can vibrate the walls and nothing wakes her up." He dropped a pan into the sink as if to make a point, and the clang had me wincing and my head aching. Though Tink didn't even twitch. John shot me an apologetic look, and I even managed to summon a smile.

It wasn't long before he set a plate in front of me with buttered toast with bacon stacked high in between the bread. The smell was fabulous. I didn't waste time thinking about it, I just bit right into it and let the mini-foodgasm detonate in my mouth. Oh, that was really good.

I made the mistake of flicking my gaze up toward John as I took another bite and the intensity in his gaze threatened to set me on fire. I sucked some of the bacon grease off my lip, then shoved more food in my mouth. Right, if my mouth was full, I wouldn't suggest morning sex to try and cure my hangover or whatever else was ailing me.

"Not bad," Bram said as he took a bite of his own. There was still more bacon, presumably for Tink, or maybe for seconds. I didn't look too close at it. John refilled my coffee and the three of us stood around the tiny kitchen, eating, drinking coffee, and being almost companionable in the silence.

A soft whirr sound. Just the faintest, muffled bump-bump went off, and Tink sat straight up and fished her phone out from the covers.

"That woke her up?" Bram said, staring at her in shock. I had to admit, I was a little surprised too. Because nothing else had.

John pulled his own phone from his pocket and grunted. "Eight o'clock."

"What happens at eight o'clock?" I asked, glancing from John to Tink, who was now sitting up and looking at her phone with an intense frown. Her hair, I was pleased to note, looked even worse than mine, and the creases down the side of her face suggested she had slept in the same position all night.

"New Game piece gets revealed," she announced,

rising to her feet without even a groan. Bitch. I bet she wasn't even hungover, too. "Or, sort of. They give us clues and a time limit and…" she waved her hand, tossing her phone onto the table and sliding into one of the vacant chairs. "Oooh bacon sandwiches. Yum. Bram, baby, coffee me."

Curiosity sparked, and I inspected the two of them in a new light. Were they fucking? The pink tint in Bram's cheeks suggested yes. Or if not already, then soon.

"So, what's the new piece?" I asked, steering the conversation back on track.

John tipped his head, his gaze intense. "Are you sure you want to—"

"I'm sure. What do we need to steal?" I grabbed more bacon before Tink could inhale it all and waited to hear that we had to steal a Rembrandt or Warhol or something.

Tink cleared her throat, looking at her phone again. "It's open to interpretation, but my best guess—based on what we know exists in Whispering Willows already—would be that fucking Nazi dude's missing sword. I can't remember what it's called, something German, but it's worth *huge* money on the weapons trade market. John, you'd know more than me about this."

"SS-Ehrendegen," he said. "Yeah, that's my guess, too."

Shock made me inhale a little piece of bacon, then nearly choke to death on it. What a way to go, asphyxiation by bacon.

John patted me firmly on the back, which did help slightly in clearing my airways, and I took a gulp of my coffee. "SS-Ehrendegen, huh? That's... different."

Tink just shrugged, not having noticed my reaction as she chewed her mouthful. "Not really. The Game has all kinds of shit. Paintings, jewelry, cars... even people sometimes. Weapons are far from unusual. We just have to work out where it is, how it's booby trapped, blah blah..." she trailed off again.

I got the impression it wasn't that she didn't want to explain, she just couldn't be bothered. Fair.

I settled back in my seat, holding my coffee to my lips as I listened to Tink and Bram speculate on the location of the sword, all the while knowing a whole hell of a lot more than I was letting on. Call me crazy, but they hadn't earned that much trust back. Not yet, anyway.

John

thirteen

Tris was hiding something, I was almost positive. She'd been quiet all morning and while I'd first shrugged it off as her hangover in full force, the longer it continued and the less interested she seemed with the whole heist plan, the more suspicious I grew.

When the Game text came, though, I'd been hesitant to jump into planning with Tink. The Game was the source of all the bad shit going on with Tris, so to continue playing so soon after what happened to Nelson? It didn't sit comfortably. But Tris insisted that playing the Game was the best way to end it, and to find Nelson's killer. And she was right.

Bram made himself useful by making coffee, tea, and

snacks throughout the morning, then cooking lunch for everyone around midday. It wasn't until we were all sitting down and eating the chicken pesto paninis he'd prepared, that Tink had connected the dots on why his presence felt strange.

"Bram..." Tink said. "Why are you still here?"

The younger man paused, food halfway to his mouth. "Um, should I not be? This is my cabin."

Tink narrowed her eyes. "Is it?"

Bram sighed and put down his lunch before shooting me a look. "As much as it matters for relevance, yes. Last I checked, John, I was doing my job." His brow lifted in a pointed expression. "You hired me to keep Tris alive."

A crash echoed through the room as Tris dropped her glass of water, but thankfully the cup didn't break. I still winced, though, because I basically lit the fuse myself on that truth bomb. Then again, I had promised her no more secrets.

"*You* hired Bram?" she squeaked, frowning.

Tink's smirk vanished before it even formed. Little shit wanted that out in the open. Fine. Better out than in. I nodded, accepting responsibility. "I did. I was worried Grimaldi would hold you responsible for *Poppy Flowers* so wanted to make sure someone was looking out for you."

"Bram's a mercenary, babe," Tink informed my girl. "He's like... hired muscle. Aren't you, hot stuff?" She squeezed Bram's biceps and he shot her a reproachful look. Yeah, he caught her less than subtle outing like I did. They were definitely fucking.

Tris licked her lips, then gave a shake of her head. "Okay. Thanks, I guess." She sent a small smile at Bram, whose expression softened and he nodded to her. What was *that* about? Had he needed to protect her more than I realized? A simmering rage threatened to boil over. Who had hurt her—or *tried* to hurt her?

"Back to my original point, though," Tink continued, waving her fork thoughtfully. "You're not playing the Game. Are you?"

Bram shook his head, answering her question. "No, I'm not. Nor do I have any interest, to be honest. I'm nowhere near stealthy enough for your line of work."

"Seems counterproductive for a mercenary," Tris murmured, her eyes on the water she was mopping up from her spilled glass. It was hard to tell if she was teasing or serious, but I agreed with her observation nonetheless. Then again, I always knew Bram wasn't *the best* the Guild could offer, he was just the only one available on short notice.

"Okay..." Tink continued, her eyes narrowed with suspicion. "But then surely we shouldn't be talking about anything Game related in front of you? Have we totally fucked the rules here or what?"

"Bram's mom is on your Game Council thing," Tris informed us with a shrug, "so I'm pretty sure he gets a nepotism free pass or whatever. Right?"

Well shit. *I* knew that, but how did *she*? Although now that made sense how she found out about Tink offering her apartment up as collateral. Bram hadn't told her——Carol had. And if anyone could make the rules up as they went along, it was Carol fucking Atwood.

Tink gasped dramatically, looking from Tris to Bram, then to me, and back to Bram. Then she scowled. "Seriously? I was the only one who didn't know? You guys suck."

I almost smirked. Served her right, wanting to throw me out there for the bus to hit, even if I needed it to hit me.

"I think maybe we're getting sidetracked here," Bram said, attempting to smooth things over. "You two were discussing how to get into Grimaldi's property again, and I was about to go for a trip to the store for dinner supplies."

"I'll come with you," Tris offered, pushing back from the table.

I gave her a sharp look, reminded again how

strangely quiet she'd been all day. "No, that's not a good idea. You're currently wanted for questioning, not to mention the Grimaldis are probably not happy with your sudden disappearance."

Tris grimaced, looking ill as she carried her plate and glass to the kitchen. "Good point. In that case, I might just go lie down for a bit. I'm still feeling like I got run over by a party bus then tossed into a washing machine on spin cycle."

She disappeared before I could argue, and I stared after her with confusion. Maybe it was just her hangover after all? Or maybe she was feeling off balance after our talk this morning? It hadn't escaped my notice when she'd eyed me with desire in the bathroom, but I could appreciate she was still working through her feelings of betrayal and distrust.

"I'm gonna go with Bram," Tink announced, grabbing her half-eaten lunch and taking it with her as she stuffed her feet into boots. "Have fun with the make-up sex, big guy. Or hate sex. Whatever."

I didn't comment as she sailed out the door with Bram like they'd coordinated it. Maybe they had. Whatever. If they were fucking, maybe it would give me some time with Tris. I stared at the closed bedroom door.

Let it go or pursue it?

After checking that the doors were locked and the system armed, I double-checked the windows. Bram had left the blinds open. I closed them. The location was remote. Still, I wanted to minimize any exposure.

At the bedroom door, I knocked once and then wrapped my hand on the handle.

"Come in," she called. Relief spilled through me at the welcome. She lay on top of the comforter, hands on her stomach and her eyes half-closed, but she didn't look remotely like she was going to sleep. "I wondered if you would follow me."

Brows raised, I closed the door and walked over to the bed. Hangover or not, she was still absolutely stunning, and I drank in her relaxed pose. "Do you want to read me in on what you're thinking?"

As much as I wanted to demand, I couldn't. I needed to keep the tone even for her as much as for me. "Where are Bram and Tink?"

Fair question.

"They left. Supply run." Probably to get laid too. "Don't really care about them at the moment, though."

"No?" The challenge was right there. Yes, she didn't trust me yet. But she wasn't throwing me out. Baby steps.

"No." I nodded to the bed and she planted her hands

against the cover and pushed herself up to a seated position before she motioned for me to join her. "Talk to me, Venus," I said, keeping it a request as I sat. Tempting fate, I wrapped a hand around her ankle.

"The SS-Ehrendegen," she said, the tilt of her lips forming an almost sad smile.

The Game piece. "Nazi sword." The provenance indicated it was once Himmler's, though there were rumors he'd traded his for Heydrich's, and that was way more than I wanted to know about those bastards. My grandfather had always been particularly interested in missing relics from the WW2 era, so he made me study them all. The fact that it was somewhere in the Grimaldi collection, though, was enough to make me shake my head in disgust. "What about it?"

She ran her tongue over her lower lip. It pulled all of my attention to the lushness of her mouth, but I yanked my gaze upward to fix on hers. The last thing she needed was me stripping her naked and trying to burn some of this need off no matter how good it would feel.

"You're sure we're alone?" She cut a gaze to the door. Was she thinking what I was thinking? No. *Fuck*. Focus, dickhead. She just wants privacy to *talk*.

"Yes, but if you want to check, I can wait." Trust had to be earned. Bridges needed work from both sides, and I needed to earn back her faith. Our sources indicated Grimaldi was keeping the sword within his family crypt, which was even harder to break into than his fucking art gallery. Maybe that was what she was worried about? "We still haven't quite figured out how to get into the Grimaldi tomb—"

"You don't need to get in the tomb." She pulled her knees up to her chest and wrapped her arms around them. The action pulled her ankle from my grip. "The real one isn't in Mr. Grimaldi's tomb."

The real one. I blinked.

One corner of her mouth kicked a little higher, but if anything her smile seemed—sadder. "Hank loves Nazi-era lost treasures. It—was his passion." She sighed. "So Nelson and I replaced it months ago."

Months.

"The one in the tomb is a forgery." I scrubbed a hand over my face and she nodded slowly.

"He really wanted it," she admitted and the elements of grief in her voice and her eyes resonated with me. "Nelson would do anything for him so...while I was earning my place with RBD—" She lifted her hands as if to say, *of course we did,* and I blew out a breath.

It made sense. When I'd been invited to dinner at Nelson and Hank's house, they'd used a Sutton Hoo replica to cut the cake. One of them—probably Nelson—

was a skilled bladesmith. "Tris, I'm so fucking sorry that all of this keeps happening to you—"

She sniffed, giving the barest of shrugs that she clearly didn't feel. The hangover disguised some of the pain, but this was a heartsickness that went too damn deep.

"I wish I could go back and change how I did all of this. Winning the Game has never seemed so important and so fucking not important before." Blowing out a breath, I shifted on the bed so I could extend a hand to her, and she eyed it for the longest moment.

The doubt and suspicion were well deserved. Today's Game piece was literally ripping open a wound she'd barely had time to treat much less heal.

"I want to hold you for a moment," I told her, offering her as much up front as I possibly could. "I need to tell you why it's all mattered. Why I did this. And you can choose to believe me or not. But—I want to tell you."

She deserved to know. "You're not going to ask me where the sword is?"

"Tell me, don't tell me—that is your choice, Venus." I kept my hand out there for her. "I'm not going to demand it of you. You don't owe me a damn thing."

Surprise made a brief appearance and then her palm glided over mine. I was up, tugging her to me, and then I had her wrapped up in my arms before I moved to take her spot on the bed and settled her in my lap.

Lips pressed to the top of her beautiful head, I took a deep breath. Eyes closed, I drank in her closeness for a few heady seconds. Then I said, "My grandfather's name was Christophe Valenshek. He—was the best man I've ever known. Smarter than everyone—so fucking smart. He lived for the puzzle and the hunt. He lived for me—his family. He took me in, he trained me—" I couldn't even begin to describe it all. "I had no idea how goddamn lonely I was before I met him. Before he took me away from the piece of shit who was my father and took over my education. Everything I am—it's because of him."

Tris said nothing, but her arms tightened around me. I'd told her a little bit about my family before, but I needed to reiterate which parts were true.

"This Game—it's not about just winning. Don't get me wrong, I've won the Game before and I fucking loved winning it. But this is the first one since he died and the winner—they get his legacy. To everyone else playing the Game, even to Tink, it's just about treasure. My grandfather found—and stole—a great deal of priceless items in his time, and that's what everyone else is hoping to win."

Tris shifted in my arms, tilting her head to look up at me. "Not you, though?"

I gave a sad smile. "Sort of. No, not really. If you'd asked me six months ago, then I'd have said I was just in it for the treasure, but if I'm honest *with myself* then no." I paused to take a breath, still processing the shift in my own head. "My grandfather always told me that a man's treasure was about more than just money. That sometimes what one person holds most sacred is less than worthless to another. The more I think about it, the more I'm convinced we aren't just playing for riches. It's about his *actual* legacy, his journals, his notes—his letters that he wrote to his one true love. He always fancied the idea that one day he might publish his own memoir, even though he never mailed his letters to Nadia. I needed to win this Game..."

I couldn't quite push the words out past the sudden lump. Tris pulled from me, and as much as I wanted to hold onto her, I forced myself to loosen my grip. But she didn't move away. Instead, she brought those delicate hands up to cradle my face and the fact she was crying hit me.

She was crying and so was I.

Fuck.

"I—I need to get those letters. Those pieces of him." Goddammit I missed the old man. "All my warmest moments with Christophe were when he told me stories of Nadia. I'd like to maybe give them to her, and let her know he never forgot. If Igor gets them, though..."

"Your father?" Tris asked softly. "What would he do?"

I gave a bitter laugh. "Burn them." Of that, I had no doubt.

Tris

fourteen

Frowning, I shifted my position once more, this time straddling his lap so I could face him fully. Wetness coated his cheeks, making his dark lashes stick together in clumps, but otherwise there was no sign of his emotion. No snotty nose or puffy eyes. It was totally unfair, but that was a thought for another time.

"Why would he do that?" I asked instead, focusing on the story he was sharing with me. Now, more than ever, I felt like he was actually being real with me. He'd meant what he said, while I was drunk and half asleep last night. No more lies, and no more secrets. "Surely he would know it'd hurt you?"

John drew a deep breath, his eyes sad on mine. His hands clasped my waist loosely and I ached to feel him hold me tighter once more. "He would. I'm sure you've already worked out the fact that Igor and I don't get along... That's largely due to my grandfather. It's a whole sad mess, to be honest. Boring long story short, Igor would gleefully burn those letters and erase any trace of my grandfather from existence."

I chewed the edge of my lip, thinking it over. What a spiteful human Igor must be, to deliberately hurt his son just to piss on the memory of his father. "Well, then we need to ensure he never lays hands on the Legacy, don't we?"

John's lips curled up in a smile. "I guess we do. For a while there I dismissed him as any real threat to the Game. Just an annoyance more than anything. But now... I have a bad feeling, and whether he's working with..." He trailed off, his expression pained.

I shook my head. "It's not Hank. I know what you *think* you saw, but it's not him. You were mistaken."

John didn't try to argue, but his face said it all. He thought I was just in denial, but he didn't know Hank like I did. Not only would he never hurt Nelson, he wouldn't betray *me* like that.

"You think I'm being naive by believing he's innocent," I said in the absence of John's response. "Will you tell me what exactly happened? Why you're so sure it was Hank, and not just someone who maybe looked like him at a glance?" I wanted to know, because if I knew the details I could point out why John was wrong. But at the same time, I really didn't want to know.

What if he wasn't wrong?

"Tris..." John whispered on a sigh, raising a hand to stroke the hair back from my face. "Venus, my love... I promised you I wouldn't lie, and I meant it. But I don't think you really want all the details right now. It's all still so raw and you're grieving... please don't ask me to hurt you any more than you already are."

Fuck. His refusal alone gutted me, so he was probably right. It was too soon.

Swallowing back my emotions, I nodded and lowered my gaze. Suddenly, I felt way too exposed. Too vulnerable and open. I needed my walls back and some distance between us.

"You're right," I managed to say even if it came out a little more guttural than I meant. Fuck, I didn't want to start crying again. When he lifted one of those huge hands to cup my cheek, it was everything I could do not to lean into the contact.

He wiped away the tears with his thumb, just a gentle stroke that had me lifting my gaze once more. He wore the faintest of smiles, one filled with open amusement and no small amount of affection.

133

It made my insides flutter far too much when he stared at me like that.

What it did to my pussy was downright embarrassing.

Clearing my throat, I reached for normal. Or at least as normal as we could get considering everything. "What?"

It came out a little harsher than intended, and maybe more than a little raw. But, I raised my chin. Maybe I was grumpy, but fuck, my heart hurt, and considering I wasn't alone in shedding tears—he clearly got it.

"You said I was right," he murmured, as if turning those words over and savoring them. That actually jerked a little laugh out of me and his smile grew. "I need to write this day down...Tris said I was right."

I snorted. "I said you were right about one thing."

"I only need to be right about one thing." The warmth in his manner wrapped around me almost as easily as he slid his hand from my cheek to my nape. Those fingers dug into the tense muscles, and I had to close my eyes as he found a particularly stubborn knot.

"Fuck..." The groan slipped out, but John only chuckled. "Tempting."

Don't respond, I told myself. *Just don't.* Didn't matter

that my whole body clenched at the way he delivered the word "tempting."

"Have I ever mentioned I like your accent?" In the great grand scheme of things, it wasn't the worst thing I could have said.

"A compliment," John said. "I'm right and you gave me a compliment..."

"I'm going to take it back."

"No, Venus," he whispered, his lips suddenly at my ear, and a shudder rippled over me. It shivered from the roots of my hair to my nipples all the way to my thighs. Awareness of how I was sitting on his lap became almost visceral. "No take-backs. Just do-overs."

It wasn't funny.

It wasn't.

Still, I laughed. "Do-overs? What kind of do-over? I'm pretty sure we've done each other over a few times."

"Hmm..." Just that single syllable and then he nipped my earlobe. It was a scrape of a touch, a bite and a tug. It was too much and not enough.

"Goddammit, John..." I fisted his shirt. He pulled back, and when I opened my eyes, his face was right there. The deep, dark brown of his gaze threatened to drown me, and I was ready to dive right the fuck in.

The whisper of his breath against my lips was right there. I started to ease forward and then stopped. The heat of him burned my hands, and he flexed his fingers against my hip and my nape.

"I need to know one thing..." I needed a lot more than that, but right now? "Right now I want to know one thing."

"What's that Venus?"

"What's your real name?"

He chuckled, his breath feathering my lips and making me moan internally. Shit's sake, I was getting all kinds of distracted. With monumental effort, I sat back to create some breathing space between us.

John must have known perfectly well what I was doing, because his lips tightened briefly and his hand slipped away from my nape once more. "Ivan," he said quietly. "Ivan Valenshek. Technically my surname doesn't follow the Slavic structure, but Christophe was arrogant enough, and British enough, to keep his surname for his descendants."

"Ivan?" I repeated, wrinkling my nose as I tried to make it fit the man in front of me. "Isn't that just *John* in another language?" His answering grin was pure mischief, and I rolled my eyes. "Okay, I guess that makes sense. Is it weird if I stick with John, though?"

He shook his head. "Not weird at all. I've used this alias for a *long* time, it feels more like me than my real name ever does."

I shifted my gaze away from his, inspecting the wall behind his head for a moment while I weighed my emotions and trust levels. He'd done so much to deceive me, and caused so much hurt... but there was no way I was getting through this alone. I needed him on my side.

More than that, I *wanted* him on my side.

"The sword. The SS-Ehrendegen. It's in a storage facility." I blurted it out quickly, before I could change my mind. "It's crazy secure, not even you could break into it."

John scoffed. "Wanna try me?"

My eyes darted back to his, and I gave a small glare. "No, I really don't. Hank, Nelson, and I designed it to be impenetrable, and more than that, if anyone *does* try to tamper with the locks it's set to incinerate the contents of the locker. Which would really suck because it's holding a lot more than just a dead guy's sword."

He gave a thoughtful hum. "You said you switched them months ago... Are you sure it's still in the locker?"

I wet my lips and nodded. "I'm sure. It takes three keys to access the locker. Anything less, and..." I made a whooshing sound, imitating flames with my hands. "We usually just store things there for a few months between heist and sale, so the trail runs cold on anyone following the items, but we also use it for storage of personal acquisitions. Which this one was, for Hank." A sour taste coated my tongue, and I frowned. "He said he was just waiting for the right buyer, but we always knew he would keep it."

"Three keys," John mused, his hands cupping my waist once more and his thumbs finding my bare skin above the waistband of my pants. A shiver of desire ran through me, and it took all my control not to grind against him. "One for each of you, I presume? So you all have to agree to access the locker? That makes sense... but how will *we* access it if you only have one key? Even if you know where Nelson's is, we don't have Hank's."

I tugged my lower lip between my teeth, heat rising in my cheeks. "Um, we don't need Hank's." John quirked one brow at me and I groaned. "I might have made a copy of his *and* Nelson's a while back... It was necessary because sometimes there were projects that Nelson and I grew a little too personally attached to and needed to, uh... you know..."

He absolutely did know, because the scandalized look on his face said it all. "Tristian Ives," he said in mock outrage, "you double forged some of the paintings and let Hank sell your forgeries while sneaking the originals into your personal hidden art gallery?"

"It sounds worse when you say it like that," I mumbled.

"I'm not judging you, Venus. I'm actually impressed.

So, you have all three keys?" His thumbs started stroking the skin of my waist again, distracting me.

I nodded. "Yeah... or I do in my apartment."

A startled look crossed John's face, but he smoothed it away quickly as he slowly shook his head. "That makes a lot of sense," he murmured, looking thoughtful. "So if we can get back into your apartment, we can get the keys and then just access the locker?"

"Yep," I replied, offering a sheepish smile. "Sorry I let you spend all morning plotting how to break into Grimaldi's tomb. Trust me when I say none of those plans would have worked." That tomb was where he kept the priceless artifacts he *didn't* want on display. It may look like a tomb—complete with stone angels guarding the entrance—but it was actually a vault more secure than a Swiss bank.

After having made the switch for the sword, Nelson, Hank, and I all agreed it was too dangerous to attempt a second time, which was why we stuck to the art gallery where I not only had access to the originals, I had time to really study them.

"You have nothing to apologize for, Venus," John murmured, his hand coming back up to cup the back of my neck. "We all have so much work to do in building trust, it's understandable you needed to think things over. Besides, if you're the only one with all three keys, and Hank is the only other person who knows the sword was switched, then we aren't in a hurry—except..."

"Except?"

His faint wince told me he didn't want to ask this next question. "Did Nelson also have—"

I sighed. "He did, but Hank didn't know. And Hank has no reason to go there. I can't imagine the sword is going to be the thing on his mind." It couldn't possibly be.

"Okay," he said, as if acquiescing. "Then we have time."

That was true. Tink had said they'd been given four days to complete this level of the Game, which sounded *insane* if they really were going to attempt RBD's tomb. But when it was just a matter of us collecting the keys, then driving to the locker... different story.

"Thank you," I whispered, raising my gaze back to his once more.

"For what?"

For so much more than I was willing to say. But I needed to answer him, so I just went with the first truth. "For trusting me with your name...John."

The pure mischief in his eyes dissolved into liquid heat. I couldn't tell you which of us reached forward first. Maybe we moved at the same time. Then his lips were on mine and I was drowning in the taste of him.

John

fifteen

Kissing Tris was like coming home. The soft caress of her lips against mine confirmed everything I'd been thinking for weeks. Somehow in the tangled web of lies, deceptions, and betrayals, I'd fallen hopelessly in love, and Tristian Ives was now the center of my universe. I existed only due to her gravitational pull.

I groaned, my fingers flexing in the back of her hair as I pulled her closer, devouring her with my kiss as she met me with equal fervor. For the first time since that heartbreaking scene in her apartment—when she'd walked in on me kneeling beside Nelson's dying form—I actually felt hopeful.

The sensible, cautious part of me knew that this was

too soon. She was still emotional and grieving. My sharing so much about my grandfather had peeled back a layer of the distrust still sitting between us, but it hadn't just magically healed all the wounds. But for all my best intentions, I couldn't push her away. I couldn't stop kissing her any more than I could stop breathing.

One hand still tangled in the silken strands of her hair, I slipped my other beneath her tank to cup her ribs. Unable to stop myself, my thumb brushed the underside of her breast through the thin mesh of the bra I'd bought her. In hindsight, I wished I'd forgotten to buy that particular item.

Tris gave the sweetest little moan as I sucked her lower lip, the sound shooting through me and landing right in my crotch. Fucking hell, I was so hard it hurt, and the way her ass shifted against my thighs said she was just moments away from grinding against me... and then I really would be lost.

If I was going to stop things before they got carried away—and I badly didn't want to—it needed to be now. Because if she got her delicate fingers wrapped around my cock, I'd probably have an aneurysm.

"Tris," I gritted out, barely giving a breath of space between our lips. "We should—"

"Shut up," she snapped, crushing another hard kiss to my lips, and I melted. It was so hot when she took charge, and the way her nails dug into my neck made me shiver with delight and anticipation.

I kissed her back, tangling our tongues together and cupping her breast firmly as she leaned into my touch. Fucking hell, she was perfect. Made for me.

"Damn it," I groaned, moving both hands to grip her waist. The only way I'd have the strength to press pause was if I created some *physical* distance, so I lifted her off my lap and quickly stood up before I could change my mind. "Tris—"

"What the hell, John?" she snapped, scowling up at me from the bed. Her lips flushed and her eyes glassy with arousal. Was I insane? Yes. But the trust between us was still so fragile, I couldn't risk her regretting things after the fact.

"Trust me on this one, Tris, I want nothing more than to rip your clothes off right now," I told her, reaching down to rearrange my pants. I tried to ignore the steel shaft of my dick, but the way her eyes followed my movement made me give it a little squeeze.

Tris licked her lips and I nearly died.

"So why don't you?" she asked, her voice husky with desire. Her eyes dipped back to my crotch where I was still grasping my dick through my pants, and I cursed all my own bad decisions.

If we were in a better place, this wouldn't even be a question. The fact that we weren't was entirely on me.

I forced myself to release my grip, or I really would lose my resolve. "If you ask me again tomorrow, you won't even be able to get the full question past those gorgeous lips before I have you naked and screaming."

Her brow dipped. "Tomorrow, but not right now? Why?"

I wet my lips. "Because honestly, right now I feel like I'd be taking advantage of you. Or taking advantage of the situation. We just went deep on the emotions and sharing our secrets, and it's totally normal, I think, to misplace grief and loss into sexual energy and I just... I don't want you to regret it the moment you climax."

Her eyes narrowed, and I got a trickle of dread that maybe I'd said the wrong thing. "You think you're taking advantage of me?" she repeated slowly, carefully.

I gave a cautious nod. "Yes. You're feeling confused and vulnerable right now, so maybe the emotions are heightened. And I want to earn your trust and love back before we go... you know..." I trailed off because her expression had shifted from burning desire to glacial frost.

"Let me get this straight," she said, clearing her throat as she pushed to sit up straighter. "I kissed *you* first. I made the first move to show *I* was ready to make amends *physically* because I'm insanely worked up and desperately need to get railed so hard I forget my name. But *you* think I'm too... emotional... to fuck."

Ah shit. I'd messed up. "That's not... no, that's not what I meant."

"But it's what you said," she pointed out. "Also, I'm here to point out that us fucking in no way translates to forgiveness for everything you've done. It's a *first step* but not the only step. But you clearly seem to think you know more about my fragile emotional state right now, John, so I guess we can put all those steps on ice for the time being, hmm?"

My mouth opened, but no words came out. How the *fuck* did I mess that up when I was trying to do the right thing by her? Trying to protect the thin, fresh bond between us?

Tris drew a deep breath, her frown set with frustration. "Sometimes, Ivan, a girl just wants to fuck. Sometimes, the best way to heal is to give your partner seven back-to-back orgasms and let her pass out from sensory overload. Sometimes... it's okay to think with your dick."

Okay. I'd definitely missed the mark. "Tris, I was just trying—"

145

"You were trying to piss me off by making me feel embarrassed about being horny as fuck, and you succeeded. Well, joke's on you big guy, I'm plenty capable of handling my own *silly emotions* all by myself." She gripped the hem of her shirt and lifted it over her head, tossing it aside.

My brain short circuited. "What are you doing?"

She quirked a brow, meeting my gaze as she unclipped her bra and freed those perfect breasts that I longed to hold. "Exactly what I said. Dealing with my own emotions." She tugged her pants down, taking her underwear along with them, and I bit back a groan. "You can leave now, John. I'd hate to make you uncomfortable in my vulnerable state."

"Tris..." I protested, unable to tear my gaze away as she spread her legs wide.

"If you're staying, you'd better be willing to participate in my therapy session." One of her hands cupped her breast, her fingers tweaking her nipple just like I ached to do. Every second I stood there watching, it became harder and harder to leave. "Well...?" she prompted, sliding her hand down to her exposed cunt and spreading her smooth lips apart.

I stopped breathing. Maybe I could just... lend a hand?

With a groan, I tore my gaze away and turned to the

door. "No, I can't. Ask me again tomorrow, *please* ask me again tomorrow, but right now after all we just shared, and the emotions and everything... I respect you too much to take advantage." Before I could lose my resolve, I stepped out into the hallway and shut the door behind me, creating a physical barrier to weaken her gravitational pull.

The thin door wasn't enough to muffle her reply though.

"What if I want to be disrespected, John? What if I'm lying here literally asking you to take advantage of me?"

Fuck.

My body moved before I even fully formed the thought, the door slamming back open as I crossed the floor to where she waited with two fingers already buried inside her own pussy.

"Did you just kick the door open?" she asked in a shocked squeak.

I shrugged, unbuckling my belt and jerking it free of my pants with one hand. "I have no idea. What did you just fucking say about being disrespected?"

Her lips curved in a wicked grin, her sultry gaze inviting. "Show me what you've got, Valenshek. Show me why I don't need to replace all those vibrators you stole."

I gave a chuckle as I freed my throbbing erection

from my pants and gave it a firm stroke. "You're never going to let me off the hook for that, are you?"

She gave a one shoulder shrug. "We'll see."

Any further smart remarks dissolved into a gasp as I batted her hand aside and slammed into her with one smooth movement. The tight grip of her body nearly made my soul leave my damn body, and I bit my tongue to bring myself back from the edge of a full blown blackout. It hadn't been *that* long, had it?

"Oh my god," Tris moaned beneath me, her fingers digging into my forearms where I braced against the headboard. "Thank you. *Thank you.*"

I wet my lips, drawing back to thrust back in and delighting in the way her body convulsed. "You're welcome?" I wasn't *super* sure what she was thanking me for, but I'd take it.

Tris gave a low chuckle, her breathing already ragged. "Harder. Fuck me harder, John. Make it hurt."

My brows raised, but shit if I wasn't a slave to Tristian Ives's every desire at this stage. If she commanded, I was here to serve. And right now, she didn't want me to make love to her. She wanted to get fucked. Hard and dirty. She wanted exactly what she'd said... to be disrespected. It was hot... but only because I was confident she knew that I loved her more than life itself at this point. Maybe she wasn't in a position to admit it, to me or to herself, but she knew. She *had* to know.

Releasing one hand from the headboard, I wrapped it around her throat and nearly stopped breathing when her pussy instantly contracted around my cock. "Hold on, baby girl, this won't be fast."

"No?" she squeaked, holding my wrist where I held her throat. She wasn't trying to push me away, just holding on. Good.

The corners of my lips curled as I met her excited gaze. "Definitely not." I drew out of her slowly, then slammed in *hard*, shoving her whole body up the bed slightly and making her eyes roll back in her head. "What did you ask for, Venus? Seven back-to-back orgasms?"

I thrust a couple more times, finding a punishing pace as she crossed her ankles behind me. "It was a figure of speech," she squeaked, moaning as her tits bounced violently with my thrusts.

A dark laugh rumbled out of me and I leaned down to kiss her, using my grip on her throat to hold her still even as I fucked her hard. "Tough. Count them, Venus, out loud. I reckon number one is almost here already."

Her pulse thundered under my fingers, and I traced

the outline of her gorgeous lips with my tongue, her breath mixing with mine like we were sharing one set of lungs. Perfect. One more thrust into her hot little body and she gave a shocked sound.

There it was. Fuck. *Fuck.* It felt so good. The way her inner muscles contracted, squeezing my dick like a velvet vice-grip...

Think unsexy thoughts, John. Dean Lawrence and his foot fetish. Yes, perfect, think about sweaty old Dean Lawrence with his little micropenis in hand, jerking off over pictures of my feet with purple sparkly nail polish.

"John..." Tris moaned, making my eyes pop back open. Thank fuck it was my raven-haired beauty spread out beneath me, but the visuals had saved me from blowing my load too soon. "Fuck you feel so good inside me."

Christ. How many times was I going to have to picture Dean Lawrence before I could let myself come? Too many. Way too fucking many, I already knew it.

"Tris..." I prompted, licking my lips as I seated myself deep and waited there.

She frowned her confusion for only a moment before her lips curled in a smile. "One," she uttered in a husky voice.

I winked. "Good girl. Let's do that again. By the time

we're done here, you won't even remember why you ever bought toys in the first place."

Or... maybe I'd buy her some replacements and see how she liked both at the same time. Oh, that was a good idea. I liked that. But first... a certain someone owed me six more screaming orgasms and I intended to collect every last drop, no matter how long it took.

Tris

sixteen

Lessons had been learned. Don't *joke* with John about multiple back-to-back orgasms because he would—and did—take it as a challenge. And if there was one thing that John'd always been honest about, it was his inability to back down from a challenge. It was—he told me some hours later as we lay in a tangle of sweaty limbs and a puddle of our combined explosive releases—the reason he'd started competing in the Game at such a young age. It was why he'd become so very good at what he did, because there had always been the underlying challenge to better his grandfather's legacy.

"You really loved him, didn't you?" I whispered, my cheek against his bare chest. He'd given me a moment of reprieve after orgasm number two, but only long enough to take all his clothes off. I liked a hot dirty fuck where neither of us even took the time to strip, but I *loved* being skin to skin with him.

His hum rumbled beneath my ear and his fingers stroked through my tangled hair. "Yeah. He was by no means a good man, and half his issues with Igor were of his own doing, but to me... he was my hero. As a child, I idolized him... then as an adult, I aspired to be just like him. To me, he was never anything but caring and supportive. I honestly felt like he was destined to live forever."

Grief and loss slid over my skin like a damp blanket, and I shivered. "That's how I feel about Nelson. Felt." The correction to past tense made my chest ache. "How I *felt...*"

John's arms tightened around me, his fingers that'd been playing with my hair now tangled in the matted mess. "It's okay to cry, Tris," he whispered in a hoarse voice. "It's okay to miss him."

I sniffled, feeling my tears pooling on his chest beneath my cheek. Part of me suspected he wasn't only reassuring me but himself too.

We lay together like that for a long time. I'd have happily stayed like that forever, but the sound of a car pulling up on the gravel driveway made me reluctantly sit up. Then I realized how badly I needed to pee, so I quickly grabbed my clothes and bolted for the bathroom before Bram and Tink could come inside and catch me making a nude dash.

"We're back!" Tink called out loudly just as I finished my pee. I grinned at how deliberately noisy she was being, like she knew what John and I had been doing in their absence. I flushed, then turned on the shower, because I was sweaty, sticky, and exhausted. Maybe a shower would wake me up a little.

"Got room in there for two?" John asked in a quiet rumble just after I stepped into the steamy cubicle.

I glanced over my shoulder, finding him leaning against the closed door, totally naked. His lips kicked up in a sly smile as I raked my gaze over him from top to toe, then tipped my head for him to join me. He stepped in, crowding me against the shower wall and cupping my face in his hand. He leaned my head back, bringing my lips to his, and I groaned into his kiss.

A sharp knock on the door made me gasp, and John released my jaw from his grip.

"These walls are thin!" Tink called out. "And we have a solid lead on the sword that we need to discuss!"

I rolled my eyes, chuckling. "No you don't." I said it quietly, and John shared my smile, kissing me again softly.

"Let me help you with your hair, Venus, then we can

go tell Tink about the change of plans." He spun me around with firm hands on my shoulders and nudged me into the shower stream to soak my tangled hair.

I didn't even give the smallest protest, I just let John gently manhandle me as he went to work giving my hair a thorough shampooing, then carefully worked conditioner through the lengths and used his fingers to work through some of the knots. It wasn't perfect when he eventually rinsed the conditioner out, but it was a hell of a lot better than it had been.

He didn't even try to slip a quickie in, despite how hard his cock had grown throughout the shower, and I wasn't sure if I was disappointed or relieved. I wanted him, but my pussy was throbbing and sore from overuse already. A break probably wasn't the worst idea.

"You good?" I asked in a sleepy voice as I stepped out to dry off. He stayed behind under the running water, his shoulders against the wall and his eyes closed.

"So good," he replied with a lopsided smile, one eye cracking to look at me while I toweled off. "I just need a minute."

I watched him in the mirror as his hand curled around his cock, and I gave a small groan. Shit. If I stayed to watch, I was definitely getting back in there.

"Um, I should get dressed..." I mumbled, unable to

155

tear my gaze away from his hand pumping up and down his thick length. "Unless...?"

He laughed, reaching forward to close the shower door. "Get dressed, Venus, before I bend you over that sink and fuck your ass."

My eyes widened and my lips parted, but Tink—with impeccable timing—knocked on the door again. "Hurry up, you two! Other players are already putting their plans in motion to break into Grimaldi's and if—"

She cut off as I pulled the door open and slipped out, towel wrapped around my body and my pile of clothes in my arms. "They won't get it," I told her with a small smile. "Promise."

Tink frowned, following me as I headed for the bedroom to dress. If I'd stayed in the bathroom even a second longer, I'd have begged John to follow through on his threat. And then probably regretted it for the next few days because ass-fucking needed lube and we had none.

"Ew, crack a window or something," Tink complained, gagging dramatically as she eyed the messed up bed. She crossed the room and grunted with effort as she hauled the old sash window up to let a breeze in. "What do you mean that they won't get the sword? Do you know something?"

I flashed her a quick grin as I tossed my towel aside

and pulled my clothes on. "Maybe."

Tink huffed, parking her hands on her hips. "Friends don't keep secrets."

A startled laugh barked out of me as I pulled my tank top over my wet hair. "Oh really? If that isn't the pot calling the kettle black, I dunno what is."

Tink had the grace to blush at that, and wrinkle her nose. "Point taken. Want a drink? We picked up more wine."

My stomach clenched, and I made a gagging sound. "No. No wine yet. Do we have any soda? Bubbles would really do wonders."

She nodded. "Sure do. I grabbed some burgers and fries for you, too. Lunch was delicious but way too fucking healthy for a hangover, am I right?"

"God yes," I groaned, following her through to the dining table where Bram was setting out greasy food on bone china plates.

"Tell us you were raised wealthy without telling us," Tink muttered under her breath, shooting me a grin as she sat down in front of a plate.

Bram didn't correct her, just giving a shrug as he held up two bottles of soda to give me options. I pointed to the Coke, and he poured me a glass. "Tink suggested this was better hangover food than the Thai beef salad I had planned."

"Tink was right," I replied, shoving five fries into my mouth and practically melting at the salty deliciousness.

"Tris has information for us," Tink told Bram, giving me a pointed look. "About the sword."

Bram gave me a surprised look. "Seriously? We just assumed you guys spent the last few hours fucking, not researching."

My cheeks heated, and I shot the two of them a hard look. "I could say the same. But this was, um, prior knowledge." I took a few big bites of my burger, washed it down with Coke, then started giving them very brief, bare-bones information about the *actual* location of the sword.

John joined us just after I started spilling my guts, taking the seat beside mine and laying a reassuring hand on my knee under the table. I was okay, though. By sticking to facts and not diving into the memories, I was able to detach from the hurt and loss of Nelson.

"Well fuck," Tink breathed when I was done. "You couldn't have told us this when we got the text?"

I shrugged, picking up another fry. "I could have." I met her gaze without flinching, not apologizing.

"Trust issues," Tink murmured, nodding her understanding. "Got it. But it's nice to see you two are good again."

"We're not," I replied before really thinking it

through. John flinched ever so slightly, and I winced internally at how harsh I'd sounded. "But we're better than we were."

John gave my knee a squeeze, silently telling me that he was okay with that. That he understood the path to reparation wasn't as simple as just great sex. He still needed to prove his trustworthiness in more than just theoreticals.

"So we need to break into Tris's apartment?" Tink asked, tapping her nails on the tabletop as she thought it through. "It's still an active crime scene. We took a little drive past while we were in town to check on things. But it's not impossible."

"How confident are you that the keys are where you left them?" Bram asked me, refilling my glass with fresh Coke. "They could be in evidence."

I shook my head. "Unlikely. Not impossible, obviously, but unlikely. The cops weren't looking for hidden keys in a murder scene." My mind flashed back to that night, and I quickly shoved it aside. I'd rather blackness than the high-definition playback of Nelson's death.

"I can get in and out without being seen," John said with confidence, and I shot him a glare.

"I'm well aware."

He grinned, his hand sliding higher on my thigh.

"And aren't we glad for it now? Your neighbors are not generally night owls but after midnight is always safest. I can stake it out, though, and go in earlier if it looks possible."

"I'm coming with you," I announced, narrowing my eyes at him. "You need my fingerprint to access the keys." I had them in a false bottom of my bedside table, but it was locked with a hidden fingerprint scanner to prevent anyone accidentally finding them. Say if the police were searching my apartment.

John's fingers flexed on my leg. "I have that handled."

Tink gave a snort of laughter, shaking her head. "Oooh John stole your prints already, Tris babe."

My jaw dropped, and John gave me an apologetic smile. "Besides," he said, not denying Tink's claim, "you're not the best at sneaking in or out of places. Or need I remind you of the drain-pipe incident?"

My cheeks heated and I glowered. "I see your point," I muttered reluctantly. "I don't *like* your point, but in light of my current status with both the police and the Grimaldis... I guess it makes sense."

John's hand moved to the back of my neck, a touch that was fast becoming a favorite for me. "I won't let you down, Venus."

"*We* won't," Tink corrected. "Last I checked there

were two highly skilled thieves in this cabin. And a second set of eyes might not be the worst idea, since we know the council has boobytrapped things."

I nodded, giving a small sigh. "You're right. Take Tink with you, John. Watch each other's back and all that shit. Bram and I will be fine here alone, right?"

He just quirked one brow, looking from me to John and back again. "Of course. It's almost like I'm paid to keep you safe, Tris. Oh wait..."

"I don't remember paying for sarcasm, Bram Atwood," John remarked in a dry voice and I grinned. I should have been mad at him for the whole *hired a mercenary* thing, but I couldn't get past the sweet intent. He wanted to keep me safe, which said a lot for how much he cared even before absconding with the fake *Poppy Flowers*.

I'd meant what I said to Tink; we weren't *good* all of a sudden... but we were on the right track. It made my heart happy to let go of some of the anger and resentment. We just had to keep looking forward and not back.

Maybe, just maybe, we had time to figure this out. We were being ourselves. Finally.

That had to count for something, right?

John

seventeen

My boots hit the floor of Tris's home with a soft thud, and I moved out of the way to allow Tink to follow me inside. She landed almost silently, and I grunted with envy at how easy small thieves had it.

"So that's how you've been breaking in all this time, huh?" she murmured, glancing around. The whole place still smelled of gunpowder, drywall, and blood. "I would have just picked the lock."

"Thanks for your feedback, Katinka," I muttered with a sharp edge of sarcasm. "I never thought of that." The fact remained that it was the seventh floor of a building, with a secure lobby and keyed elevator. It wasn't as simple as just picking the lock, and the risk of being caught bypassing all that security was too great.

Much easier to rig one of Tris's windows and drop in from the roof.

"Bedside table, right?" Tink asked, ignoring my snarky tone. She stepped carefully, not disturbing the scene, and crossed to Tris's bedroom. She already had a pair of gloves on her hands and tugged open the top drawer to peer inside. "Looks like a normal drawer."

I scoffed. "That's the point. Do me a favor and pack a bag of clothes for Tris? Grab her hairbrush, too."

"Can do," Tink replied, leaving me to deal with the keys in their hiding place. I followed Tris's instructions, removing all the bits and pieces out of her drawer—mostly charging cables, toy cleaner, and lip balm—then pulled my toolkit from my bag. I'd made a cast of Tris's index finger weeks ago, when I needed to access Grimaldi's gallery, and for some reason I'd kept it in my kit. Just in case.

So I used the rubbery fake finger to unlock the false bottom of the drawer and quickly scooped up the three keys laying on the padded base below. It took no time at all to tuck them safely away in my bag and put the drawer back exactly as it'd been when we arrived.

"How are we doing?" I called out quietly to Tink.

"Good," she replied. "You got the keys?"

"Sure do," I confirmed, glancing around the rest of Tris's apartment. Nelson's body was gone, of course, but the blood stains remained. As did the debris from the exploded wall and the empty room beyond. Surely the cops could see this was a robbery gone wrong, not a personal vendetta. At least, it wasn't my girl's vendetta. The same couldn't be said for Hank, because his parting words to Nelson sure sounded personal.

To my disappointment, most of her art supplies were mixed up in the mess of debris, so I didn't want to pick through and disrupt it all. Taking some clothes and personal items for Tris was one thing, but I was reluctant to touch the actual scene of Nelson's death.

"Done!" Tink announced a moment later. "We good?"

I jerked a nod. "Yeah, let's go. The sooner we can get back to the cabin, the better."

"Oooh John baby, you having withdrawal symptoms already? She's got you good, huh?" Tink was teasing, I knew that. But she wasn't wrong.

"Heart and soul," I agreed, popping the window open for us to exit the way we'd entered. Tink slung the duffle bag of Tris's belongings over her shoulder and climbed out first, scaling the side of the building with enviable ease. I followed, and we didn't speak again until we were safely back to the car a block away.

"Actually, can we make a quick stop in town before we head back?" Tink asked, stowing the bag in the back and buckling her seat belt. "I want to buy something for Tris."

I arched a brow in curiosity but followed her directions to the shop she had in mind. It was almost one in the morning, so I was confused about what was even open, but Tink was confident as she hopped out and told me to wait with the car.

Frowning, I followed her with my eyes, then groaned when I saw which doorway she disappeared through. Fucking hell... I wasn't sure if I should be annoyed or excited. Either way, I had to sit there and drum my fingers impatiently on the steering wheel while waiting for Tink to reappear.

At one stage while waiting, I thought I spotted Igor strolling down the street toward Tink's former place of work—The Slippery Lips. It wouldn't shock me: he'd been lurking around there playing the part of Grimaldi henchman, but I was pretty sure he'd dropped his cover after the *Poppy Flowers* forgery like the rest of us. When the man stepped into a pool of light from a store display, I let out a breath. It wasn't him.

The paranoia remained, though. Why had Igor been so quiet since the snake incident? Could he be working with Hank? That'd just be... typical. Two peas in a pod, considering how two-faced Hank turned out to be.

The passenger door popped open and I nearly

jumped out of my skin before registering Tink's petite frame climbing inside.

"You good?" she asked, giving me a skeptical squint. "You look like you just lost at Bean-Boozled."

I gave an ick face, knowing exactly what game she was talking about. Once was enough, playing that and being unlucky enough to eat the vomit jelly bean instead of watermelon. Whoever designed those flavors was a true sadist.

"Yeah. Did you get what you wanted?" I directed my gaze to the large shopping bag in her lap. There was definitely more than one item in that bag.

She grinned broadly. "I did. Why? Are you worried she won't want you if she has other options for her O?"

I glowered, refusing to rise to her teasing. "It just seems like an odd gift to buy for a friend, that's all."

"Not when that friend is Tris. I needed to get her a *sorry I lost you a billion dollars worth of art* gift, and the florist isn't open at this time of night, so I got her a different sort of rose. One I'm sure she will appreciate a whole lot more." She deposited the shopping bag into the back with Tris's other belongings and waved for me to drive. "Besides. Now if she has her collection of toys restored, you'll be able to know for sure."

I frowned, focusing on the street as I drove away from the sex shop. "Know what?"

"Whether she fucked you because she wanted you... or if she was just super horny and needed an easy O. Obviously. Thank me later, champ." She adjusted her seat to recline a little, and cracked open the can of energy drink she must have just bought.

I shot her a scowl. "Did you get me one of those?"

Her response was just to loudly slurp the drink, and I rolled my eyes. Brat.

As much as she was teasing, there was an uncomfortable truth to what she was saying. Had Tris made that first move because she was willing to make amends with *us*? Or had she just wanted sex with no emotional attachment, and fucking me was better than just her own fingers?

I hated that Tink's off-hand insult was getting under my skin... and I made up my mind. Tris was just going to have to see that she *could* have her cake and eat it too. I was secure enough not to be threatened by her vibrators. Wasn't I?

"Uh, I'm sure you've already noticed this," Tink said, cutting through my thoughts about vibrators and bedroom play, "but we're being followed."

I jerked, casting a quick look in my rearview mirror and noting the car following us some distance behind. "Are you sure?"

She narrowed her eyes. "Are you *joking*? Yes, I'm sure. I thought you'd seen them too."

I licked my lips, dread rolling through me. "Any idea who it could be?"

"Literally anyone," she shot back, her tone dry. "Another Game player? Igor? Hank? Cops? One of the Grimaldis? Someone else entirely? Unfortunately I left my x-ray vision goggles at the cabin and my psychic powers only work during a full moon, so I can't give you much more than that."

"Right," I agreed, glancing in the mirror again. She had a point... At this stage there were so many possibilities for who could be tailing us, it was ridiculous. All I knew was that I couldn't risk leading them back to Tris. "Got your seatbelt on?"

Tink snorted a laugh. "Of course I do. Only idiots who have a death wish don't use their seatbelt regardless of who is driving."

I shot her a grin then jerked the steering wheel swiftly to the right. Tink gave a startled squeak as she splattered against the door, flailing as she righted herself and gripped the door handle.

"Try not to kill us," she suggested in a strangled voice, looking like she was trying to press an imaginary brake pedal in the passenger footwell.

I huffed a short laugh, shaking my head. "Drama queen. This isn't my first car chase." Because that's exactly what it was, with the car trailing behind speeding up to keep us in his—or her—sights. Hmm, they seemed determined and didn't much care that we'd spotted them.

"Seriously? You need to work on being more stealthy if you have people chasing you on the regular," Tink muttered, still holding onto the door with a white-knuckled grip. "I don't think I've ever needed to perform evasive maneuvers to get away from a heist. Maybe that makes me better than you?"

Adrenaline pumped through my veins as the needle of my speedometer climbed higher. At least they'd picked a good time of night to pull this shit, when there was significantly less risk of hitting a pedestrian and very little other traffic on the roads.

"You wish," I replied. "It just means you play it too safe, Tinkerbell. Up the stakes a bit and I guarantee you'll get a taste of the chase. Besides, I'm not the one who wanted to stop at the sex shop. Maybe you picked up more than toys."

"Eww," she complained. "You think I got an STD or—"

I shot her a brief look. For real?

"Oh. The tail. Right." She made a little shrugging

motion even as she gripped the oh shit handle tighter. "Fair call."

I snorted, Although in fairness, I preferred to get in and out unnoticed. This *did* remind me of how I'd needed to run from Carol not so long ago, and I frowned as I glanced at the mirror.

She had no reason to tail us, though. Did she? According to Tris, she'd already been to the cabin and told Tris all about the Game and its rules, so she didn't need us to lead her there... or was I misreading the situation? What if it was just someone following me—or Tink—and nothing to do with Tris? Either way, I had to lose them before returning to the cabin.

"Good thing we have plenty of gas," I murmured, performing another swift corner turn and noting that our tail followed with ease. "This guy could be hard to shake."

"Amazing," Tink groaned. "Is now a good time to mention I get car sick?"

A quick glance over at her showed she was already pale and sweaty. Fucking hell. "Better grab one of those bags, because we aren't stopping."

She grimaced but a moment later leaned over to dump out the sex shop bag and clutch the empty plastic in front of her. So dramatic. My driving wasn't *that* bad.

Tris

eighteen

For the first half hour that John and Tink were gone, I paced with restless energy, worrying about an endless list of *what ifs*. Then when I started yawning, I decided to make better use of my time and sleep instead. As soon as they got back, they'd want to go to the locker to collect the sword, and that was a solid three- to four-hour drive away.

I told Bram I was heading to bed, and he assured me he was keeping watch, so I snuggled into the sheets that still smelled of John to sleep.

The startling shriek of an alarm ripped me viciously out of my slumber, and I tripped on the sheets as I tried to launch myself out of bed in a blind panic. I hit the floor *hard* and Bram burst in with a gun in hand, like he was expecting to find an intruder.

"Are you okay?" he yelled over the sound of the alarm.

"What's happening?" I shouted back, untangling myself from the bedding so I could cover my ears.

Bram replied, but between the alarm and my hands over my ears, I couldn't hear him. Pretty sure he said *alarm,* which was sort of obvious, then he gave a frustrated gesture and disappeared back out of the bedroom. I followed, breathing a sigh of relief as he shut off the noise on a keypad inside the pantry.

"What the hell was that?" I asked in the now deafening silence.

He arched a brow at me, sliding out a little screen with a set of numbers and two flashing lights displaying. "An alarm," he said, making me roll my eyes. "Someone has turned into the access road without deactivating the system, which means it's not John."

I nodded slowly, vaguely recalling Bram giving John the codes and instructions before he left earlier. Glancing at the clock on the wall, I realized I'd only slept for an hour at most. No wonder I was all groggy and confused.

Bram watched the panel with blinking lights for another minute or two, but nothing changed.

"What are we waiting for?" I finally asked, when the curiosity got too much.

He glanced at me, tucking his gun back into his waist holster. "To see if any other sensor points activated closer to us. But these two are the furthest from the cabin so now I'm wondering if someone just got lost and turned around or... something. If anyone was coming all the way to the cabin, all these would be lighting up." He ran a finger down the dark numbers.

I started at the panel with him for a moment, then rubbed my upper arms because it was *cold*. "Um, so... what now?"

Bram scratched the back of his neck. "I need to check it out, I think. Just in case... we can't just ignore it. Right?"

"Why are you asking me? You're the professional."

"I wasn't asking," he retorted, his tone droll, but there was a serious glint in his eyes. "But I don't want to leave you here alone. Can you handle a gun?"

My smart-ass response collided with the memory of the gun RBD pressed into my hands and the instruction to kill that guy. It was him or me.

I chose me.

"Yes," I said, forcing the words past the lump in my throat. Flashes of hot and cold skated over my skin. It wasn't all that long ago, and yet it seemed both like years and minutes. The uneven feeling left me off-center. "Yes," I repeated. "I can use a gun."

He nodded then flipped open a door to the cabinet next to the tea and coffee station. Then popped the side of a plastic container that opened to reveal a gun. It was tucked neatly in there.

"Easy access. I'm just gonna leave it open for you. Stay inside, be smart. If you aren't sure who it is or you don't recognize them—shoot them."

"What if—"

Bram shook his head once. "If you don't know them, they probably mean you harm. If they're cops, trust me, they are going to identify themselves. Can you do this?"

All his easy-going manner had vanished, and in its place was a cool professional with an appraising look in his eyes. Honestly, the change was unnerving. "I can do this." Yeah, that came out a little weaker than I intended, and I gave myself a solid mental shake. "I can do this."

"Good." He checked his own weapon then handed me a key fob. "Panic button. If something happens, hit it. I'll get back here. But remember what I said..."

"Shoot first."

He winked then entered a code into the door. "It'll lock behind me. Enter that in again if you need to open it. Don't need to open it." Then he was gone. The dark outside seemed a great deal darker. Even venturing closer to the windows, I couldn't see Bram at all. It was like he stepped outside and just vanished.

So, he was really good at his job. I supposed that should make me feel better. As it was, I rubbed my upper arms to try and chase away the chill. Coffee. I needed coffee. It would help. I was tired, I was cold, and—why weren't John and Tink back? What if something—

The knock on the door had me spinning around to stare at it.

Bram *just* left.

John and Tink wouldn't have knocked. They had the codes—and a key. I'd seen Bram give John a key, but he'd proved more than once he didn't need *keys*. I stared at the door, torn between going to peek out the window and pretending I wasn't here.

"Tris..."

The voice calling from the other side of the door stunned me. Was he for *real?* Shock collapsed into fury. After yanking the gun out of the cabinet, I hid it behind me as I peeked out through the window.

Yep. Sin *fucking* Grimaldi stood on the porch like he was just stopping over to share a nightcap in the middle of the goddamn night. His eyes fixed on mine as he stared at me.

"Let me in, Tris."

"Why the fuck would I do that?" Cause, I really wanted the answer to that question. Needed it.

"Because I'm here to rescue you..."

Here to— "Are you *high?*"

"Let me inside, Tris. I don't want to argue through the window."

He had a valid point, and I rolled my eyes as I unlocked the door and held it open. I blocked his entry with my arm, though, and made sure he got an eye full of the gun in my hand. "Sin Grimaldi, you'd better be here with good intentions, or I swear to fuck, I will shoot you."

His brows hitched and the corner of his mouth twitched, but he wisely didn't smile. "Understood. I come in peace, Tris. I swear."

I gave him a long look, then stepped aside to let him enter. Despite the whole unpleasantness back at RBD's when he literally locked me in the bedroom, he'd never been anything but respectful toward me. Nothing about him made me worry for my safety, and besides... I had a gun.

"Are you going to put that down?" he asked, eyeing the weapon in question.

I shook my head. "Nope."

"Fair enough," he murmured, glancing around the cabin. "This is where you've been staying?"

My eyes narrowed. "Clearly. Don't be such a snob, Sin. It's safe."

"Okay, I'm just saying there's an actual company who rents out safe houses that are a whole lot nicer than staying in Grandma's cabin from the sixties. Where'd you even find this place?" He scratched at his stubble, giving the floral sofa a critical look.

"Cut to the point. Why are you here?"

"I already said," he replied, spreading his hands defensively, "I'm here to save you."

"I don't *need* saving," I informed him. "Unlike some people I know, John isn't holding me prisoner."

Sin at least had the grace to look apologetic at that. "Ah yeah, look... I'm sorry about that. It wasn't my finest moment, I freely admit. You escaped before I could apologize the other day, so please understand I felt awful about the whole thing."

I scowled. "That's it? You locked me in your bedroom."

"I panicked," he admitted. "This deal you had going with my father really worked in my favor, and when it seemed like you were going to try and back out..." he trailed off with a shrug. "I fully acknowledge it was stupid, but I hope you know you were never in any danger?"

I shook my head. "No, Sin, I didn't know that. You

locked me up like an animal, and considering my history with your family, with your father forcing me to kill a man, and your brother attempting to rape me? Yeah, I was scared. Can you blame me?"

He winced. "Point taken. But, I'm here now, come to save you. Surely that counts for something?"

I went to cross my arms then remembered I was holding a gun so ended up doing an awkward one arm wrap around myself. "Like I told you, I don't need saving."

Sin frowned. "Okay. Noted. But would you *like* saving? Because I have both John and Bram well distracted right now. They don't need to know you're gone until we're miles away."

My jaw dropped. "Miles away? What about my deal with your father? I still owe him a forgery."

Sin shrugged. "We tell him that we eloped. He'll be thrilled and give us space until the whole police mess sorts itself out here in Whispering Willows. By that time, this whole... *Game*... will have moved on."

"How do you know—" I cut myself off shaking my head. "Nope. Doesn't matter. I don't care. I'm not going back there with you, Sin, so unless you planned to force me...?" I raised a brow, but he quickly shook his head.

"Wouldn't dream of it," he assured me.

"I want to believe you," I said. "But I've been lied to so damn much lately."

"Yeah, lies don't encourage trust," he said with a grimace. "Especially when they come from someone who *was* trusted."

Pointed comment or not, I sighed. "I know, I betrayed your father's trust."

Sin gave a little shrug. "Honestly, he'll get over it. Eventually. Maybe. Especially if you finish the job for him and give him back *Poppy Flowers*."

Tears burned in the back of my eyes at the mention of that damn painting. "I really wish I'd never seen it." I meant it.

His gaze was measuring as he nodded, then something way too close to sympathy drifted through his expression. "I can imagine." That was it. No platitudes or empty words of comfort. "Right now, he's distracted because of what's going on in Whispering Willows."

"He has to know I'm gone—or that I snuck out." It had been days. Well, a couple of days. The weight of the past few days collapsed against me, and all the weariness and grief I'd been fighting threatened to smother me.

"He might believe it has something to do with a piece—and the *Game*..." The comment startled me, and no way I hid it because Sin actually smiled. "Not the first time I've needed to cover someone's exit, Tris. Maybe we're not getting married—my loss, clearly—but you're still my fiancée, so I'll still look after you."

"Why?" Probably not the most politic of responses.

"I have my reasons," he said, then studied the cabin around me. "I'm going to leave my private number. If you need me—for anything—you call. I'll get help for you."

"You don't have to—"

"Let me." It seemed almost a command, and I raised my brows. He let out a dark little chuckle. "I owe you one for locking you up."

No, he didn't. He knew it. I knew it. "Your father?"

"You still owe him. That debt will need to be paid. I can do a lot, but I can't take care of that one."

Fair call. "It's my debt."

"Yes, it is." At least he didn't try to sugar coat it. "I'm reaching into my pocket," he continued after giving his watch a glance. "We have maybe five minutes of privacy left before Bram gets back here. I'm impressed that you turned one of my father's guards."

If he was fishing, I wasn't biting.

Sin's smirk said he figured as much. He pulled out a card and then set it down on the counter. "My numbers.

I mean it—you need anything—even if it's just an ear, you call me."

"I don't understand you," I finally admitted.

"Good." Then he winked. "Enigmatic is sexy, no?"

I snorted a laugh and shook my head. "Not really."

"Liar," he teased, but at least he wasn't insulted. "Take care of yourself, Tris. You make sure that John takes care of you too."

With that, he slipped out into the night leaving me alone—just like he said.

"Weirdo," I muttered before I went to grab his card. Honestly, I wasn't sure which of us I was referring to with that name. Maybe all of us.

John

nineteen

"I think I've lost him," I said for what felt like the twentieth time, easing my foot off the gas ever so slightly. "Surely, this time I've lost him. This is getting fucking ridiculous."

Tink turned around in her seat, peering through the back window in search of our mystery, persistent tail once more. She was silent for a few moments, and I started to relax. Then she groaned, and every muscle in my body tightened up once more.

"Does he have a tracking device on us or something?" Tink exclaimed, throwing her hands up. It wasn't the first time she'd asked it, either, but we'd already tried stopping the car to check and found nothing. The tail had disappeared entirely, too, so we couldn't even approach them and work out who it was.

Then, once we set off again they were right there on us once more.

"We need to get back to the cabin. We've been gone way too long, Tris will probably be freaking out." I glanced at the time, then grunted. "Or she's asleep and hasn't noticed."

Tink snickered. "She did look rather exhausted. Almost like she spent the afternoon *exercising*, hmm? I guess those bridges weren't burned quite as badly as we thought they were?"

I tried to hide my smile, but I was too smug. I was too happy.

"Wait. Wait, wait, what? They're gone," Tink announced.

Startled, I glanced in my mirrors to check. "Huh?"

"I don't know! They just... turned off down that street to the left."

"What the fuck?" I slowed the car, twisting to look over my shoulder. Behind us it was all just dark. No headlights from another car... nothing. Darkness. "He's gone?"

"Or she," Tink corrected. "But yes. I think so? Sure seems that way."

Confusion rendered me speechless. I'd been trying to shake that tail for over an hour and now they just... gave up? It didn't make sense. Unless... "Could that have been a diversion? Keeping us away from the cabin...?"

Tink gasped. "Tris!"

"Fuck," I whispered. Every instinct screamed at me to go to her, but what if it was a trap? "Try calling Bram, let him know what's going on. I'll... drive around a bit longer. Just in case."

"Right. Yes. Good thinking," Tink agreed, pulling out her phone. "Could we maybe stop somewhere? I'm dying to pee."

I cast a long sideways glance at her and sighed. "Sure. Even if we have dropped our tail, I'd feel better if we switched cars. Just in case there was a tracker we couldn't find."

Tink gave a childish snort laugh.

"What?" I asked, already knowing it would be a stupid answer.

"Like we're a lizard," she said with a loopy smile. "Dropping our tail. Like how lizards... never mind." She grumbled under her breath about my lack of humor and turned her attention out the window.

I shook my head silently, not wanting to encourage her bad jokes. But at the same time, I hoped we *weren't* like a lizard, because they eventually regrew their tails. I'd rather be done with evasive maneuvers for one night.

Ten minutes later we were back in the main strip of

Whispering Willows, and I pulled into a multi-story parking lot where I had a spare car parked. We made the switch, driving back out of the building barely three minutes later in our replacement vehicle.

"I'll stop at the gas station over on Acorn Ave," I told Tink, who was wiggling like a three year old in her seat. "Just hold it, would you?"

"I'm *trying*," she whined.

When we arrived at the gas station, she practically flew out of the car and I laughed to myself at her antics while getting out to fill up the car. Just in case we *did* regrow our tail, I wanted to have a full tank of gas.

I leaned against the car as I waited for the gas to pump, my gaze scanning our surroundings in search of anyone or anything even slightly suspicious. We were just a block from The Slippery Lips, so it wasn't surprising to see several of Grimaldi's men cruise past and a group of drunk businessmen heading in that direction.

As I finished up and hung the pump on its rack, I narrowed my eyes at the car pulling in behind mine. It was a nondescript black sedan, but we were the *only* car at the pumps. They had their choice of plenty of vacant pumps to use... but chose to pull up there.

When the driver climbed out, I didn't even try to hide my irritation.

"Really?" I snapped. "You had nothing better to do with your night, old man? What were you hoping I'd do, lead you to the sword so you could take it at gunpoint? Oh wait, that feels familiar."

Igor gave me a tight smile, tucking his hands in his pockets. "Holding grudges will give you gray hair, son."

I leveled a hard glare his way. "Why were you following me?"

Igor shook his head. "I wasn't. I was on my way out of town and saw you here so figured it was fate pushing me to extend an olive branch rather than just disappearing without a word."

"What do you mean? Where were you going?"

He shrugged. "Not sure yet, but I'm bowing out on this *Game*. You were right, this whole thing is way over my head, and as much as I'd love to set fire to Christophe's legacy... it's not worth everything that's happened lately." He shook his head, looking ten years older than the last time we'd crossed paths. "If your mother saw the man I'd become... she'd be disgusted."

He was right about that. "You'll forgive me for being suspicious, but just a week ago you were willing to let me die of snake venom just to get a leg up in the Game. What changed?"

Igor scrubbed a hand over his gray whiskers. "I wouldn't have let you die, son. You know that. But that shit with *Poppy Flowers...*" he grimaced, shaking his head. "I thought no one hated my father more than I did, but Hank sure proved me wrong. I don't have the stomach to stay mixed up with his vendetta, and if you were smart you'd let him have it."

I wet my lips, reading between the lines. "You were working with him. He's the reason you made it into the final round in the first place, isn't he?" The tightness in Igor's expression confirmed my guess, and I sighed. "Was he the one who planted that tracker on me?"

My father just grimaced. "He's unstable, son. You cross his path, you get the fuck out of his way, you hear me?"

Frowning and fucking *confused*, I just nodded.

"Good," Igor murmured, "Maybe I'll see you around sometime. Maybe not. Just... make better choices than I have in life, Ivan. Make your mother proud."

With that, he slid back into his car, reversed out of the gas station and drove away down the street. I stood there in some level of shock, staring at his taillights disappearing into the darkness until Tink came back out with her hands full of snacks.

"What'd I miss?" she asked, glancing in the direction I was staring. "You look like you've seen a ghost."

I ran my hand over my face, trying to shake off the eerie feeling of dread Igor had left with me in his total absence of usual Igor bullshit. He'd seemed... genuine. Remorseful. That wasn't a version of my father I knew or ever expected to meet. It was unnerving, to say the least.

"Hello? Earth to John?" Tink waved her hand in front of my eyes. "You still with me?"

"Yeah," I sighed, glancing into the darkness again, like I was waiting for Igor to circle back and tell me he was just fucking around. "Yeah. Let's go."

Once back in my seat, I paused for a moment with my finger on the ignition button. Had Igor been distracting me while tampering with the car? Planting another tracker? I cast the whole interaction through my mind, dissecting it. He hadn't touched my car, though. He hadn't even touched me. He'd been careful to remain at a safe distance, and he'd been alone. There was no way he could have done anything... but maybe it wouldn't hurt to be safe.

"Let's change cars again." I grunted, making up my mind.

Tink arched a brow in question then just nodded. "Alright. Better safe than sorry, huh?"

I grimaced. "Exactly."

The only other safe vehicle I had in Whispering Willows, though, was back at the safe house Tink and I had been renting. She took the opportunity to grab some of her own clothes, and insisted I do the same, so by the time we got back to the cabin the sun was rising over the horizon.

"I'm wrecked," Tink muttered as I passed the alarm sensor points, using the access codes Bram had shared with us. "My butt hurts. So much for a quick heist. I'm not cut out for the car chase business."

"It was hardly a *chase*." I breathed a sigh of relief as the cabin came into view through the trees. Bram's car sat in front and the lights were on inside. Was Tris awake already? Or just Bram keeping watch?

"Whatever it was, it sucked. I need to nap before we set out for the mysterious storage locker, alright?" She groaned like an old lady as she climbed out of her seat, and I rolled my eyes at the drama.

I got out myself and closed the car door with a heavy *thunk* just a moment before the front door of the cabin burst open and Tris came flying out.

"Where the hell have you been?" she shrieked. "You've been gone for *hours*, do you have any idea how worried we were?"

"We?" Tink asked, grinning. "Bramble, baby, you were worried?"

The mercenary standing on the porch glowered in her direction. "You text me saying *someone's following us, not safe, ttyl*. Then didn't answer any of my calls after that. Yes, Tink, I was worried."

My little scatterbrained accomplice pulled out her phone and winced. "Oops, must have put it on airplane mode by accident. My bad."

Small, cold hands grabbed my face, jerking me down until I was nose to nose with Tristian Ives.

"John. Are you okay? Did they hurt you? What the hell took you so long? He left here like two hours ago, I've been going out of my mind..."

As gently as I could, I peeled her claws from my face, holding onto her hands as I pressed a kiss to her forehead. "I'm fine, Venus. We're both fine. We were just —" I broke off, realizing what she'd just said, my spine prickling with fear. "Who? Who was here, Tris?"

"Sin," she replied with a heavy exhale. "Sin was here."

Of *fucking* course he was.

Tris

twenty

John's whole face clouded over with fury at the mention of Sin's unexpected visit, and it dimly occurred to me that I could have shared that information more tactfully. It was done now, though, so fuck it.

Besides, the flash of jealous possessiveness that crossed his face was hot as *fuck,* so I had no regrets. Hell, I almost wanted to rub salt in the wound just to see his head explode a little more.

"Grimaldi?" John snarled, his head whipping around to glare at Bram. "You let *a Grimaldi* know where to find her? Are you insane?"

"Whoa, I did nothing of the sort," Bram replied, holding up his hands.

"John," I snapped, grabbing his face again. "Don't

jump to conclusions. Sin didn't come here to hurt me, and he isn't going to tell his father how to find me, so just take a breath. I'm fine. Are you?"

A look of bewilderment furrowed his brow. "Am I? What? Tris, you—"

Unable to help myself, I crushed my lips to his, cutting off whatever he was saying with my kiss. I only meant it to be quick, just to reassure myself he was okay because I'd been going out of my mind worrying about how Sin had *distracted* him and Tink, but now he was here...

John groaned, parting my lips with his own to deepen the kiss and before I knew it, he was lifting me up by the thighs and wrapping my legs around his waist.

"Okay, I think that's our cue to leave," Bram announced, giving an awkward laugh. "Tink, maybe we should go into town for supplies and leave these two to chat in private."

I didn't look over, nor even attempt to answer him. How could I, when John was devouring my soul with his deep, drugging kisses and his dick was rapidly hardening between us?

"What?" Tink whined. "We already got supplies yesterday and I've been sitting in the car for like four hours already, I don't wanna—"

"Katinka, get in the car," Bram growled, and a scuffle

of shoes implied he was pushing her in the direction of his vehicle.

I groaned as John bit my lower lip, then repaid the favor and delighted at his own moan of arousal as I sucked his tongue. My hips rocked against him, totally forgetting where we were, or the fact that he was holding me entirely off the ground.

"John, don't forget the presents I got for Tris!" Tink called out just a moment before Bram's engine started up. They drove away, and I tilted my head back just far enough to peer at John through heavy lids.

"Presents?" I asked, my lips puffy and tingling from his kisses.

"Mm hmm," he replied, kissing my throat as he carried me up the porch steps and pushed open the door with his foot. "We made sure to pick up some essentials while we were in town."

I gasped, remembering the whole point of their trip. "You got the keys, right?"

John jerked back, his eyes wide. "Oh fuck. The keys!"

"What?" I squeaked, slithering out of his arms. "You didn't get them? Why? What? How?"

His horrified expression melted into a teasing smile, and my eyes instantly narrowed.

"You're not fucking funny, John Smith."

"Aw come on, Venus, I'm pretty funny." He tried to

reach for me again, and I danced out of reach. Fuck that, he could have a taste of hard-to-get after pulling that stunt. "You want me to chase you, hmm?"

A flash of excitement lit me up inside and I batted my lashes. "Would you? If I ran, would you catch me?"

Moving faster than I thought such a big man was capable, John snatched me around the waist, pulling me against his body as his mouth closed over mine. He kissed me until I was weak and breathless, then whispered his response against my lips like a prayer.

"Always and forever, Venus. You're worth the chase, no matter how long it takes."

Be still my heart. This man...

He scooped me up, carrying me through to the bedroom without a word then set me gently down on the messy bed sheets.

"Are you going to tell me what happened?" he asked in a low voice, while lifting my shirt up and over my head.

I let him toss it aside, then tugged his loose to repay the favor. "With Sin?"

An angry noise rumbled through John's chest, and I grinned, running my fingernails down his smooth pecs. "Jealousy looks good on you, Professor. But there's nothing to be worried about. He was just here to save me."

"Save you?" he repeated, sounding genuinely offended. "From what?"

I grinned then booped him on the nose with my finger. "From you, silly. He was under the impression I was here against my will, which I guess he *technically* wasn't wrong about when you think it through. There was the whole handcuffed to your bed incident."

John frowned. "You tried to kill me."

"With good reason," I reminded him, shifting away slightly. Oh yeah, the mood had just soured really quickly.

John must have felt it, too, because he exhaled heavily and hung his head. "I'm sorry, Venus. I didn't... I shouldn't be acting so possessive when we're still on shaky ground."

A lump of guilt formed in my throat. "I don't mind you acting possessive," I admitted, "so long as you know, deep down, that I'm no one's possession."

His head raised, his eyes meeting mine with a fiery heat. "Understood."

Words failed me as I stared back at him, letting the intensity of his gaze warm me and spark the mood back to life. I wet my lips. "So, um, what was Tink saying about presents?"

He leaned in, his hand grabbing the back of my neck as he tilted my face back to kiss. His mouth claimed mine with raw demand. I scraped my teeth over his lower lip. His rumble of a growl was my only warning before he captured my lower lip, then nipped it hard enough to make it sting.

Liquid heat flooded my veins, and the scorching temperature made the clothes we were wearing way too much. The worry and the exhaustion that had consumed me all night burned up along with the frustration. Somewhere my panties vanished and John's pants were open. Hands roving all over his chest, I couldn't make up my mind what I wanted to do first.

With some actual effort, John yanked himself backward, leaving me to stare at him panting. "What are you doing?" Why the fuck was he over there? I was on the bed and he was by the door.

But instead of answering me, he just held up one finger then stalked back out of the bedroom.

"What—?" I pushed up off the bed. "Where are you...?"

I'd barely made it to the edge of the bed when he stalked back inside and closed the door to the other room with a thump. In his hand was a plastic bag. He toed off his shoes and then pointed me at the bed. "Get back on there, Venus."

Command licked over every single syllable. Fuck,

Professor John was hot, but then, I'd been panting after him in class for how long?

Scrabbling backward, I didn't stop until I hit the headboard. Instead of following me, John stood there, shirtless with his pants open and that Adonis belt on display with just the hint of his erection that I could almost taste peeking out but still tucked away. The heated look in his eyes raked over me and traced fire everywhere he studied me.

Well, except for my nipples, cause those just went taut. After a long, wordless pulse of pure lust bounced between us, I raised my eyebrows.

"You coming to get me or what?"

Cause, as much shit as I wanted to give him, I was definitely a sure thing right now. I wanted him to just fuck me until I saw stars.

Then do it again.

Though, I might hold off on that seven back-to-back orgasm challenge.

He licked his lips.

Or maybe not.

"I'm debating something here, Venus."

"With yourself?" Because he wasn't saying anything.

"Uh huh." Then he opened that paper bag.

"My presents?" I swallowed, even if my mouth had gone abruptly dry and my stomach bottomed out.

"Hmm-hmm," he hummed. The bag was a decent size, and I kind of wanted to see, but then John pulled out a package and his expression was the hottest, hilarious thing I'd ever seen. "I'm going to kill Tink."

"Sure, kill Tink later, fuck me now." Whatever he needed. Then 'cause, *I* needed to know, I shifted to my hands and knees and crawled toward him. He didn't complain once about me leaving the headboard. If anything, his eyes went positively molten. "What's in the package?"

He turned the box around and my jaw dropped. I'd seen those but...

"Is that a cock sleeve?"

A half-snort, half-laugh escaped him. "Trust that you would know what that is."

"I mean, it's on the package." I reached for it, and he surrendered it. The instructions were pretty clear. There were five different textures available, all ribbed in some fashion for my pleasure, and it had a little insert where we could put in a vibe.

"What do you say, Venus?" John's voice was low, hot, and hard. It did purely illegal things to me. "Want me to try that on for you?"

"Your willingness to incorporate toys into the bedroom is a turn on, Professor Smith, I won't lie. What else is in there? Also, why the fuck did Tink buy us sex toys?" My mind had glossed over that odd detail until now.

John shrugged. "She said she wanted to get you a gift, but since it was two in the morning, there wasn't a whole lot open." He tossed the cock sleeve onto the comforter and peered back into the shopping bag. "Uh, she got you a beauty blender?" He pulled out the little box, reading the side of it and I grinned.

"Uh huh, she's a gem." I took it from him and tossed it onto the bedside table. Despite its appearance, it was not for applying makeup. "What else? If there's handcuffs, it's a hard *no*, just so we're clear."

John winced, shaking his head. "No handcuffs, but there is *this* sizable thing called... *Thrust*. Well... I think I know what that does, but I'd like to see it in action just to be sure." Another scorching gaze that made my pussy flutter. "Okay last items are a thing that looks like a bougie blue Christmas ornament, and... oh this looks fun. Edible body paints."

He held the last two items up with a suggestive eyebrow waggle, and I chuckled at the "Christmas ornament" which was definitely a long bumpy shaped vibrator with a finger loop at the end designed for ass play. Tink must have been feeling really guilty because this was a shopping spree.

"Did she include any lube?" I enquired sweetly,

batting my lashes as I wriggled out of my pants. "Because I want to try that bougie blue thing in my back door."

I wished I could have captured John's expression on camera because it was *priceless*.

"Seriously?" he asked after a moment of shock. "Okay, shit, um, let's see if..." He practically dived head first into the bag, checking for anything he might have missed. To my relief, he pulled out a handful of sample packets, all of which contained some form of lube.

"Pants off," I ordered, flipping over on the bed and getting onto my hands and knees. I didn't have the patience for long drawn out foreplay, I was already soaking and on the edge of climax just anticipating all the fun we could have with Tink's presents.

John gave a groan, kicking his clothing away then climbing onto the bed behind me, one big hand grasping my ass cheek firmly. "Holy shit, Venus, are you trying to kill me?"

"I will, if you don't hurry up and get me off," I snapped back, arching my back until my elbows rested on the bed, waggling my rear at him in what I hoped was a suggestive, inviting way.

John made a growly noise then gripped both my cheeks, spreading me wide as his mouth latched onto my pussy. His tongue lashed at my clit, and I needed to ball the sheets up in my fists to keep from collapsing.

"Fuck," I moaned, rocking back on his face. "John..."

"You taste so fucking sweet, Venus," he murmured, playfully biting my inner thigh. "I can't get enough." He dove back in for another taste, tongue fucking my cunt until I exploded with a startled cry, but he just buried his face deeper like he wanted to suffocate within my folds.

It was all I could do to gasp lungfuls of air as my orgasm shuddered through me, but John was only just getting started. He surfaced for air a moment later, only to tear open one of the little lube samples with his teeth and squeeze it out directly over my tight hole.

"You sure this is okay?" he asked, sounding breathless as he massaged the lube in with his index finger, pushing the tip in, ever so slightly, like he was testing my reaction.

I moaned, rocking back onto his finger and mentally willing my body to relax. "Yes," I gasped as his thick index slipped deeper. "Please, John..."

"Have you played with these before?" he asked with sexy curiosity, keeping his finger where it was while reaching for the knobby blue wand. "When you're at home, alone? I know you love the rabbit clit vibes, but I never pictured... *this*..." He withdrew his finger, replacing it with the smooth silicone tip of the anal vibe. Ever so slowly, he pushed it inside, his breathing heavy as he undoubtedly watched it disappear.

My own breath hitched as the intense sensation washed over me, making my head swirl and my pussy flutter, and he hadn't even turned the toy on yet. So good.

"Tris," John murmured, pausing his action. "I asked a question."

Oh god, the authority in his tone made me tighten up, and I needed to wet my lips before I could formulate my reply.

"Yes," I admitted. "But this is better. You being in control is so much better."

He bent down, kissing my ass cheek as he pushed the vibe deeper as a reward. "Good girl," he purred, and I nearly came right then and there. It was unclear if he was praising my eagerness for ass play or my honesty in answering him, but it didn't matter. It was hot as fuck, and I was here for it.

Then he turned it on and I turned into a puddle of liquid.

"Is that good?" he murmured, giving the toy a tug, pulling it out one bump then pushing it back in. Fucking me with it.

My answer was incoherent noises as my fingers

twisted in the sheets and my hips rocked back and forth, begging for more. More would be *divine*.

"John," I gasped out loud. "John, I need you. Fuck me, please."

He didn't need to be told twice, quickly shifting his position to line up the head of his huge cock with my soaking pussy. "Thank fuck," he moaned, pushing inside without removing the vibe from my ass like I'd been expecting. "Oh my god, Tris... you're so tight right now. Does that feel good?"

Words failed me as fireworks went off inside my brain, the endorphin high so intense I was seeing stars. I just moaned and panted as he thrust deeper into my cunt.

John was in an authoritative mood, though, and grabbed a handful of my hair, jerking my head back until I was bent at an awkward angle. "Venus, my love, I asked you a question. Does" —*thrust*— "that" —*thrust* — "feel" —*thrust*— "good?"—*slam*.

"Yes!" I screamed, my whole body lit up with way too many sensations and the pleasure so high I was sure I might burst. "Yes, it feels amazing! Fuck, John, I'm going to—"

He turned the vibe in my ass up a level, and I convulsed. The climax that rocked through me from my ass and pussy both was so strong I blacked out momentarily. John released my hair, letting me fall to the bed as he gripped my ass and pumped hard. His long shaft got me in all the right places, prolonging my climax as he went harder, faster, rougher, until hot jets of his cum painted my insides white.

Thankfully, he withdrew the anal vibe then, turning it off and tossing it aside as I twitched and shuddered through what seemed like an hour-long orgasm. My hips were still hitched in the air, despite the way my face remained buried in the sheets, and John took his sweet time pulling out of my cunt.

"Beautiful," he murmured in a husky voice, his fingers swiping up some of his cum leaking from my pussy. Then he pushed it back inside. "Fucking perfect."

I squirmed, riding his fingers playfully when he didn't immediately pull them out again, and he gave a dark chuckle. He knew damn well I didn't have the energy to go again quite so soon. Maybe just a little rest... then I wanted to try all the other toys.

As he arranged us on the bed, his naked body curled around mine, I made a mental note to buy Tink a thank-you cake.

John

twenty-one

The wet glide of a paintbrush on my skin woke me at some stage, but Tris kissed me softly and whispered to go back to sleep, so I did. If she wanted to decorate my flesh, I wouldn't stop her. But I'd forgotten that the body paints were edible, until I started dreaming about getting the best blowjob of my life...

"Venus?" I murmured, shaking off the haze of sleep to find her lush lips wrapped around my rock hard dick. "Oh fuck, yeah I could get used to this." I lifted my hands to her head, threading my fingers into her silken hair as her tongue swirled around my tip.

Through half-open eyes, I noted the array of designs painted all over my torso and thighs, and the swirl of filigree decorating the base of my cock. She'd really let out her creativity and was now cleaning it up... with her mouth.

"Mmmm," I moaned, my hips rising off the bed as she took my cock deeper into her mouth. "Yeah, like that. Can you take more?"

Her dark glare up at me through her lashes said it all, then she sank down further, taking my tip into her throat. She swallowed around me, relaxing her gag reflex, and I whispered curses at how good it felt, which only spurred her on.

Those delicate fingers of hers wrapped around my base, pumping my shaft in time with her mouth, and I fought with myself not to take over and fuck her face. She wanted to be in control, so I had to let her... for now.

"Holy shit, Tris," I moaned, my ass cheeks tight as I fought to last longer. She had a way of making me come so fucking fast it was embarrassing. My fingers tightened in her hair, my hands no longer on board with letting her set the pace, and I found myself pushing her down harder than ever.

Then she did something totally unexpected. While I was busy panting and groaning, fucking her throat, she slipped a finger between my cheeks. I startled and paused but didn't jerk away, and she took that as permission.

The next thing I knew, her finger was in my ass—a

totally foreign but not unpleasant sensation—and her mouth had created a vacuum seal around my cock. Then her finger wiggled, finding my prostate from the inside, and I came harder than I thought I'd ever come in my life. Buckets. It just kept going, in load after load until I worried I would drown her.

"Baby," I gasped, collapsing back into the pillows to let her up. "Are you okay? That was—"

I cut off, realizing that she was smirking up at me with her lips tight and her cheeks full. Was she holding a mouthful of my semen right now? Why was that sort of hot?

She held my gaze as she reached for the big peach colored vibrator that had been named *Thrust*, then slowly as deliberately, without blinking, dribbled my fluid out of her mouth and onto the toy.

My jaw dropped, and I lay there transfixed, watching in awe as she smeared my cum all over the huge toy, then proceeded to sit back on my thighs to insert it into her pussy. Holy fuck, my girl was filthy.

"Show me how it works," I demanded, my voice rough as she pushed it in fully. She did as she was told, switching it on. Initially, all I could hear was the hum of the vibration and the movement of the clit stimulator, but the way she tossed her head back and moaned said I was missing out on something more. "Show me," I said again, with more force.

She returned her gaze to mine, then slowly pulled the toy out once more. Sure enough, the whole thing was *thrusting*, but it also had a ring around the middle of spinning bumps. No wonder she'd reacted like that.

When I said nothing, she put it back in her pussy, holding eye contact with me as she fucked herself with the clever device, then came with a gasping moan. The fact she'd done it all using my cum as lube? Icing on the cake. Insane.

"Shower?" I suggested, noting how sticky we both were. Tink and Bram would be back any minute, and I already had plans to fuck Tris again before they were. If we did it in the shower, then it'd be like multitasking.

She nodded, her eyes glassy and disoriented like she always looked after a great orgasm. It was an addictive look on her, and one I wanted to keep there as long as humanly possible.

Scooping her up, I indulged myself in one of my favorite activities where this delicate dynamo was concerned. I cradled her. She was so much smaller than me, but it didn't diminish her one whit. If anything, she could take me to my knees with just a compression of her lips.

I could handle just about anything, except her pain.

That—that gutted me. Too soon to wallow in those memories. The rawness of her grief was right there, but maybe we'd eased off the edge with the sex and the orgasms. We could sand down quite a few more of those jagged pieces in the shower.

The weight of her breasts teasing my chest was definitely something to savor. I carried her all the way into the bathroom, then shut the door with my foot. I held onto her, greedy for the contact, while I got the shower started.

"You're turning into a caveman, John," she teased, and I chuckled.

"Where you're concerned? Absolutely, Venus. I treasure the priceless art, after all." There was nothing more priceless than her smile except for maybe the glow of satisfaction in her eyes or the low, almost soundless cry that preceded her real screams of pleasure.

Speaking of which, as soon as the water was warm enough, I thrust us both under it and filled her in the same moment. Her gasp dazzled as she lifted widened eyes to meet mine. "John…" Was that wonder?

Oh, my Venus… "You have no idea how much I want you," I told her. It was a constant burn, and she had her legs wrapped around my hips and our mouths fused as I fucked into her with a rhythm designed to drive us both mad. Considering she played with my ass earlier, I enjoyed pressing one finger against the rim of her ass, and she came with a startled if strangled shriek.

The clamp of her muscles fisting me seemed determined to milk me dry. We leaned into each other, trading gasping kisses as we fought for breath. Eventually, she slid down to stand on shaking legs, and I couldn't say mine weren't trembling. The spread of her fingers against my chest just reminded me of how close she was. How much closer I wanted her.

Everything about her was perfect. Her delicate little toes where they curled against the tile. The jut of her hip when she caught me watching her, and the lazy smile on her kiss-swollen lips when I took over working the shampoo through her hair.

"How are you doing, big guy?" She practically purred as I continued to massage the shampoo into her scalp.

"Good. How about you, Venus?"

"Hmm." It came out on the lowest groan. "You can stop that sometime around never."

I chuckled. Yes, the most priceless of items needed to be handled with the most exquisite of care. I'd made mistakes. Too many. But she was made of the finest materials, as strong as she was beautiful.

Just—perfection. I nudged her under the water and helped her rinse out her hair, then I went to work with the conditioner.

"I was thinking I'd have bedhead," she said in a throaty tone that just wrapped around my cock and gave it a gentle caress. "But now I think I'm just going to be a puddle."

It was my turn to chuckle. I enjoyed lavishing this care on her. While the conditioner soaked, I soaped up a washcloth and moved it over her. It gave me the time to explore every curve from the sweet swell of her breasts to the magnificence of her ass. She took that toy and me at the same time so goddamn sweetly.

The thought of sinking balls deep into her ass was definitely making my dick twitch. Even as I wondered if she would be up for it, I answered my own question. Tris was up for everything. Defiant. Intelligent. Cunning. Determined.

She was the perfect match for me.

So damn perfect. Eventually it was time to rinse everything off and we were slipping out of the shower. She leaned against the vanity in a towel as I helped with squeezing the excess water out of her hair. Her gaze held mine captive in the mirror, and when she passed me a comb, I couldn't hold back my smile.

Smooth down all the snarls so I could take advantage of a handful later? I didn't mind in the slightest. This—this was the kind of thing I'd never imagined having in my life, and suddenly I understood what had been missing.

What *I* had never been able to fill with a single job. I was Hermes. I was the best goddamn thief in the world. There was nothing I couldn't steal. Nothing I couldn't get to—nothing I hadn't attempted. Except this.

She raised her eyebrows at me, and I pressed my lips to her damp hair. "I love you, Venus." The admission fell out of me like a prayer, to be offered up to my goddess.

Tris smiled. "Thank you."

This whole day was utterly perfect, I just—

"Sorry?" Did she just say what I thought she said?

Her smile was pure sunshine in the mirror. "Thank you, John, that means a lot."

My lips parted but no sound came out. *Thank you?* Not *I love you, too.*

Panic flooded my body, and in an instant I reexamined all our interactions from the moment I'd arrived at the cabin. Were we mending bridges and moving forward together? Or was Tris just using me for sex because I'd stolen all her vibrators and she was horny?

Holy shit. Had I totally misread everything?

Tris spun around in my arms, reaching up to cup my cheek as she pressed a sweet kiss to my lips. "I think I heard a car pulling up. Tink and Bram must be back."

She patted my cheek then slipped out of the bathroom with her towel tucked around that luscious body of hers, leaving me standing there staring at my reflection like a fucking moron.

Of course she hadn't said it back. Why the fuck did I think she should have? It'd only been a handful of days since her whole life imploded thanks to yours truly. Sure, she might be on the *road* to forgiveness with me, but that didn't mean it was a done deal. It was a work in progress, and that realization was like a bucket of ice water to the face.

I was an asshole for thinking the wounds I cut into her heart and soul could be healed with great dick and back-to-back orgasms. If I was going to eventually earn her forgiveness—earn her *love*—then I had to accept that it needed time. I had to be patient, and I would be. She was worth everything and more, so I'd finish the Game... then spend however long it took to win her back, even if it took an eternity.

That was my strongest certainty right now.

She was worth it.

Tris

twenty-two

It was a three-and-a-half-hour drive from the cabin to the storage locker, and by the time we got there my back was aching and my nerves were on edge. John had been *weird* the whole time, too. Not distant but also not *all over me* like he'd been in the shower. Maybe my *thank you* had hit home harder than I'd anticipated?

Whatever. He needed to understand where we stood, because he had clearly been thinking all his lies were forgiven and forgotten. Far from it, but I was open to the process so long as he realized that's what it was. A process.

"Shadow Grove Secure," Bram muttered, parking the car in front of the enormous self-storage unit I'd directed him to. "Probably the best city in the world to lock up priceless stolen art, I'll admit. What does the rent on one of these units cost?"

I gave a short laugh. "Too much. There were a whole bunch of additional fees before we could install our own security on the unit, to protect other renters. As it is, the fail safe we ended up using is designed to incinerate the entire contents of our unit, but not damage anything *outside* the locker."

Bram looked thoughtful, glancing around as we headed inside the building. "Huh," he murmured. "Who installed that for you?"

I frowned, thinking. "I thought Nelson had done it, but now I'm wondering if he might have contracted someone to do the work."

Bram just hummed a sound in response, following as I led the way down a long corridor lined with roller doors on either side. The building seemed empty, but I couldn't ignore the nervous anticipation curling inside me. Had someone else discovered the locker already? Surely not. Only three of us knew about it, and one was dead. So unless Hank told someone...

"Just up here," I muttered, trying to distract myself from the uncomfortable thoughts in my head. "Locker 802."

At a glance, the locker looked no different from the other hundreds of lockers inside the storage facility. The roller door was secured with a simple combination padlock, which I unlocked and removed, allowing John to raise the metal roller.

"Ah, that looks more like I expected," he commented, inspecting the internal door that'd been hidden by the roller. It was solid steel, no visible hinges, and just one keyhole. "Tris?"

I huffed a quick sigh. "Yep." I pulled the ring of three keys from my pocket and set about unlocking the unit. One key after the other, one full turn clockwise for each. As always, I held my breath as the last key—my key—turned in the lock, deactivating the failsafe measures.

"We good?" Tink asked when I just stood there unmoving for a moment.

Her words jolted me out of my trace and I exhaled in relief. "Yeah, we're good." I withdrew my key, then pushed the door open with only a slight hesitation. Inside, the climate controlled, dust free locker was cool and dark. No flames or piles of ash. As always, my replica keys had worked flawlessly.

Swallowing back my anxiety, I rubbed my arms and stepped forward. "This way."

Tink let out a whistle as she followed behind me, and I glanced over my shoulder to see her wide eyes scanning the room. Nothing was immediately identifiable, each piece stored within its own protective case, but the sheer quantity of treasure was undeniable.

"What do you do with all this stuff?" Bram asked, sounding genuinely curious. "Is it just a personal collection?"

I shook my head. "No, that was in my apartment... This locker is just a holding room. We store things here for a minimum of six months before flipping it on the black market, so there is less chance of it being connected to us *if* anyone was tracking the sales."

"How do you vet your buyers?" John questioned, his voice edged with concern. "How do you know you're not selling to Art Crimes, or worse?"

"That was Hank's job. I created the forgeries, Nelson made the switch, and Hank sold them." With the occasional exception for jobs that Nelson was better at forging or Hank was better placed for stealing... My job was only ever forging, though.

I stopped in front of the shelving unit that held a handful of long, flat storage cases. The blades and weapons that Nelson had so much fun forging in his metalworking phase. My hand trembled as I placed it on the case that I knew held Heydrich's sword.

"Hey, you don't have to go through with this," John said quietly, his hand resting gently on the small of my back as I stared transfixed at the case. "You don't have to play the Game. We can find another way."

Tink gave a spluttering sound from the next shelf over where she'd opened an art case to check out the contents. "Whoa, hey, uh... no? I thought we agreed to *win* this bitch?"

John gave a frustrated sound. "Private conversation, Tink. Butt out."

"Private conversation inside a four-hundred-square-foot storage locker? Okay sure. Super private." She grumbled something else under her breath, then Bram hissed at her to shut up.

"Tris, baby, I mean it," John murmured, his thumb stroking my skin beneath my shirt. "No one knows this sword is here. We can just let them steal the fake from Grimaldi's crypt and say nothing."

I bit my lip, thinking it over. But there was no reason to hesitate, really. The sword meant nothing to me, now. It had been Hank's obsession to steal World War Two era artifacts, and Nelson's hobby to recreate swords. Truthfully, the only person I'd be stealing from was Hank, and he'd understand. Especially if this took us one step closer to finding who'd really killed Nelson...

"We're doing it," I said, grabbing the case handle and pulling it from the shelf. "Here." I handed it to John with determination. Even if it wasn't about my own vengeance, it was about his grandfather's legacy. Those precious memories he wanted to preserve and the love letters he wanted to finally mail out.

"Thank fuck for that," Tink exclaimed. "So um, what are you doing with the rest of this stuff now?" She waved a hand around at the shelves of stolen stuff and flashed me a wide grin.

"Out!" John ordered her, pointing to the exit. "No stealing from Tris."

"Oh that's rich, coming from you," Tink muttered with a sullen pout. "How many vibrators did you steal?"

"She's got a point," I chuckled, but still eyed them all carefully as we exited to ensure no one had taken a souvenir. They waited while I locked up once more, activating the failsafe then closing the roller door. Still, the uneasy feeling sat heavy in my stomach as we returned to the car.

John must have noticed, because he pinned me against the door before I could get in. "Venus, are you sure you're okay with this?" he asked with a deep frown of concern set across his features.

I jerked a nod. "Yes, definitely. I just... can't help feeling like someone is watching us or something. After everything, this is all kind of anticlimactic. But then again, no one else knows about this locker, so why did I think it would be any more dramatic than this?"

"Except Hank," he replied, his eyes searching my face.

I swallowed hard. "Right. But he only has one key, and even if he had more... he's not in the Game. I know what you *think* you saw, John, but I know Hank. He didn't murder Nelson."

Bram snapped his fingers, drawing my attention. "That explains why you could fix my apartment key," he exclaimed. "Makes sense now. Also, it feels like we're being watched because we are. This is Shadow Grove, Tris. Someone is always watching."

That sent a shiver through me, and I rubbed my arms.

"And on that ominous note, we should go," Tink suggested. "I want to check out what's going on at Grimaldi's place, see if any competition has been eliminated there."

John gave me another concerned look, so I mustered up a reassuring smile. "She's right, we should go."

He gave a nod, stepping back to give me space to open the door and slide into the backseat. He stowed the sword case in the trunk, then joined me in the back of the car while Bram and Tink took the front.

As we drove out of the storage compound, we needed to key in a code to open the gates. Another car was waiting to enter, so Bram waited for them to drive through and pass us before leaving, and I just happened to glance out my window as the car rolled past.

All of a sudden, it felt like I'd been dipped in dry ice as my eyes locked on the driver whose window was still open from keying in his own access code. He didn't see me, not even glancing our way, but I sure as fuck saw him.

There was no mistake. No room for denial left after laying my own eyes on him in the flesh. It was Hank... unquestionably Hank.

My heart thudded frantically in my chest, and my palms broke out in sweat, so I squeezed my eyes shut tight as Bram drove us away from the storage facility. Away from Hank.

There had to be another explanation for why he was there. It didn't need to be what it seemed... right? Maybe he was there to retrieve a sale item or... or something? But if that were true, he'd have asked me to accompany him with my key. If that were true, he'd have reached out about Nelson's death by now. Right? He'd be *heartbroken*, like I was.

The man driving that car had not seemed grief stricken. He'd seemed cold and distant, to the point I nearly second guessed myself.

Denial was strong, but it wasn't *that* strong. Hank was the one driving that car, so it stood to reason that

Hank was also the one John had seen the night Nelson died. But how the fuck was I supposed to process that information? How the *fuck* was I supposed to swallow that undeniable gut punch, that somehow Hank was involved in Nelson's death?

I had lost them both that night, and I was all alone in this world. That was my knee-jerk reaction and the voice that'd yelled it inside my head was *loud*. But it was also wrong. Blinking back the tears burning my eyeballs, I looked around the car. At Tink and Bram in the front seat, bickering over which radio station was better, and at John. John Smith... Ivan Valenshek... the man who loved me.

I wasn't alone, but Hank would have to answer for his sins nonetheless.

That thought still gutted me, though, and I curled my knees up to my chest on the car seat. John reached out, linking his fingers with mine between us, and I squeezed back. Thank fuck he was here.

John

twenty-three

Tris was totally consuming my mind. I didn't even notice how intensely I was focusing on her every move until she stiffened up and her face paled. What had just spurred that reaction from her? Was she changing her mind about the sword?

No, that wasn't it. She'd been resolute and determined. A car had just passed us as we left the facility, but I had barely even noticed it. Had she recognized the driver?

I waited for her to say so, but she remained silent. Seemingly lost in her own thoughts, she drew her knees up to her chest, and I couldn't stop myself reaching out to take her hand. The way she squeezed my fingers said I did the right thing.

Whatever was going on inside her head, she clearly

wanted to deal with it privately, but I kept my hand in hers, letting her know she wasn't alone. Even when she fell asleep with silent tears tracking down her cheeks, I didn't let go. Maybe subconsciously she would rest assured that I was there for her, and always would be.

She slept for most of the drive back to Whispering Willows, and I told Bram to head back to the cabin. She'd done her part in giving us the sword, and we could spare her from being involved every step of the way.

"You sure she won't want to be the one handing in the Game piece?" Tink asked quietly, turning around in her seat after I said as much out loud.

I shook my head. "It needs to be one of us; otherwise we can't overtake Hank on the leaderboard."

"Wait, how'd he overtake us with only one win?" she asked, wrinkling her nose in confusion. "Or are we thinking he'd been working with someone?"

I stared at her a moment, then realized I never told her about my chat with Igor. "Yeah. Pretty sure he was. Anyway, she's still wanted for questioning by the Whispering Willows police for Nelson's death, and the Grimaldis probably have a price on her head by now. I'd feel a whole lot better if she was safe at the cabin." The cops probably wanted Hank too, but I hadn't heard of any sightings of that prick yet.

"Are we still considering the cabin safe?" Bram

asked, glancing in the mirror at me. "After her visitor last night?"

It was a good point. Then again, Sin Grimaldi had too much on the line to risk Tris's safety right now. If anything, he'd be motivated to keep her *safe*... like he would hope I'd do for him.

"As safe as anywhere right now," I replied after a beat. "She knows how to handle a gun, and so long as she doesn't go opening the door to anyone..."

"I'll stay with her, too," Tink offered. "It's probably better if Bram goes with you to the turn-in point to watch your back. Now that people are actively killing to win the Game, you never know what might be lurking around the corner."

I grimaced, the memory of Hank pushing his gun against Nelson's head still fresh in my mind. Would he do the same to Tris if he caught her? It was a sickening thought. "I'd prefer Bram stay to protect Tris."

"No," a small, husky voice interjected, startling me. "No, Bram's going with you. Tink is right, and we are perfectly capable of looking after ourselves in the cabin."

I frowned, taking in Tris's disheveled appearance. Her eyes were rimmed with red, and the tip of her nose had a pink flush from her silent tears. "Venus, I don't think—"

"John, I mean this in the kindest way I can, but your

thinking hasn't got an amazing track record thus far. How about you let me think for myself this time?" She cocked a brow in challenge, and my mouth went dry.

Tink gave a strangled laugh from the front seat, and I shot her a death glare.

Tris paid no mind to Tink's behavior, focusing her tired eyes on me. "I'm an adult, John, not a child. You don't get to overrule me when it comes to my personal safety, and right now I'm telling you that I feel one hundred percent confident in my and Tink's abilities to remain safe. Sin wouldn't have told anyone where to find me, so unless someone has seen me during this little expedition... where's the risk?"

"Girl's got a point," Tink agreed, inserting herself in our conversation yet again. This was why I never worked with a partner. Annoying brat. "You're stuck between a rock and a hard place right now, Johnny baby, better off just nodding and smiling, maybe offer a polite *yes, ma'am*, and kiss her hand. Anything less will see you castrated."

"Not helping, Stinkerbell," Bram said, but we were back at the cabin. "Let's give them a minute." And he didn't wait for Tink to answer, just swung around the car and hauled her out. "We'll get the coffee started." Then they were both heading toward the cabin while

Tink kept arguing with a combination of wild gesticulations and sulky looks.

A wet laugh escaped Tris, and I shifted my attention back to her. "She means well," Tris said and I shrugged.

"She's a pain in the ass." But I didn't want to talk about her. "Look me in the eye and tell me you're okay with me and Bram going to turn in the sword while you stay here?"

Confusion clouded her expression as she sat up and faced me more fully. "I—"

I waited.

"This isn't about trust," Tris said slowly. "Is it?"

"No. This is about me keeping promises that I made to you." That was part of it. The other was keeping promises to myself. "So, tell me you're really okay with it and that you'll be safe while I'm gone."

She searched my face, the heat in her eyes intensifying, and then the corners of her mouth softened into a suggestion of a smile. "I'm sure. We want to win the Game so we can get—Nelson's killer and your grandfather's letters. We're in this *together*."

Yes we were. But even if I walked away tonight with only Tris, I'd won. I hated the idea of risking her for even a moment.

"I can use a gun," she reminded me, and that made

me smile for real. "And Tink seems capable of annoying someone to death."

That made me laugh for real.

"Now, Mr. Smith," she continued, smoothing down my shirt before she cupped my face and leaned up to kiss me. It was a brush, there and gone again. The brief contact seared me down to my soul. A brand. Fuck, I wanted her to claim me. So I'd take what I could get, even if the kiss tasted of salt and sadness amidst the teasing. "Go score some points and piss off the soon-to-be losers."

"We'll be back soon." Then I gave her another kiss before we both climbed out of the car. The air out here was a lot chillier than it had been in the cocoon inside the car. Arms folded, she winked one her red-rimmed eyes at me before she turned to head up the path toward the cabin.

Bram had to have been watching because he stepped out to meet her. He paused next to her and said something to her. Probably details on where the weapons were or the security system. If it had been anyone else who'd come up here, I'd have said we should move them before we went.

Sin Grimaldi though? As much as I didn't like him, I trusted him with Tris' safety in mind. Particularly because I had something he wanted, and Tris being safe was what *I* wanted. Dragging my gaze off of Tris, I studied the area around us. There were cameras. I'd been picking them out with every trip. The camouflage on them was excellent.

As safe houses went, this cabin was isolated, secure, and had plenty of surveillance. They could also see anything coming at them before it got here. When I checked on Tris again, she was disappearing into the cabin, and Bram strode toward me.

"Where are we going?" was all he said before he climbed behind the wheel. With one last glance at the cabin, I slid into the passenger seat. Tink had the seat all the way forward so I moved it back. I needed the leg room whether I was in the front or the back.

"Head toward Whispering Willows," I told him as I dug my phone out. I needed to send the turn-in code and get the location.

"Brief on how these turn-ins go?" He'd already turned the car around, and we followed the winding road away from the cabin. I focused on *not* thinking about leaving Tris *behind* so much as leaving her secure with Tink. They could look after themselves. This was where Tris wanted to be while Bram covered my ass on a milk run to turn in the item.

To be fair, how much of this Game had been a damn milk run? I still had a bruised area around the taipan bite. I had bruises from being jumped. Others from being near explosions. None of the physical injuries could touch the pain of damn near losing Tris. None of them.

So maybe a milk-and-cookies run? That didn't sound right either.

"John?" Bram prodded and I shook off the melancholic introspection. Head in the Game.

Literally.

"Generally we're given coordinates—we never know where they are. But there is a safe cordon set around the turn-in point. Once we're inside the perimeter, we're safe from interference."

"But we have to be inside the perimeter?" Bram verified, and I grimaced.

"Yeah, we do. This usually isn't an issue, and no one is watching us." Even on the drive to Shadow Grove and back, Bram had employed counter measures, not that any of us spotted a tail. Then again, none of us were aware of how Sin Grimaldi had tracked the cabin either.

A matter for another day. My phone pinged as we passed the first mile marker sign telling us Whispering Willows in ten miles.

"Got it." I put the coordinates into the car's GPS and the location popped on the far side of Whispering Willows, near the university. They really needed to leave that school alone. The amount of cleanup we were going to have to do when this was over and done with might end up closing that place.

Then again, once this was done, I was getting Tris the hell out of here.

"Thirty minutes," Bram said, but he moved his head from side to side, cracking his neck before he continued, "Do we want to go straight there or vary our route?"

"We have an hour from the message to get there."

"So, thirty-minute window of play." Bram nodded. "We'll take a longer way around Whispering Willows and come in from the other side, which puts us closer to the school."

It seemed reasonable. Paranoid was reasonable in this case. As much as I told myself it was fine, my own agitation seemed to increase with every passing mile. The GPS altered itself as Bram hit the highway and circled the town. He cut his gaze to the rearview regularly, and I kept watch on the side mirror.

Traffic joined us and peeled away again. No one seemed "suspicious." No one followed too close; in fact, we stayed out of the fast lane so we got passed a lot. Good plan, anyone pacing us would stand out with Bram going—I leaned slightly to check. Fuck, he was going eight miles under the speed limit. That explained the people blowing past.

Still a solid plan.

I was flexing my hands to keep from digging my fingers into my palms as we found our exit. We were two blocks from the turn-in point. This was going fine. It was going...

Headlights flooded the interior of the car from the back and then the side.

"Brace," Bram ordered even as he floored the car. We avoided the impact from the car that suddenly sped past us and slammed into the side of a building, but not the car that caught us from the side as we swung through the intersection.

It T-boned the car, hitting right at the rear passenger door, and we spun. Airbags deployed. The burn sucked, but I had the oh-shit handle in one hand and the rest of my body pressed back against the seat to fight the urge to rock forward.

Bram turned into the spin as the cars locked together. The crash of metal screaming on metal joined the crunch of glass. It was like something out of a cartoon as we came to an abrupt halt against a light pole.

"Get the sword," Bram ordered, then he was out of the car. My ears were still ringing but the pop of gunfire galvanized me. I snagged the case from the back seat—we'd moved it out of the trunk after dropping off the girls, and now I was glad for easy access—and went out the driver's side door. It wasn't a graceful exit, but it was faster, and I hit the ground with the cars between me and the shooters.

Tucked down against the front driver's side tire, Bram glanced over his shoulder at me. Then he held up five fingers. Two to our right—on the other side of the car. Two ahead and then one behind.

I nodded.

He pointed to me, then the one behind and said, in a low voice, "Count of three, on the three."

Worked for me. I moved the strap of the case over my shoulder then crossbody with care. I didn't have a gun, but I wasn't a huge fan of them anyway. Instead, I stayed where I was, crouched, and ready to move. My ears were still ringing, but the report of guns was hard to miss. They weren't even trying to be quiet.

"Come out and give us the sword," someone yelled —someone with a very distinct New England accent. Farthingway. Ernest Farthingway. What an ass. "We might even let you walk away from this."

Right. I looked at Bram and he nodded then mouthed, *one*. I said, *two*. We both said, *three*, or maybe we just did in our heads, because Bram was up on his feet and firing and I was on the move. I stayed crouched, because guy number five was standing and taking aim at Bram.

I hit him mid-body and slammed him back into his car. The guy was five-eight, maybe, but he was built. Didn't matter. I was bigger. I didn't give him time to recover before I slammed my fist into his stomach, then into his jaw. As he staggered upward, I caught his gun arm, twisted and spun him around. Wrenching his arm upward, I kept going until it popped and the guy let out a small shriek of pain.

He also let go of the gun. Then I knocked his head into the hood of the car and turned to check on Bram, gun in hand. The last of his four went down with two in the head. I scanned the area and then looked to where the other car had crashed into the side of the building. Bram was checking the bodies, then he looked at mine.

"He's out," I told him.

"Leave him for clean-up," Bram said, already reloading his weapon. He'd been so damn swift and smooth. I might have to change my opinion of his skills. "Let's go. We've got two blocks to go on foot."

We weren't getting his car out of that smash-up.

"Stay right with me," Bram ordered. "If I tell you to get down, you get down. Clear?"

"Yes, sir," I said, not quite saluting, though I would admit to some fresh respect. "You know," I told him as we crossed the street and headed away from the accident. "Tris is going to say she told me so."

Bram chuckled. "And you're going to be a good boy and agree."

Yes, yes I was. "Good point."

One more block and we'd be inside the cordon. I couldn't wait for this Game to be over. Well and truly over. I wanted Hank to pay for what he did, I wanted my grandfather's letters, and I fucking wanted away from the insane crews this Game had pulled out.

My phone chirped when we were inside the cordon, but I didn't let down my guard, nor did Bram. We also didn't leave cover as we made our way down the street. The shadows weren't perfect, but they would do.

"So, Stinkerbell?" I had to know.

"It pisses her off," Bram said, a grin in his voice.

I chuckled. "It's amusing."

"I know."

Ahead, there were three people waiting, but they weren't alone. More appeared along the street and above. Snipers.

Fuck, this Game was out of hand. Christophe would be rolling in his grave if he could see this mess.

But these points were ours.

Tris

twenty-four

After napping for most of the drive from Shadow Grove, I was way too awake to go to bed. Besides, I doubted I'd be able to sleep until John and Bram returned all in one piece, so I happily accepted the coffee Tink handed me.

"So..." she started, giving me a sly look as we sat down on the sofa together. "You and John seem awfully cozy again. How's that all going?"

I couldn't stop my smile as I thought back to our adventurous afternoon while Tink and Bram were gone. "Um, it's good. Thank you for the presents, by the way. Much appreciated."

Tink grinned. "It seemed like the least I could do, after all the bullshit. Besides, his dumb obsession with stealing your vibes was totally uncool. A girl needs her toys."

"Agreed," I laughed, sipping my coffee. "So, is this the last step in the Game? Once they get the sword turned in, it's all... done?"

Tink wrinkled her nose. "Doubt it. I think there will be at least one more stage."

"How do you not know? Aren't there rules?"

"Hah! Yeah, you'd think, huh? There *usually* are. There's *usually* so many rules it's borderline not even fun to play, and everyone is hardcore about toeing the line, too. But this Game? Total shit show. I mean, *complete clusterfuck*. I legit question the sanity of whoever is running it all this year." Tink sighed heavily, shaking her head. "It's never meant to be this messy. The collateral damage has been totally unprecedented, and I swear the Council are just making shit up as they go along. And we're all just... letting them."

I blinked in surprise. "That's insane."

Tink shrugged. "Most of us are, to a degree. But back to your love life... John is, of course, all fucking anime heart eyes around you, but you seem a little more reserved. Are you guys actually good, or is it a sex thing?"

With a groan, I dragged my lower lip through my

teeth. "Uh, it's complicated. A little bit of both? I *want* to forgive him, but it's just..."

"Too soon?" she guessed, nodding. "I get that."

I shrugged. "Yeah. Too soon. So in the meantime, I'm just..."

"Scratching an itch?" Tink grinned wickedly. "A deep, delicious itch that can only be satiated with a long, thick, hard *scratch*?"

Despite the warmth in my face, I grinned back. "Well... yeah. Pretty much. Does that make me a bad person? I know he thinks we're moving on and all—and we are—but it's just not that easy for me."

"You're not a bad person, Tristian Ives," Tink assured me with a firm head shake. "You're the furthest fucking thing from a bad person—except maybe for the sneaky forgery shit, but I can totally overlook that for how sweet you are. Using John for sex while letting him think you're committing to forever? That just makes you *human*, girl. He hurt you. Big time. That can't be forgotten with a couple of good orgasms, you know? It takes time."

A loopy laugh bubbled out of me before I could hold it in. "A couple? Yeah. Yep. Just a couple."

She groaned. "I hate you. I swear to god, if Bram doesn't fuck me soon, I'll die of blue-ovaries."

"What? I thought you guys were already fucking? I'm in shock. What's the problem?"

Tink rolled her eyes. "He has some arbitrary rule about not fucking around while he's working, and since he's *technically* under contract to keep you alive until John releases him..." she sighed. "We haven't even kissed. Isn't that crazy? I feel like we're... you know... like... *dating* or something."

I laughed, a lightness filling my chest with the sound. I was glad to have her around, amidst all the doom and gloom. She was a breath of fresh air, even when she was accidently handing all my art over to a band of thieves.

"Tink... you're hilarious. Have you guys even—"

Beep beep beep!

A shrill alarm interrupted our gossip session, and my heart leapt into my throat. I'd heard that siren before, so I knew immediately what it was. I scrambled out of my seat on the sofa, knocking my coffee flying and paying it no mind as I raced to the kitchen.

"Tris, what's going on?" Tink yelled, covering her ears with her hands.

I flung the pantry open and clawed open the control panel with my fingernails like I'd seen Bram do. Almost every signal light was flashing red, and my head swirled as the blood drained out.

What the fuck did we do? Who was it? Sin?

No, this wasn't him. This was something much worse, I was sure of it. Gun. I needed a gun. Where had Bram kept it again?

Frantic, I started opening containers, my fingers closing around the butt of a gun right as the front door burst open with a bang so loud I startled and ducked. I didn't wait to see who was bursting through, instead just aiming my weapon and firing.

Three shots rang out, and I had no idea if any of them landed before someone tackled me and twisted the gun out of my grip. A scream wrenched out of me as my wrist protested, but my attacker kicked the weapon away with a heavy boot and terror coursed through me.

"Hold her!" someone barked, and the man hauled me up to my feet, my wrists pinned behind me. I struggled and thrashed, but the guy restraining me was at least twice my size. What in the actual fuck was I thinking when I said I could handle my own safety? Clearly, I could not.

Tink cried out in pain, and I jerked in my captor's grip, frantic to help my friend. What I saw nearly made me faint, though. She was bloody and on the ground, making me think for a second that I'd shot her in the madness. But then the man looming over her knelt down to punch her right in the face, and I screamed again.

He paid me no mind, hitting her again and again until she was like a bloody rag doll and I was choking on my tears as I thrashed, kicked, and sobbed.

Eventually he straightened up, pulling a fabric handkerchief from his pocket and wiping his bloody hands as he approached. "Well, well, well. Look who I found, Tristian Ives, alive and well."

"Dex," I cried, my vision blurry and my whole body aching with grief and fear. "Why?"

"Why?" he repeated, arching a brow as he stepped closer still. "Why the fuck not? Now... do we think my father will want you back alive? Probably, hmm? I wonder if he'll mind alive but broken?"

I didn't reply. What the fuck could I even say that would make a difference? Begging would only encourage him further, so I locked my lips and shut him out. He said something more, but when I didn't give even a flicker of reaction, he ordered the guy restraining me to take me to their car.

Dex was a fucking psycho, and volatile as hell, but he wasn't totally stupid. He knew he'd set off alarms and that it was only a matter of time before reinforcements arrived. Within moments, I was stuffed into the trunk of a car and we were on our way back to RBD's.

I just prayed that John and Bram would return to the cabin soon. Maybe if they did, they could save Tink. As I'd been manhandled out the door, I could have sworn I saw her blink... but maybe that was just my own wishful thinking.

The drive back to the Grimaldi house—or that was where I assumed he was taking me—was all a blur. Nothing but the hum of the car engine until we eventually slowed to a stop and the trunk popped open.

Rough hands lifted me out, and I went limp. Fuck them. If they wanted me somewhere they could damn well work for it, but to my disappointment, the guy just dragged my feet along the ground without seeming to break a sweat.

"What the hell is going on down here?" a familiar voice roared, right as we passed by the Grecian statue in the foyer. "Dexter, what the fuck are you doing in the middle of the night with—" Mr. Grimaldi broke off with a gasp. "Is that Tristian?"

"The little thief you've been searching for? Why yes, Father, it is. I found her for you and actually brought her back... unlike your other son." Dex's voice was stacked high with hatred and smug satisfaction, and it turned my stomach.

There was a long pause, and I couldn't bring myself to look up at Mr. Grimaldi. He terrified me, but at the same time I hated feeling like I'd let him down when he'd extended so much trust. It was complicated, to say the least, but now that I'd run... now that I'd welched on our deal... I was doomed.

"Take her to the sitting room," Mr. Grimaldi ordered, snapping his fingers to the man holding me up.

Dex gave an uneasy laugh. "You mean the ballroom, right, Father?"

"If I did, then I would have said that," Mr. Grimaldi replied, his tone ice cold. "Move. Now. All of you. I need to make a call, but so help me if any of you lay so much as a finger on that girl, you'll answer to me. Am I clear?"

A rumble of agreement came from Dexter's henchmen, but Mr. Grimaldi didn't leave.

"I said... *am I clear?*"

Dex gave a low, frustrated growl. "Clear," he gritted out, sounding like he wanted to strangle someone. Probably his father. Or me.

"Good." With that, my former employer stalked away and my captor hauled me along the marble corridor toward the sitting room opposite the ballroom. Thank fuck for small mercies. I'd never seen anyone beaten bloody or killed in the sitting room, and I could imagine what a nightmare it'd be to get blood out of the thick woolen carpet.

Once inside, I was unceremoniously dropped onto

the sofa and then left there while the henchman retreated to the hallway and closed the door. Cautiously, I sat up to look around. Then with a sniffle I pulled my knees up to my chest and wrapped my arms around them.

I had to count myself lucky that Dex was more interested in winning his father's favor than in harming me. The same couldn't be said for Tink.

Time passed—I had no idea how much—and then finally the door opened, and in strode my handsome fake fiancé.

He stopped dead in his tracks when he saw me sitting there, the shock undeniable across his face. He hadn't known.

"Honey, I'm home," I tried to joke in a watery voice, then immediately burst out crying. Fuck I was a mess.

John

twenty-five

Not that I would go admitting it out loud any time soon, but I was enormously grateful Tris had made me take Bram with me to the drop-off point. By the time we finally delivered the cursed thing, we'd left a trail of bodies in our wake and barely kept our own skins attached in the process.

It was an easy enough process to pick up a new car, and Bram made some calls on the way back to the cabin, requesting urgent cleanups. All in all, the trip took about four times longer than it should have, and my anxiety about being away from Tris built by the second as we drove the long, winding dirt tracks back.

About a half mile from the cabin, Bram slowed the car and rolled down his window to key in the alarm deactivation code. Then he paused.

"What's wrong?" I asked, instantly paranoid.

"I don't know..." he replied, but at the same time he pressed his foot down on the gas, accelerating us up the road at high speed. "The sensor has been tripped and not turned off."

Fuck. That meant...

"Either it was an animal and the girls just haven't turned it off yet, or something worse."

Thank you, Bram, I'd already come to that conclusion myself. God, I hoped it was a dumb-ass animal that'd tripped the sensor, but surely the system was designed to know the difference or it would be constantly going off.

My gut told me it was something worse.

"Faster," I growled, my bruised knuckles turning white as I gripped the door.

Bram didn't fire back a quick retort, which told me he *also* suspected the "something worse" option had happened.

We heard the alarm before we could see the cabin, and I leapt from the car before Bram even fully stopped. Even in the darkness of the driveway I could see the front door wide open and all the lights on inside.

Something was really wrong.

"Tris!" I shouted, flying up the porch steps and

through the open—no, broken—front door. "Tristian! Where are you?"

I barely made it halfway over to the kitchen when I found Tink.

"Shit," I gasped, crouching down beside her seemingly lifeless form. A deep slice of pain and sorrow cut through me, the idea of losing my only friend too painful to comprehend for a moment. Then I found her weak pulse, thumping softly in her throat against my fingers, and I exhaled heavily.

Bram's boots on the floor behind me reminded me I wasn't alone, and I looked up at him with a frown. "She's still alive," I reassured him, because it really looked like she wasn't. "She needs to get to a hospital, though."

"Tris?" Bram asked while checking Tink's pulse for himself.

I swallowed hard, glancing around. "Not here... I hope." Because if she was, she was likely in a similar state to Tink. Or worse. I passed him my phone, since his had been lost in the car wreck earlier. "I'm going to check, you call an ambulance."

Not waiting for Bram's response, I was on my feet and searching the rest of the small cabin for any sign of my girl. When I found nothing, I wasn't sure whether to be relieved or not. Clearly whoever had damn near killed Tink now had Tris and had taken her God knew where.

"Medic is on the way," Bram told me in a clipped voice, crossing over to the kitchen and leaving Tink where she lay in a small pool of her own blood. "Don't move her. She might have a neck injury or something."

"I'm not an idiot," I muttered, but the desire to pick her up was strong. It just felt *wrong* leaving her there on the floor, even if the logic was sound. "Tell me you have recordings from all those surveillance cameras to explain what the fuck happened here."

He'd turned off the alarm, thank fuck, and my ears rang as he pulled a laptop from behind the toaster and plugged it into the control panel for the security system. His shoulders betrayed how tense he was as he brought up the hidden camera feeds. He scrolled back to about half an hour after we'd left the girls alone, and we found the culprit.

"That *motherfucker!*" I roared, losing my grip on calm and punching my already bruised fist through a kitchen cabinet. "Fuck!"

"Do you feel better?" Bram drawled, eyeing my now bleeding hand. "Talk about counterproductive acts of anger."

"Is that attitude fucking helpful?" I barked back, practically steaming with fury. "Give me my phone."

He arched a brow but handed it over. "Who are you calling?"

The sound of helicopter blades whirred in the distance and I frowned. "Is that—"

"Medic," he confirmed with a nod. "I wasn't waiting for a road ambulance. Who are you calling?"

"Luther Grimaldi," I replied with a grimace. "He has something I want, and I have something *he* wants. Maybe we can arrange a trade before..." *before she gets hurt. If she isn't already.*

Bram nodded, crossing back to Tink to check her pulse again. "Good. She's still hanging in there. Do you think Dexter took Tris to his father?"

"I have to hope he did. Or at very least, Luther will know where to find him and pull him in line." I brought up the old man's phone number—his personal one that he'd given me when we were bonding over art—and hit dial.

Bram strode outside to meet the helicopter which was louder than ever. They'd be landing on the grass beside the driveway, so I moved through to the bedroom to dampen the noise as much as possible while the phone rang.

It went to voicemail, and I needed to resist the urge to hurl my phone at the wall. Instead I pressed redial and listened to my blood pressure rise with each dial tone. It took two more attempts, but then *finally* the call connected.

"John, this is a surprise," Luther Grimaldi said when he answered. "I'm a little busy right—"

"Do you have her?" I snapped, cutting him off.

A tense silence filled the line. Then he gave a short sigh. "I do."

A rush of breath exited my chest, and I sagged to sit on the edge of the bed. Luther Grimaldi was a bad guy, no question, but he had a huge soft spot for my girl. He wouldn't harm her... I didn't think.

"Is she... hurt?" I had to ask. Because Dex was the one who took her, and Tink was barely clinging to life. Any man who could do that...

"She doesn't appear to be, no," Grimaldi replied, his tone clipped. "Do you think I'm the kind of man who would assault a young woman?"

I grimaced. "Assault? No. Kill? Yes. But I wasn't asking if *you* had hurt her."

He made a grunt of understanding. "Dexter is... unpredictable. But it seems that he was more interested in gaining my favor than harming her."

"Because he already got his fix damn near beating another woman to death," I growled, my fingers tightening around my phone.

Grimaldi paused a moment before replying. "I see."

"I'll cut to the chase," I continued, anxious to make the deal to get my girl back. "You have Tris, I have your painting. Let's arrange a trade and clear the debt."

A creak sounded on the phone line, like he'd just sat up in a leather office chair. "You have my Van Gogh? The original?"

I swiped a hand over my face, praying he would take my offer. "Not *Poppy Flowers*. I have the Picasso that you wanted Tris to forge. I have the original *Le pigeon aux petits pois*. It's yours, in exchange for Tristian."

This time the silence stretched so long I wondered if the call had disconnected, and glanced at my phone to check that it wasn't.

"You have the original?" Grimaldi repeated slowly, with a heavy dose of disbelief. "*You* have it, personally? Or you know who has it?"

"I have it," I gritted out. "In my private collection."

Luther Grimaldi let out a low whistle. "Well. This changes things, doesn't it?"

"So, you accept my deal? Picasso for Tristian?"

"I accept," he replied quickly.

"Unharmed," I specified with a firm tone. "She needs to be *wholly unharmed*, or I will set fire to the fucking painting right then and there."

Grimaldi gave a chuckle. "I understand, John. She will be my honored guest until you get here with my

251

Pigeons. You have twenty-four hours. Is that acceptable?"

I rubbed the bridge of my nose, thinking it over and doing the math. "I need longer. Thirty-six."

"Very well. I will expect to see you in thirty-six hours. In the meantime, I will guarantee Miss Ives's safety within my house." He inhaled deeply, his chair creaking again. "John, I'm sure I don't need to warn you, but if you think of double crossing me it will not end well."

I wet my lips. "I understand, Luther. Just keep her safe, and keep her the fuck away from your piece of shit woman-beating son."

"You have my word." Then the old man ended our call, filling my ear with dead air.

I breathed out another long sigh of relief, my hands shaking as I put my phone back in my pocket. Swallowing back my fear and desperation, I wiped my sweaty palms on my pants and went out to check on Tink and Bram. Fucking hell, Dex had done a number on her.

The living room was empty, just a bloody floor where she'd lain, and outside it sounded like the helicopter was taking off again. I headed through to the porch and watched the chopper lifting off, then noticed

Bram standing in the driveway beside our car, watching them leave.

"Is she going to be okay?" I called over the whirring sound.

Bram glanced back at me, his expression drawn with frustration and worry. Then he looked back to the sky where the chopper was quickly disappearing and hung his head in defeat.

"Too soon to know," he eventually replied, returning to the cabin where I waited. "It doesn't look good, though. Considering how long she was lying here..."

I nodded, hating that we'd fucked up so badly by splitting up. "You didn't want to go with them?"

He barked a sharp laugh. "Want to? Of course I did. But I'm still under contract to protect *Tris*, not Tink. And right now I'm failing pretty fucking bad, so it's not a question of what I want, is it?"

As much as I would have liked to release his obligation, as valuable as Tink was to me as a friend... Tris was always going to be more important. So I just nodded and returned inside to make the calls I needed to make. The Picasso that I was trading for my girl's life wasn't even on this continent so I needed transport. Fast.

This time when I placed a call, it was answered on the first try.

"Carol," I snapped. "I need to borrow your jet."

"John," she replied, betraying no curiosity or concern in her voice. "Which one, dear?"

I scrubbed a hand over my face, my head whirling with conspiracy theories. Did Carol already know what'd happened here tonight?

"I don't care," I replied. "Whatever is closest and can handle the distance to Luxembourg. It's an emergency."

A tap of computer keys in the background told me she was working on it. Or I hoped that was what she was doing. "Mm hmm, I have one just outside of Cloudcroft, can you get yourself there?"

"Yes. I'll leave now."

"Very well. Of course, there is the matter of cost..."

Anger flared hot in my chest. "The *cost* has already been paid, several times over, Carol. The *cost* of this fucking Game has been paid in blood, and I swear to fucking God if any more is shed before the Game is over, I will personally steal every last thing you hold valuable. Including my favorite Atwood."

Bram frantically shook his head at me, warning me that it was a fucking awful idea to threaten a woman like Carol Atwood, but I already knew that. It didn't stop me, though. Nothing was too far, when it came to rescuing Tris.

"I'd be very careful with how you speak to me, John

Smith," she said in an ice cold voice. "I understand you're emotional right now and not thinking straight. Go and do what you need to do, then we can discuss this further when we all have a cooler head. Understood?"

My teeth ground together so hard I nearly broke one. But even through my panic and anger, I could see I'd gone too far. "Understood," I growled.

She ended the call without saying anything further, and I stalked back out to the car.

"John, do you have a death wish?" Bram exclaimed, following. "You don't speak to Carol like that. Ever. Not if you value your own skin. Not even—" He broke off, frowning. "Okay, that's not true. Danny does talk to her like that, but she's an exception. *You* aren't family. You're expendable, my friend."

I knew that, but I stood by my threat. "Get in," I barked. "I'm dropping you at Grimaldi's house, you can keep watch while I fly to fucking Luxembourg."

All he needed to do was keep an eye on her from a distance. Just make sure Grimaldi stuck to his word, and no one let Dexter even breathe the same air as Tris. In thirty-six hours, she'd be free.

"If he even looks in her direction," Bram said and I didn't need to ask which he or what he would do.

That worked for me.

Tris

twenty-six

Sin had stayed true to his word, protecting me in his own father's home for the next day and a half. He'd sworn he had no idea about Dex's attack, and I believed him. After getting his guards to do some digging, we'd discovered that it wasn't Sin who led Dex to the cabin. It was Tink.

Accidentally, of course, she couldn't have known she'd been sighted by one of Dex's friends in town with Bram and had a GPS tracker stuck to her purse. He'd come to find *her* in a fit of jealousy, thinking she was dating someone new. He'd found me there entirely out of luck.

I had to guess his lack of foreknowledge was what'd spared me a similar fate to Tink. He'd been surprised enough that he tossed me straight to his daddy, rather than anything worse.

"Any word on Tink?" I asked Sin as I picked at my lunch. He'd asked Chef Tony to bring meals to his room, since he was refusing to leave my side for even a minute. I didn't think he'd even slept in the day and a half since I'd arrived.

"She's in a stable condition," he replied with a nod. "But it will still be touch and go until she wakes up and they can ascertain the extent of any brain damage."

My food stuck in my throat with guilt and worry. I'd told Sin what Dex had done, and he'd immediately asked his father to make the relevant enquiries. Bram and John had apparently got her transported to a private hospital, and she was receiving the best treatment money could buy.

"He needs to pay for what he did," I said with quiet determination. "If he gets away with this, who will he hurt next? Does he beat his wife?"

Sin's jaw tightened with fury. "He wouldn't dare."

I scoffed. "So attempted murder of a stripper is okay, but he draws the line at his spouse? Bullshit. Isn't she pregnant, too?"

His brow dipped low in a scowl, but he wasn't angry at me. Instead, he pulled out his phone and tapped his thumb over the screen. Instead of taking his call in private, he swapped it to speaker as it started to ring.

A few moments later, a woman answered. "Hello?"

Sin frowned. "Maria?"

"No, this is her sister. Maria is, um, unavailable. Can I take a message?"

Sin met my eyes and I could see the concern and dread he was processing. "This is urgent. Can you ask her to take my call, please?"

"I'm sorry, no. She isn't available right now." The woman sounded firm and cold, unwavering. In the background some machinery beeped and a muffled voice sounded over an intercom. "I have to go. I'll... I'll tell her you called."

The woman ended the call quickly and I gave a groan. "Sin... she was in a *hospital*."

He grimaced, nodding. "I noticed that, too. Fuck. I need to..." He trailed off, running a hand over his face. "If Dex has hurt her or the baby... my father will kill him."

"Good." I said it before my mind could prevent the word escaping, but it was true. I hoped Mr. Grimaldi *would* kill Dex, because he was nothing but a slug on the cabbage of life.

"I need more information about Maria. Do you mind if I...?" He gestured to his phone, and I nodded quickly.

"Yes, go ahead. I want to know, too. And I'm fine

here." There was a bite in my words that he didn't deserve. I should feel worse about the deep exhaustion on his face. He'd kept his word to me, and I appreciated it more than I could express. But I wasn't so grateful I wanted to chance letting him go whether it was just outside the door or not. Yes, he wouldn't go far, but I also hated feeling this fucking terrified.

He arched a smile. "I'm not going anywhere, Tris. I just didn't want to be rude by sitting here on my phone."

Goddammit. He really didn't deserve my snark. "Oh, geez, you're fine. I'm a big girl, Sin. I can entertain myself." And this time I meant it. I gestured to my lunch, and the sketch book he'd given me the day before.

For the next hour or so, Sin made calls and sent texts, doing his utmost to find out what'd happened to Maria. Both of us were scared Dex had done something to hurt her like he'd hurt Tink, and what that'd mean for the baby... I shuddered to think. Sin told me Maria wasn't due to give birth for another six weeks yet, so she was in a very vulnerable state.

Eventually, a knock on the door interrupted us, and one of the security guards announced that Mr. Grimaldi required our presence in the sitting room.

"At least it's not the ballroom," I muttered, voicing my same thought from the night Dex had abducted me.

Sin winced at my comment, though, and rubbed the bridge of his nose.

"You'll be fine, Tris, I promise. So long as John isn't trying to pull a fast one..." He let that thought hang in the air, and I shook my head.

"He wouldn't. Not about this. If he said he has the painting, then he does. Or he knew where to steal it from. Either way, there's no duplicity here." I was confident in that. For all the lies and betrayals, John hadn't lied when he said he loved me. He wouldn't risk my safety with a forgery. Not now.

As we headed downstairs to the sitting room, Sin received a phone call and raised his brows at me like he was asking if I'd be okay without him. I got the feeling he didn't want anyone knowing about the investigation we'd been undertaking today, so I nodded quickly.

He lagged behind, answering the call as I continued along the hallway with my guard. The dark-suited man politely held the sitting room door open for me to enter, and a rush of staggering relief washed through me when I spotted John waiting inside.

"Venus," he exclaimed, and I rushed over, leaping into his embrace. He buried his face in my hair, his arms tight around me and lifting me clear off the ground as he held me. "Are you okay? I'm so sorry I left you alone."

"I'm okay," I assured him, my arms banded around his neck. "I'm not hurt. How's Tink?"

John grimaced, and Mr. Grimaldi cleared his throat to remind us we weren't alone. I drew a deep breath, loosening my grip on John, and he reluctantly set me back on my feet. He didn't move away, though, and neither did I. I was quite comfortable staying within the loop of his arms, but I turned around to face my former employer nonetheless.

"So, you see I held my end of the agreement, yes?" The old man gestured to me and my uninjured status. "Despite what some might think, I am a man of my word."

John gave an irritated sound, but reached for an art case on the floor. "As am I, Luther. Do I have your assurance that we'll be free to leave your property without harassment? Once again, it is not you or Sinister that concerns me; it's Dexter."

As if summoned like a demon, the sick bastard in question burst through the doors with two of his own henchmen at his side. I recognized one as the man who'd restrained me while Dex beat Tink half to death.

"Father, what is this I hear about you letting Tristian go? She's not *yours* to release!"

Mr. Grimaldi leveled a hard glare at his son. "Nor is she yours, Dexter. You were not invited to attend this meeting, and I do not appreciate the interruption. Leave."

Dex's mouth dropped open, and John's arm around my waist tightened, pulling me closer into his body. Before Dexter could argue, Sin strode into the sitting room with a sly smile on his lips. He totally ignored his brother, instead heading across to where Mr. Grimaldi stood by the window.

As Sin leaned in close to whisper in his father's ear, his eyes caught mine and the satisfied glee in his gaze was palpable. Whatever that call had been, it was good news... of a sort.

Mr. Grimaldi's brows shot up in surprise, then a delighted smile curved his lips. Whatever Sin said next, though, caused his joyful expression to darken so much I shrank backward into John's protective embrace.

"What?" he roared, reaching inside his Armani suit jacket to pull his gun. "You spineless fuck. I should have done this a long damn time ago." Without any hesitation, he pulled the trigger.

The shot rang out with a deafening crack in the intimate room, and Dexter dropped like a puppet with its strings cut. For a moment, no one spoke. No one moved. Blood spread in a pool beneath Dexter, his lifeless eyes glassy and the entry point between his eyes dribbling blood down his temple.

"Sir..." one of the henchmen started, clearly in shock.

Mr. Grimaldi's eyes were hard as granite, though, as he put his gun away. "Tristian, dear, I apologize that you had to witness this mess. You are free to leave, of course. John if I find that painting is a forgery—"

"It's not," he said firmly.

"If it is," Mr. Grimaldi continued, "you will regret it. Please leave now. I have a funeral to plan, and a new grandson to welcome into my family."

I gasped, and Sin shot me a knowing glance, inclining his head slightly.

"I'll escort you out," Sin offered, motioning for us to hurry the fuck up.

We didn't need telling twice, quickly circling around Dexter's body and exiting the room without hanging around to see what RBD would do next. He really had lived up to that nickname.

"Sin," I hissed as we made our way quickly through the halls to the front of the house. "What just happened back there?"

Sin ushered us out of the house before replying, glancing over his shoulder before he spoke. "I finally got a call back from Maria. She *is* in the hospital, because her *son* was born early and has been in the NICU unit for the past week. She said Dexter didn't know about the birth, and she wanted it to stay that way. She'd used an alias name when she was admitted, and due to her injuries the hospital had been happy to go along with it."

I sucked a horrified gasp. "Her injuries?"

Sin nodded, his frown severe. "You were right about him. Thank you for pushing me to investigate. If I hadn't, Maria would have been on the run from him the rest of her life. That's no life for a child."

"Holy shit," I breathed, stunned and disgusted.

Sin sighed. "Well... it's dealt with now. You two better leave while my father is otherwise occupied. If all goes well, this might be goodbye for good. Please, Tris, try to stay out of the Game from here on out? You deserve better." The way his gaze flicked to John said he meant more than just the Game.

For his part, John said nothing, but his grip on me stayed firm until I pulled away briefly. In spite of or maybe because of the weird circumstances, Sin had become something of a friend. He welcomed my embrace, but we didn't linger.

After a quick hug, Sin returned inside.

"Let's go, Venus," John said, snagging me around the middle again and half-lifting as he hauled ass to the car in the driveway

He didn't waste time on the passenger door, just opening the driver's side and nudging me to scoot over. Car started, he braced a hand on the seat and backed up, then swung us around. "Seat belt on," John ordered, and he accelerated down the drive like we had the hounds of hell on our heels.

We didn't. Weirdly, I believed RBD. I believed Sin. I believed John. This whole damn mess blew up on me because of a forgery. John saved me with the real thing. A half-mile from the bottom of the drive, John jerked the car over to the side of the road, and Bram popped out.

A second wave of relief hit me, but I didn't have time to even wave at Bram before John dragged me in for a kiss.

Fuck.

I held onto him and didn't even mind being manhandled into the backseat while Bram took over the driving.

"Don't start fucking until we're somewhere safer."

For some reason, Bram's deadpan delivery cracked through the terrifying and icy cold bubble that had encased me since Dex exploded into the cabin.

I laughed.

I laughed until I cried, and I held onto John for all of it.

John

twenty-seven

With the cabin compromised, Bram and I decided to rent a Hestia safe house. It was our only really viable option on short notice in a town where the Grimaldis knew everyone and everything. I had confidence that Sin meant Tris no harm, and, with Dex dead, it eliminated a huge risk, but Hank was still out there somewhere. As were all the other Game players.

The only available option that met our criteria was about an hour and a half outside Whispering Willows and was a stately old manor house blanketed in creeping wisteria. The Hestia app told us the cleaners had just finished and fully stocked the kitchen in accordance with my saved preferences, and the whole place smelled like lemony cleaning product.

"Nice place," Bram commented with a low whistle, looking around the kitchen with wall-to-wall glass overlooking the back garden. He flipped open the host guide book on the counter and browsed the information. It was usually things like where to eat, safe takeout options with discreet delivery drivers, contact info for mobile arms dealers. Useful shit.

"Yeah well, it's secure. That's all that matters." I kept Tris's hand in mine as I looked around the house, checking for the panic room location, secondary exit points, gun safes...

"Cloudcroft House was built in 1876," Bram read aloud from the brochure, "and once provided safe haven for the notorious highwayman Black Bart before he was captured in 1882. I had no idea safe houses had prestige and history."

"Learn something new every day, Bram," Tris chirped with a little giggle at his version of the house's history. "So do I, come to think of it. Did they put any wine in the fridge?"

"Yes, ma'am, they did. Is Pinot Gris okay?" Bram held up a cold bottle, and Tris nodded enthusiastically. He poured her a glass, and she detached from my hand to take it from him. My fingers itched to grab her again, but I bit the inside of my cheek to resist the urge. She didn't need me clinging to her like a two-year-old.

She sipped her wine, groaning in a way that made my dick pulse, and I had to look away.

"Uh, I was thinking..." Bram said with a slight hesitation, "if you guys are cool here, I might go check in on Tink?"

I was right on the verge of telling him *no*, but Tris spoke up before I could get the word out.

"Of course you can," she assured him with a severe frown of worry. "I had Sin check in on her medical records, but I know I'd feel a shitload better if you saw her yourself. Does it take long to get there?"

Bram stifled a yawn with the back of his hand. "Yes, but I can get a lift on a helicopter to cut down travel time. There was a new Game level issued yesterday, so hopefully they take the maximum allowed time to find it, which means there won't be another until... day after tomorrow?"

He directed the question at me, and I nodded, folding my arms to keep from pawing at Tris. "Yeah, that's right. But if Ha— uh, *someone* finds it sooner they'll issue the new challenge earlier." Tris was so adamant that it wasn't Hank playing the Game, I didn't want to start an argument with her now.

"Go," Tris told Bram. "If we're not safe here, then there's not much else you can do."

He frowned, rubbing the back of his neck. "That's

not super encouraging, Tris, but I agree. You cool with this?" Again, the question was directed to me. Because I was the one holding his contract. Fucking hell, sooner or later I needed to release that.

"Sure," I agreed. "Take her a teddy bear from us or some shit."

Tris gave me a bemused smile over her wine glass, but Bram nodded. "Can do. Let me just do another sweep of this place first and make some calls." He walked away, pulling out his phone as he went, leaving Tris and me alone.

A heavy silence hung between us for a moment, and she took another sip of her wine.

"Venus, I—"

"John, you—"

We both started speaking at the same time and shared a smile.

"You go," she murmured, biting the edge of her lip like she was nervous.

I shook my head. "Please, you. What's on your mind?"

She wrinkled her nose in an adorable way. "You were right. I never should have pushed you to take Bram. I just really thought we were safe at the cabin, but maybe if he'd stayed then Tink wouldn't be..." She trailed off with a sad shrug, the guilt etched all over her face.

That was what cracked me, and I closed the gap between us, scooping her up in my arms and sitting her perfect ass on the edge of the island counter. "First of all, you are not to blame for what happened to Tink. That blame lies squarely and solely on Dex. Second of all, both Bram and I are grown-ass adults capable of disagreeing if we felt strongly about the situation. The fact remains, we both thought you'd be safe, too."

"Still..."

"No. That's facts, Venus. We were *both* wrong, because weirdly enough, neither of us is psychic." I brushed a kiss over her lips, and she gave a delicious little moan.

"It'd be so useful if we were, though," she replied with a sigh.

I smiled, my hand cupping the back of her neck and my thumb stroking her pulse point. "Well, if it makes you feel better, I probably wouldn't have made it back in one piece if not for Bram."

Her brows shot up and she sat back slightly, her gaze scanning my face. When she zeroed in on my hairline and brushed her fingers against a bruise, she gasped. "What happened?"

"Long story," I shrugged. "I'd rather use our alone time for something involving less clothes and more *hands on.*"

Her eyes narrowed. "You think you can distract me so easily, Professor Smith? I'll have you know, that I—" Her indignation was cut short as I crushed my lips to hers in a hot, hungry kiss. She moaned, kissing me back with equal ferocity while her hands made quick work of my shirt.

I had to stop kissing her just long enough to rip the buttons off the shirt she was wearing. They went flying like pieces of popcorn. There was something satisfying about the scattering sound they made as they hit the wood floor.

"John." Honestly, the way she half-moaned my name did insane things to my already hard dick. No more talking for Venus, not until we managed to ease some of the vibrant worries we'd both endured for the last two days.

I'd just barely gotten her pants undone and my fingers down to cup her sweet cunt when a knock hit the door followed by Bram calling, "Do me a favor and be dressed when I come in, yeah?"

Tris groaned as I pulled out my hand and I twisted to glare at the door as Bram stepped back inside.

"I thought you were going to the hospital to check on Tink." Yes, that was absolutely why I was pissed about him coming back early.

"She's all right, isn't she?" Tris' voice climbed with a note of alarm. "Nothing happened—"

Shit. Would they have called him? I didn't want to face the idea of losing that pain in the ass. She was—

"She's fine," Bram said. Relief had my shoulders dropping and Tris all but curved around my shoulders. "I called as soon as I got to the bottom of the drive. Visiting hours are over, and they want her to sleep. But she is sleeping. They said it's a good sign."

Sleeping. Had she woken up yet? That was what we'd been waiting on, but Bram gave me the briefest of head shakes. So, sleep was good but she still hadn't woken up. Shit.

"I want to see her," Tris admitted, "but I don't want to bring trouble to her door."

"Maybe not tonight, Venus," I said, turning to face her. The exhausted, wounded look in her eyes tore at me. "We'll make sure you see her." I'd break us both in if I had to. "You look tired."

"I am, and I'm not. I slept last night, but I woke up a lot too."

I narrowed my eyes. "But you were fine?" Cause Dex being dead was a good thing, but I hadn't been kidding about burning that damn painting.

Soft hands cupped my face and brought me back to the present. I'd never thought of myself as a particularly violent man before. For my Venus? I would willing plumb the depths of depravity to fuck shit up if necessary.

"I'm really alright. Sin never let me out of his sight, and I don't think he slept. But he was on guard duty from the moment they tossed me back into that room, and Mr. Grimaldi," she continued, "was a perfect gentleman. I know it's weird and I know he's done really bad things and he had me shoot someone... but he could have been so much worse."

I understood that. "I can see that, but I'm never going to be his biggest fan."

A faint smile touched her lips. "Agreed." A yawn caught her off-guard, and she covered that perfect mouth with her hand as Bram cleared his throat.

"Maybe you should get some sleep, Tris. I know it's not late..."

"No," she said, glancing at me. "It's not, but maybe if I had a good cuddle buddy."

On that note, I scooped her off the counter and shot Bram a look. "Yell if you need us."

"But don't need us, please," Tris called before I could close the door.

She laughed when I tossed her on the bed. "You really are tired, Venus." Because there was a darkness moving in her eyes.

"I know," she told me soberly. "Like I said, I really didn't sleep well last night, and I was worried about you and Tink and this Game and..."

Right. My girl needed some care. "Come on, let's get you ready for bed."

"And a couple of orgasms?" She batted her eyes at me like I would deny her. Twenty-five minutes later, she was sound asleep against my chest and I deserved a medal for sainthood. I went after three orgasms, and the third one knocked her out.

My dick was hard, but it could wait. Having her right there to hold was worth a little suffering on my part. Even though I didn't expect to sleep, the vibrating of my phone's alarm had my eyes snapping open. Tris was still asleep, on her stomach, arms curled under the pillow, and I had my hand on her ass. Such a lovely ass—

The phone vibrated again, and I glared but reached for it. Eight on the nose. New Game clue.

The words on the screen had to be a joke.

They had to be.

What's more valuable than the art of the ages? The forger whose impeccable work can fool madmen, criminals, and thieves alike...

The next *piece* was *Tris*.

Tris

twenty-eight

Raised, angry voices woke me from my heavy, dreamless sleep, and I groaned. The bed was still warm from John's body, and I buried my face in his pillow for a moment, breathing deeply and wondering how in the *fuck* I'd fallen so hard, so fast. He infuriated me to no end, but fuck he made me happy. He made me feel safe and treasured and totally adored.

When the shouting became increasingly heated, I sighed and scrambled out of bed to investigate. Bram's quick return last night had me suspicious. His excuse about visiting hours hadn't sat quite right, knowing him and what he did for a living. Why would he let something like "visiting hours" dictate whether he saw Tink or not?

My guess? He'd suspected some fresh danger and decided to stay close. To keep me alive, like John had contracted him to do.

I ducked into the bathroom to pee and freshen up, then dressed in John's huge t-shirt before tying my hair up in a messy bun on top of my head. His shirt was big enough that I saw no need for pants and made my way downstairs to where the guys were screaming at each other in the kitchen.

"...I don't give a rainbow rat's ass, Carol!" John was bellowing as I entered the room quietly. "I'm done. We're done. Cancel my entry, wipe the scoreboard, I don't fucking care. I *refuse* to put her in danger like this. Not after what she just went through!"

My brows shot up in shock, because I didn't think I'd ever heard John that *violently* angry before. Was Tink in danger?

"John, take a breath and calm down," a woman said from the speaker of John's phone on the counter. She didn't sound even the slightest bit sympathetic, and I dimly recognized Bram's mom who'd told me about the Game. "For one thing, you can't just *give up* like that. For another, if you don't want Tristian in danger, then it's a very simple answer. Keep her safe. You want to throw blame around? Blame yourself. You never should have threatened my child."

She ended the call, the room practically reverberating with tension in the resounding silence.

"Um, what's going on?" I asked, and John nearly leapt out of his skin. Bram just tossed me an apologetic smile, but he must have seen me come in already.

John closed the gap between us, sweeping me up in his arms until my feet dangled a solid six inches off the floor. "I'm so sorry, Venus. I'm so fucking sorry. We need to go. Now. We need to—"

"Whoa, hold up, Professor," I interrupted, pushing out of his arms and regaining some floor underfoot. "I'm not going anywhere until someone explains what the fuck is going on? What was Carol talking about? You threatened her *child?* I have to assume she doesn't mean Bram."

Bram shook his head. "Uh no. Not me. My little brother, whom my mom is *fiercely* protective over."

John scowled. "I never would have *hurt* him. It's a running joke with Carol that he'd make an amazing thief with just a little guidance."

"Yeah... Carol doesn't have a sense of humor, bro. She definitely took that as a threat."

John rolled his eyes and gave a frustrated sigh. "Yeah well... I was under a lot of stress."

Confused, I frowned as I glanced between the two of them. Then I shook my head and headed for the coffee machine on the kitchen counter. "Okay. Here's what we're gonna do. I'm going to make coffee, then the three of us are going to sit down and drink it while Bram explains what fresh hell I've just woken up into. Alright?"

John folded his arms across his bare chest, making me drool a little at the bulge of muscles. "And what am I meant to do while *he* explains?"

My lips twitched with the need to smile. "You are going to sit there and look pretty, sweetheart. Better yet, you can rub my feet while Bram talks. Okay? Good plan. Go on, sit." I gestured to the stools behind the long island counter, then turned back to the fancy automatic espresso machine.

It only took a few minutes to make lattes for all three of us, then I served them to the sulking men sitting in silence and smiled. "Go ahead, Bram. I'm listening."

He shot a warning glare at John, who scowled daggers back but didn't say anything.

Bram huffed, turning his attention back to me. "Okay so, someone must have found yesterday's piece pretty quick because they issued a new Game challenge this morning."

I nodded to show I was following along. Nothing seemed too crazy or dramatic so far, though...

"Um, so I would suspect this is the last piece for the Game because it's sort of like a *winner takes all* situation and that would mean that—" Bram was rambling and my nerves were fraying.

"Get to the point, Bramble," I snapped, using Tink's nickname for him. "What's the item?"

"You," John growled, answering for him.

I wrinkled my nose, not understanding. "Me? You mean something I have?"

Bram grimaced. "No... it's *you*."

My brow creased, then I vaguely remembered Tink mentioning that Game pieces could be *anything* and I was pretty sure she'd included *people* in her list of examples.

My lips rounded. "Oh."

"Yeah. So, you see why we need to *leave*?" John prompted, giving me a pointed look. "If we disappear and the time limit lapses, they'll be forced to issue a new clue or... I don't even know what. I don't care, either. After the absolute shit show of this Game, there won't be another and right now I'm pretty fucking happy about that fact. My grandfather would be sick to see what's happened to his legacy."

I rested my elbows on the counter, dropping my head into my hands. It was too early for all this. Hadn't I *just* been abducted by a psychopath then literally traded for a priceless work of art after my only friend got beaten practically to death? What did I have to do to get a vacation?

John's explosion at Carol on the phone made sense now. Part of me was overwhelmingly touched that he was so willing to walk away from the Game for me, knowing how much it all meant to him and his grandfather's memory. But the bigger part of me latched onto what Bram had just said.

"Why do you think this is the last Game challenge?" I asked, looking up from my hands.

His expression turned shifty and he rubbed the back of his neck. Guilty. He looked guilty. Why?

"Bram..." I warned. "Now isn't the time to play coy."

He blew out a long breath, his cheeks puffing. "A little bird told me."

That confused the hell out of me, but John cracked a grin and chuckled. "See? Eavesdropping on someone as careful and private as Carol is just the mark of a future thief. Tell me I'm wrong."

Bram rolled his eyes, and I got the impression his *little bird* was his brother that John had used to threaten Carol. Weird family.

"Oh-*kay* so... assuming that's accurate, this is

potentially our last chance to catch Hank... right?" I said it cold and matter-of-fact, refusing to let myself feel the agony associated with that admission. That I was no longer questioning John's recollection of the night Nelson died. That I believed Hank was exactly as John said... a fucking fraud. A liar. A murderer.

John's soft eyes said he understood, though. He got it. "Venus..."

I wet my lips, then cleared my throat. "So, if this is the last chance, I'm not going anywhere. If Hank wants to win this Game so badly he would kill the only person he ever loved, then he'll come for me. And when he does..." I trailed off with a shrug. "I guess when he does, then we'll... um..."

What? We'll what? Kill him?

I swallowed hard, unable to get the words out.

"We can deal with it," John assured me quietly. "You don't have to do anything."

The relief that washed over me was almost embarrassing. I wanted to be strong and fierce. I wanted to be the girl who could handle her own problems, reap her own vengeance, and not rely on men to do it for her. But deep down, that just wasn't me. Not if we were talking about hurting *or killing* someone I considered family for so much of my life.

"Maybe we could have him arrested?" I suggested in a small voice, my eyeballs hot with unshed tears.

The look that both guys gave me, though, said they didn't think it was a viable option.

John cleared his throat and turned to Bram. "Okay. If Tris has her mind made up, then let's talk about how we're keeping her safe until Hank arrives. Every other piece has been booby trapped. Is this house wired to blow if we step on the wrong floorboard?"

Bram screwed up his face. "That, John Smith, would be a travesty for such a historic safe house. No, uh, that is actually why I had to abort my mission to visit Tink. I'm the booby trap."

"You?" I repeated, puzzled. "Um..."

He gave me a *look*. "I'm more than capable, thank you. But to set your mind at ease... there may or may not also be a dozen well-paid mercenaries surrounding the house."

I breathed a sigh of relief, then caught myself when Bram pouted. "Um, not that I think we need extra help, or anything. I'm sure you're... very capable. But it can't hurt. Right?"

"Good save, Venus," John laughed.

I smiled apologetically at Bram, then crossed over to the front window and peered out at the bright sunshine. If we were surrounded, then where were they all?

"You won't see them," Bram said, reading my mind. "They're some of the Guild's best. Carol might be pissed at John, but she wouldn't want Tris actually hurt. She called in the big guns."

John gave a chuckle. "Tell your sister I said hi."

Jealousy flared hot, and I whipped around to glare at him, and his hands raised defensively. "Platonic friend. Nothing more. I'm not that insane."

"It's funny because it's true," Bram agreed.

I yawned, returning to where I'd left my coffee. "I'm confused. Is the Game run by this... guild?"

John exchanged a look with Bram before replying. "No... it's separate. Carol is the only crossover that I'm aware of. She just happens to be in upper-level management so is utilizing the resources at her disposal. Or, that's what I am gathering."

"Sounds right," Bram agreed, grinning. "But I love the mental image of Carol as *management*."

I'd only met the woman once, but she definitely didn't strike me as an office worker. I sipped my coffee and thought it all over. We weren't in Whispering Willows anymore, and the safe house was supposedly super confidential, so it could be ages before Hank found us. If he was even the first one. Someone had put that bruise on John's head, and now that I looked carefully at

Bram, I noted various cuts and scrapes he didn't have a few days ago.

"If I'm the piece and John has me, hasn't John already won? I mean—technically?"

Hope flared in John's eyes, but it was Bram who lifted his shoulders. "Above my pay grade."

When John headed for the cell phone, both Bram and I said, "Don't." That earned a bit of scowl. But Bram continued, "She's already mad. Let her get even, then we'll talk to her after."

It seemed a reasonable conclusion. John pissed her off. She made John pay. Then we could all be chill.

"Fine." John didn't seem to disagree, but he also didn't like it. That was fine; so much of this shit I hadn't *liked*. We could all deal. Bram had gotten me out of Grimaldi's, and he'd beaten the shit out of Dex for me, keeping him from hurting me. I could handle trusting Bram's assessment of this.

"So... we just hang out and wait?"

John stared at me intently, while Bram nodded. "Yep. Pretty much. You guys wanna play Uno or something?"

I scoffed and gulped the rest of my coffee. "Sorry, Bramble, you're shit out of luck. If today is ending in bloodshed and drama, I'm damn well starting it by getting my rocks off." I dropped my empty cup in the sink and started out of the kitchen. "You coming, Professor?"

"Fuck yes," he enthused, hurrying after me. "In more ways than one, I hope."

I laughed, taking the stairs at a run with him chasing behind. More ways than one and more than just *once*, hopefully.

John

twenty-nine

The most delicious little moans and whimpers escaped my girl as I plowed into her tight cunt, really doing—in my opinion—a bang up job of the task she'd assigned: to rearrange her guts from the inside.

"Oh my god…" she groaned, her inner muscles clamping around me as she came. "John… fuck… don't… yes, keep going…"

With direction like that, I didn't know how anyone got confused about what women wanted in bed. It was crystal clear. I gripped her lush hips, lifting her up off the bed and driving deeper, which she rewarded with a gasping *yessss,* and I needed to bite my cheek to keep from coming just yet. If Venus wanted to double down on that orgasm, I was damn well going to deliver.

"Fuck, you feel so good," I murmured, making the mistake of glancing down to where her pussy swallowed my dick like it was made for me. I groaned, damn near losing my control, but my girl started trembling with the spark of another climax, so I jerked my eyes back up to her face.

Her eyes were heavy, her dark lashes low, but the gleam of blue locked on my mouth, and she reached out a hand. "John, kiss me."

Yes, ma'am.

I leaned down, claiming her mouth with mine and letting her suck my lower lip like she loved to do. Then I slipped a hand down to play with her clit, and she detonated. So sweet.

"Oh..." she panted, her breath mixing with mine as our lips remained together. "Oh... yeah... John..."

"Hmm?" I replied, slowing my thrusts and staying deep. I loved being able to feel every clench and flutter of her body. I was so fucking close to exploding, but if she wanted a third...

"Come for me, Professor," she whispered, then grabbed my lip with her teeth in a teasing bite.

What my Venus wanted, she got. That was my silent oath to her every minute of every day. We still had a whole lot of restoration to be done on our relationship, but it was worth the work. *She* was worth the work.

Kissing her like she deserved to be kissed, like she was my whole reason for living—and she was—I rocked my hips and pumped faster for just a few moments before releasing my iron grip on my control.

Euphoria flooded my body, my toes curling and—

Bang!

"Fuck."

We both said it, and I braced my elbows on the pillow either side of Tris's head.

"Bram can handle it," she mumbled, her eyes sleepy and glazed. My girl was riding an orgasm high and not even the sound of gunshots outside was bringing her back to earth. I loved her so much.

Smiling, I kissed her again, then again, then when my dick twitched inside her I forced myself to withdraw. The pout she gave me was almost enough to ignore the nearly deafening pop of bullets just outside the room, but her safety came first.

"This is the end, Venus," I whispered with the weight of guilt and regret sitting heavy in my chest. "After this, we're free."

She huffed, sitting up in the messy bed. "So, what you're saying is that I need to put clothes on?"

"Regretfully, yes," I found her discarded clothing on the floor and handed it over before pulling on my own pants. "Do you want me to grab a washcloth?" As much as I loved knowing she would be dripping my cum, it seemed rude not to offer a cleanup.

She grinned, shaking her head. "Nah, I'm fine like this."

Heat rushed to my dick and I moaned, biting my knuckles as I pictured that. Damn it, we didn't have time to go another round. "Later," I promised "I'm going to fuck you so hard for so long you won't be able to walk."

"I'm counting on it," she retorted, pulling her top on and hiding those glorious breasts from view.

The gunfire seemed to be dying down somewhat outside, and I tilted my head to listen. One or two pops here and there, but otherwise... was it over? Without Tris even having to see Hank?

"Come on." She headed for the door, sweeping her inky hair up into a messy bun. "Let's get this shit finished so we can breathe easy again."

Panic flared as she reached for the handle, and I darted forward, batting her hand away. "Venus, baby, let's just... be cautious. People with guns out there, remember? I can't have you getting caught in the crossfire."

She pulled her hand to her chest with a grimace. "You make good points, Professor. I'll let you, uh, do your thing."

Grinning, I grabbed her waist and smacked a kiss on her lips. "Fuck, I love you. Let's go."

Drawing a deep breath, I opened the door just a couple of inches and peeked out. The hallway outside our room was empty and quiet, and a moment of listening said the *guests* were all downstairs. But the question was whether Bram *actually* had the situation handled or if Hank had brought backup of his own and won the upper hand.

"Stay behind me," I whispered to Tris, cautiously stepping out of the bedroom and treading softly. The house was *old,* and the floorboards could creak at any moment, but luck was on our side as we made it halfway down the stairs before I paused to listen more.

At the sound of Bram's voice—sounding relaxed and smug—some of the tension evaporated out of my shoulders.

"Bram?" I called out hesitantly.

"Yep," he replied, raising his voice, "under control."

I didn't immediately move, but Tris gave me a nudge in my side, and I clenched my jaw as I descended the last of the stairs and peered around the corner. The scene I found waiting in the open plan kitchen-dining area was... well, as Bram said. All under control.

Tris was clearly frustrated at being held back and gave me another shove, pushing me out of the way so she could enter the room, then gave a sharp gasp when she took it all in.

"Nice of you two to join us," Bram teased from his position sitting casually on the edge of the kitchen island. He was decked out in black combat gear and armed to the teeth, for the first time actually looking like the mercenary he was.

Around the room there were maybe a half dozen more anonymous mercenaries, head to toe in black and sporting more weapons than a small army. On the floor, several bodies lay lifeless and bleeding, but one intruder had been kept alive.

Just one.

Hank knelt on the pretty boho floor rug, his hands zip-tied behind him, a gag tied around his mouth, and the nose of a Glock 19 resting against the back of his head courtesy of the mercenary standing behind him.

"Holy fuck," Tris exclaimed in a strangled voice. She was deathly pale, her gaze locked on Hank, but no tears stained her cheeks. She was done crying for this traitor. "Hank."

"Bram, you're the best, we always had faith in you..." Bram muttered in a falsetto, glowering in our direction, then shifted back to his normal voice. "Aw, thanks, you guys. You don't have to gush your admiration; it's getting embarrassing."

That seemed to jerk Tris out of her trance, and she shifted her gaze over to our mercenary friend with a confused look painted over her pretty face. "I didn't see it before, but you and Tink are a match made in a psychiatrist's office."

Bram's response to that was a wide grin. Crazy fuck. He had splatters of blood on his face which I didn't think for a moment belonged to him, and his eyes held a sheen of dopamine that all Guild mercs seemed to get after some hands-on killing. It took a special type to do their job...

Tris took another step into the room, and I couldn't stop myself putting a hand on her waist. Not holding her back, just letting her know I was there for her no matter what.

"Can we take his gag off?" she asked the mercenary with a gun against Hank's head. "Please? I need some answers."

The merc didn't speak, but did reach forward and tug the black rag out of Hank's mouth.

"Thank you," Tris said in a small voice, her delicate brow furrowing as she stepped closer again. I moved with her, staying by her side in case she needed... anything.

Hank said nothing. The glare he directed at my girl held enough venom to drop a horse, so I preferred he *didn't* speak any time soon. Nothing coming from his lips could heal the wounds he'd cut across her heart.

"Hank," she whispered, her voice thick with sorrow and confusion. "Why?"

That was it. That was the one question that had torn her up inside. *Why?*

I wanted to hold him down and beat the answers out of him. Cut him over and over with the sharpest of paper until he cracked and gave Tris the closure she so badly needed.

"It has nothing to do with you," Hank growled, his voice rough. The lines of his face were deeper than ever and his gray hair more disheveled than I suspected he'd ever been seen with. For a man who routinely wore a three-piece suit, this was a drastic difference.

"Bullshit!" Tris exploded, stomping her foot sharply. "Bull. Shit. This has *everything* to do with me, Hank, because you practically fucking raised me! We were a fucking *family* and you—" Her voice caught with a sob deep in her chest. "How could you? How could you hurt *Nelson* like that?"

"We weren't a *family*, Ivy, we were a partnership. A mutually beneficial business arrangement. I'm sorry if you saw it differently, but you're mistaken." The ice in his voice chilled *me*, so I couldn't blame Tris for the way she flinched and leaned against my hand.

I wanted nothing more than to rip Hank's head from his shoulders, for twisting the knife so brutally. It took every shred of willpower to stand there silently, letting Tris handle herself in this confrontation.

Bram tipped his chin up, his eyes asking the question I was wrestling with myself... should we shoot him and be done with it?

It was so damn tempting, but Tris drew a deep breath and took a step forward. Her mind was made up, and she was standing on her own two feet to take her closure no matter how much it hurt.

All I needed to do was be there for her when it was all over.

Tris

thirty

"Y ou're a liar," I accused the old man on his knees before me. "You can tell yourself you didn't care until you're blue in the face, but I know the truth. You loved me once. And we both know you loved Nelson. No amount of denial can change that fact, nor can it change the fact that *you murdered him*."

Hank, for all his stoic anger, seemed to shrink into himself with that truth. His hard eyes saddened, and he aged before my eyes.

"I didn't murder him," he replied in a gruff voice. "He didn't need to die. None of this needed to happen, and it could have been avoided if the two of you weren't running a parallel con behind my back. You want to blame someone? Blame yourself, Ivy."

My mouth fell open, but no sound came out. What

could I even say to that? I'd done enough blaming myself already, and it had gotten me nowhere. I was no more responsible for Nelson's death than John was.

"Don't believe me?" Hank sneered. "Ask your boyfriend. He saw it all. He saw how I gave Nelson the choice. I was very reasonable when I discovered you two had been stealing from me, and that you had hidden *Poppy Flowers* in the hidden gallery. I *asked* him to simply open the door and we would have been fine. We all would have been fine. No one needed to die. Certainly not him."

John didn't move from my side, but in my peripheral I saw him cock his head in my direction. He'd told me once already that I wasn't ready for all the details, and he'd been right. Maybe now it wasn't about me being ready, though. I just needed to know, despite how much it hurt.

"You mean when you held a gun to his head?" John asked in a low, angry voice. "When you told him to open the gallery or you'd shoot him and frame Tris for the murder?"

I tried so hard not to show a reaction but couldn't stop the gasp I sucked through my nose. He was right not to tell me.

Hank glowered. "It was still a choice. He could have just *opened the damn thing*. Instead, the foolish fucking martyr deliberately tripped the booby trap wire."

Holy shit. Nelson had... *chosen* to die like that? He should have just given Hank the fucking paintings. He was more than capable of opening my gallery without tripping any wires and for the love of fuck, they were *just paintings*. As beautiful and treasured as they were, Nelson's life was more valuable.

"He didn't commit suicide, Hank, let's get that straight," John interjected. "He hoped the blast would end *you*. He never imagined you would use him as a literal human shield to protect yourself."

Oh *god*. Bile rose in my throat, and I needed to close my eyes for a moment to compose myself. The mental images assaulted me, despite having not seen it with my own eyes, and I swallowed hard. The new information lay on my skin like a coating of slime, and I suspected it would take some time before I could feel clean again.

"Why?" I asked again, hating how broken my voice came out. "Why now? Why *this* Game?"

Hank stared at me a moment, and I became acutely aware of how many people were in the room. All the faceless mercenaries who just stood at the ready, protecting us. Me. Led by Bram and ready to take action should Hank try anything sneaky. I was safe... but I'd never felt more vulnerable.

I wondered if maybe Hank had decided not to answer. I met his eyes, pleading with my own gaze. "Just tell me the truth," I whispered. "Please, help me understand why you ruined it all. Was any of it real?"

He wet his lips, his gaze dipping to the floor. "Yes. Of course it was, Ivy. But the Game was always meant to be played like this. Bloody, brutal, ruthless. Christophe imposed too many rules to keep players *safe* when natural selection should have thinned the herd."

Surprise rocked through me, and I glanced up at John. Shock had his eyes wide, so I had to assume he didn't know Hank and his grandfather knew one another.

"How'd you know him?" I asked when John remained silent. "Christophe, I mean."

Hank's lips curled in a cruel smile. "That's irrelevant now. He's dead, and I've been playing this stupid Game to regain the treasure that he stole from me fifty years ago."

My mind whirled, and I reached for John's hand, linking our fingers together. This was the closure I needed from Hank about Nelson's death and the duplicity of his entire fake life... but it was about John, too. About his grandfather's legacy that he was fighting so hard to keep. We were in it together, and as guilty as it made me feel, I was glad.

John gave my hand a little squeeze of support, and it filled my chest with warmth. I couldn't imagine a better partner in crime—because there was no way crimes weren't being committed here.

"What did he steal?" John asked when my mind remained blank. "What did my grandfather take from you that caused you to play *such* a long Game to get it back? And how did this all culminate with Tris and Nelson?"

Hank startled, bewilderment rippling across his face, quickly followed by realization, and he gave a low chuckle. "John Smith. I knew it was a fake name all along. Ivan, I presume?" He eyed John with a shrewd expression. "I see the resemblance now. I should have seen it sooner, but that's on me for being too distracted with the Game."

He tipped his head to the side as if checking whether there was a gun still to his head. Shocker, there was. The mercenary made no sound, just tapped Hank's skull with the barrel as if telling him to speak up and answer John's questions.

Apparently we weren't the only ones interested in hearing Hank's confessions.

"Sure, fuck it, may as well take my moment to correct history while I can, I guess. Better than leaving that double-crossing bastard Christophe as some kind of legend."

Hearing Hank swear was like a cheese grater against my brain. It wasn't *him*, but that only served as more evidence that I never really knew who he was after all these years.

"Christophe and I were friends once. Partners. We shared a passion for treasure hunting and spent a lot of our time searching for one treasure in particular. The S.S. Minden. A ship full of priceless works of art and jewels, sunk somewhere between the Faroe Islands and Iceland in 1939. We found it, *together*, then..." He shrugged, shaking his head. "Poof. It was all gone."

John let out a low, bitter laugh. "*Faroeice*. Faroe Islands, Iceland. Your Game alias."

"Don't feel bad, Ivan. Only Christophe would have made the connection, and he's dead." Hank said in a tone so cold and matter-of-fact. It was such a harsh contrast to the warm, caring man I knew.

The mercenary with a gun to Hank's head laughed. Actually laughed. It was the first sound I'd heard from any of them—aside from Bram—and it startled me a little.

"Unless," a man's voice came from the masked face, "he isn't. Unless, he used this Game to smoke you out once and for all, knowing you wouldn't be able to resist the lure of the Valenshek Legacy... *Hans Künsberg*."

The masked mercenary used his free hand to peel the black mask off and revealed a handsome older man... who I'd never met in my life. What the—

"Christophe?" John exclaimed in a horrified whisper.

The man turned a warm smile in John's direction, his eyes creasing with sincerity. "My apologies, Ivan. Needs be as needs must."

"No!" Hank barked, spinning on his knees to get a better look at the man who'd been right behind him this whole time. "No, this isn't possible. You're *dead*! You *died*! I paid good money—"

"To the wrong organization, Hans," Christophe sneered. "You spent so very long hiding from me, you missed out on a lot of vital information. Like how Nadia earned a trusted position within the very same Guild you paid to have me assassinated."

Hank's whole face went gray, and I leaned into John's side. He had to be in shock. He'd *grieved* his grandfather's death, taking his loss so hard, and it was all a ruse? Unforgivable.

"I have a lot to make up for, Ivan, and I apologize. But this vendetta between Hans and me is about a lot more than stolen treasure." Christophe turned his attention back to Hank. "Which is why I won't feel even the slightest bit of guilt for what I'm about to do, old friend."

It all seemed to happen in slow motion. Christophe reached out a hand to one of the other mercenaries, who smoothly tossed him a sword. I screamed, already predicting what he was about to do, but it was useless. The sword swung, and Hank's head toppled from his body, rolling across the rug until it stopped on my feet.

My entire body convulsed, and I turned away, desperate to create some distance as all my coffee came back up and I vomited into an indoor plant pot. It was as I heaved, my mind looping what had just happened over and over, that I recognized the sword.

SS-Ehrendegen. As if we needed any further confirmation that Christophe was behind the Game this whole damn time, he'd used the SS-Ehrendegen to behead his arch nemesis.

I was never getting over this. Not even with the best therapy money could buy.

"Well, fuck," Bram commented from his lazy perch on the island counter. "I didn't see that coming, did you?" He gave me and John a loopy smile, then winced. "Ah, I guess not. No. That makes sense. I'll just... shut up. Yeah?"

My head swirled. Was I about to faint? God, I hoped not.

"Again, I do apologize," Christophe said politely, picking up Hank's decapitated head by his gray hair. "This is not the first impression I would have liked to make on my grandson's girlfriend. Tristian, if it's any consolation, I've been admiring your talents from afar for quite some time. Forcing you two together was one of the best things I've achieved in all my years orchestrating the Game, I must say."

John flinched, like he was being slapped out of the trance he'd fallen into with his grandfather's resurrection. "You... *what?*"

"Story for another day, Ivan," Christophe said, brushing off what was—in my opinion—a pretty fucking valid question. "Do we have the plate?" That question was directed to the mercenary who'd provided the sword. From a backpack, an ornate silver serving platter was produced and Christophe carefully placed Hank's head in the center of it, blood and all.

"There. Perfect. I do hate to kill and run, but there is a very special lady that I promised this to a very long time ago." Christophe flashed a dazzling smile to John and me, then indicated for the same mercenary assistant to carry the plate for him. "I'm so very proud of the man you've grown into during this Game, Ivan. I'll be in touch soon."

"Don't," John barked, his voice thick with emotion. "Don't fucking bother."

Christophe frowned but then nodded. "Very well. Take care of Tristian. You wouldn't believe the lengths a man can go to if he loses his one true love."

With that, he was gone and took all the anonymous mercenaries with him.

"Well, I think I speak for all of us when I say this whole Game did *not* turn out like I expected," Bram announced into the resulting silence. "They could have at least taken the rest of him."

That was when I made the mistake of glancing down. Hank's headless body was still bleeding out all over the floor, and my bare feet were coated red. My stomach lurched, and this time, I really did pass out.

John

thirty-one

It took nearly a full two weeks after Hank's death —and Christophe's resurrection—before Nelson's body was released for burial. Tris had finally been cleared of any wrongdoing in his suspicious death, and the police had officially issued a warrant for Hank's arrest, thanks to some damning video footage that had been anonymously submitted.

Of course, they'd never find him. After Tris fainted that night, Bram extorted me for an eye-watering amount of money to make the headless body disappear. And he did. While I carried Tris back to the bedroom and washed her bloody feet, Bram went to work loading the body into his car and scrubbing the floor so clean you could perform surgery on it. The rug, sadly, couldn't be saved. Hestia customer service informed me the cost would be deducted from my security bond, as would the repairs to the brick cladding where multiple bullets had become lodged.

By the time Tris woke, the house was spotless and Bram was long gone. His contract was fully discharged.

Fourteen days after that night at Cloudcroft House, Nelson was finally laid to rest in the Whispering Willows cemetery. The turnout was impressive, with what seemed to be half the population in attendance to bid their tearful farewells to an extraordinary old man.

Aware *now of what* I knew of his decades of art heists and replica swaps, it didn't surprise me in the least to spot dozens of familiar faces from the criminal underground. Tris didn't pay any attention, though. Her grief had manifested twofold the morning after Hank's death. Suddenly she was no longer simply mourning Nelson, but also the man *she'd* known as Hank... because no matter who he turned out to be underneath it all, to her he was family.

She was so strong, though. My girl was made of steel and refused to let crippling grief stop her from giving Nelson the funeral he deserved. She stood behind the casket, reading Nelson's eulogy with tears streaming down her face, but she never faltered.

I'd never believed how much a person could love another, until I met her. She was my everything, and my heart overflowed with pride as I stood back and listened to her sharing her raw emotions with the mourners.

As she finished, the dark clouds above opened up and the sky echoed Tris's tears. Everyone gathered around the grave site and opened umbrellas, blanketing the congregation in a sea of black domes, but I just stood to the side to wait as Tris accepted condolences from an elderly couple from her building.

In the distance, standing beneath an enormous willow, a woman caught my eye.

Glancing back to Tris, I found her locked in an intense conversation with Luther Grimaldi, whose presence at Nelson's funeral surprised me. Then again, I suspected he just wanted to check in on Tris; for all his violent actions, he genuinely seemed to care about Venus. He was also a man of his word. So I headed across the grass to where the woman stood.

"John, dear," she greeted me with a warm smile, despite our never having been formally introduced. "It was a lovely service. Tristian is a beautiful speaker, creating such emotive art with her words."

I pushed my hands into the pockets of my heavy black coat, ignoring the way rain dripped into my eyes. "Why are you here, Nadia?"

My grandfather's long lost love just looked over to the gathering of mourners and sighed. "I felt it was a visit long overdue. So very many mistakes were made, and I regret that your generation has paid the price for sins you had no hand in."

I huffed a bitter laugh, shaking my head. "That's an understatement. Why are *you* here, and not him?"

Her brows rose in her weathered face. "Christophe will respect your wishes and stay away until you're ready to hear him out."

"But you won't?"

She shrugged. "I owed you a thank you and should have offered it a long time ago." When I frowned, she chuckled. "For my egg. You returned a priceless Fabergé egg to me some years ago, and it changed the course of my remaining years in the most dramatic way."

Now I remembered. It'd been an offhand mention from Christophe one night after too many whiskies. Or so I thought. I'd decided to track down a gift he'd given his love when they were young and dumb and return it to her. It was the sort of thing I often did, to keep my skills sharp and sort of give back to the universe... After everything though, I was second guessing how staged that "offhand comment" had really been. He'd manipulated me, and I hadn't even noticed.

"John," the old woman said, reaching out to place a hand on my forearm. "Thank you. I can never express how much I needed that gesture at that point of my life."

I was *seething* mad at my grandfather, but I couldn't muster the same vitriol against Nadia. She seemed so... warm. Caring. Like I imagined a grandmother would be.

"Can you tell me what happened with Christophe and Hank—uh, Hans?" I glanced over to check on Tris, but she was still speaking with Luther under the canopy of an umbrella held by a henchman.

I expected Nadia to tell me no. That it wasn't her story to tell. But instead she nodded and gave my arm a squeeze. "Of course I can, John. It's a conflict that you and Tristian have been so rudely dragged into, the least we can offer is our truth. Our origin story, the three of us." Her smile was sad, and an uncomfortable feeling twisted in my chest. "Shall we talk at the wake? This rain is a bit miserable, and I think your young lady should hear this tale, too."

Nodding, I took a step away, then a sliver of sunlight caused a dazzling sparkle on Nadia's hand. It was an antique engagement ring that I recognized almost as well as the palm of my own hand. It had sat on Christophe's nightstand for as long as I could remember. I always thought it was Magdelena's—my grandmother's—but now I knew better. It had always been Nadia's, just waiting for the day he could put it on her finger.

Turning my back on her, I made my way back to Tris

and politely extracted her from Luther Grimaldi's clutches as he told her to *consider his offer* with a very pointed look.

Tris was smiling when we walked away, though, so I didn't think he was threatening her... this time.

"All okay?" I asked, taking her hand in mine then cupping my other hand below hers. Holding her close and safe, like I always would. "That evidence of you shooting his guy *was* erased, right?" It was one of the first things I'd dealt with while Tris grieved. It'd taken some tech assistance, but it should be gone from existence now.

"Yes, totally gone. He's very puzzled about how his server got fried, but it's gone and he no longer has anything over me. That was just a very generous offer to come back and work for him full-time." She grinned wide, and curiosity got the better of me.

"How generous?"

She pulled a folded piece of paper from her pocket and handed it to me. On it, a number had been scrawled in elegant handwriting, and while it was a lot for a college student, it wasn't a fraction of what she was worth.

"Per month," she added, and my eyes widened.

"Oh I see. That *is* generous, then. Are you considering it?"

She shook her head. "No. But it's nice to have my talent recognized, you know?"

I did know, but I'd known how talented she was from the moment I laid eyes on her *Literary Woman*. Grimaldi was late to the party, and I was more than prepared to double his offer just to keep her to myself. And then some. Could she be swayed by the freedom to paint naked all day every day? What if I threw in hourly orgasms to foster creativity? Lifetime subscription to a toy store?

Smiling at my own dirty thoughts, I took her umbrella and held it over us both.

"He did ask me if I'd heard from Sin. Apparently he's dropped off the radar."

"Huh." Didn't really surprise me. I had made good on one promise.

"Do you know where he is?"

I had promised no more lies. "I might have some ideas." Of course, the blonde was already long gone, but I did tell him where the photograph came from.

"Planning to share?" She looked at me.

"Later," I promised. I didn't want to think about the Grimaldis at the moment. Or any moment, really. "There's someone who wants to meet you at the wake, if you're feeling up for it," I told her, remembering our impending chat with Nadia. "She might be able to lay some of those lingering questions about Hank to rest."

Tris nodded then leaned against me as we walked back to our car. "I'd like that. I know it's technically your family's story, but Hank..."

"He was *your* family. Even if the whole thing was fake for him, it was real for you. No one can take that away, Venus." I pressed a kiss to her hair and opened the passenger side door for her, keeping the umbrella above until she was seated then closing the door firmly.

It was a quick drive over to the wine bar where Nelson's wake was being held, and I spotted Nadia as soon as we made it through the front door. She'd arrived just before us, still taking off her coat and looking around the room, so I guided Tris directly to her. Better we get that story than spend hours making small talk with townsfolk I had no interest interacting with. Or worse still, dealing with professional colleagues who I preferred know nothing about me.. or Tris, for that matter.

"Let's sit outside," Tris suggested, gesturing to the covered verandah. "It'll be quieter with the rain keeping everyone indoors."

Once Nadia and Tris were seated comfortably, I ducked back inside to get them drinks then returned to find them laughing in a slightly delirious way. Like a laugh or cry sort of vibe.

"What'd I miss?" I asked, unable to fight my curiosity.

"Oh, nothing important, dear," Nadia replied as I took a seat across from her. "Tristian noticed my engagement ring and asked how Christophe proposed."

I was still confused and glanced at Tris, who was smiling genuinely but also a little gray with nausea. Oh. Now I got it. "Hank's head on a silver platter, huh? That's... unique."

Nadia gave a little shrug. "When Christophe reentered my life after so long, he tried to propose immediately. We aren't young, and we lost so many years to heartbreak... but time doesn't heal all wounds. We could never live our happily ever after—so to speak —until Hans was dealt with. So Christophe started searching for him, and when Hans found out he was being hunted, he decided to strike first."

"He tried to pay a hitman to kill Christophe?" Tris asked in a quiet, pensive voice.

Nadia's lips tipped in a smile. "Mercenary, *malyshka*, not hitman. But yes, he did. What he didn't realize was that I spent a lot of years in Guild service and fostered some invaluable relationships within the Circle. That's the management."

"So they helped Christophe fake his own death and then... he started this Game to smoke Hans out of hiding? Because he knew he'd come for his legacy if he thought Christophe was gone for good?" I tried to make sense of it all in my head, but there were so many missing pieces of the puzzle.

"In simple terms, yes. Hans went to extreme lengths to hide himself over the years, and it wasn't until the night of Nelson's death that we were sure of his new identity. And by then, he was in the wind and we had to draw him out by continuing the Game." Nadia sighed, reaching out to pat Tris's hand. "I am truly sorry you were put in danger, *malyshka*, but we were improvising on the fly."

"And Carol wanted to teach me a lesson," I muttered, still pissed as hell.

Nadia dipped her head. "Yes. That too."

"That explains the Game," Tris said thoughtfully, "sort of, I guess. But what caused it all? What happened all those years ago that was worth holding a grudge for *so very long*? Fifty years? That's a lifetime."

Nadia reached for her glass of cognac and took a sip before replying. "Fifty-eight years, actually. And it was a grudge worth holding, since Hans was the reason I never knew my son." She paused, seeming to lose herself in the painful memories for a moment. "When we were all young, and dumb... we were inseparable. With Christophe... it was love at first sight. Wild, passionate, undeniable love that our families very much disapproved of. Hans was his best friend, and became mine too. The two of them were so very talented, fast becoming quite notorious for their heists and treasure hunts."

That lined up with the story I'd always heard from my grandfather, without Hans. But now that I thought about it, he had occasionally made mention of a friend who hunted for the SS Minden with him.

"I won't bore you two with the gritty details," Nadia said with deep sadness, "but I fell pregnant. It was a terrible scandal, since we weren't married and my father would *never* allow us to. So we ran away and I gave birth in secret. The baby was stillborn, and I broke. The grief was too much to bear, Christophe and I started fighting, and I returned to my family. I ran away from the hurt, thinking I could somehow pretend it hadn't happened. Before my body even healed, my father had arranged a marriage to another man, and I was relocated to America."

Tris leaned forward, very obviously hooked on Nadia's story. I was... confused. It was the same story Christophe had told me, but with a lot more information. Facts that dramatically darkened the wistful star-crossed lovers tale he used to spin.

"So, how did that all relate to Hans?" Tris asked, carefully using Hank's real name. Maybe it was helping her separate the two in her mind.

Nadia sipped her drink again, her eyes distant. Lost in the past. "A few years after I married and moved to America, Christophe and Hans found their white whale. The S.S. Minden. Under heavy intoxication during their celebration, Hans confessed to Christophe what he'd done. How he'd *saved* his friend from an unexceptional life by dealing with the *Nadia problem*. Jealousy and greed had convinced him that if Christophe and I ran away together with our child, Hans would be left behind. Cut out of future wins. So he took a hefty payoff from my father to ensure I would return home, by whatever means necessary. He stole my baby and swapped him with the stillborn baby in the next room."

Holy shit.

"Hans made me think my baby was dead, when in fact he was alive and well being raised by a couple in the very same town as my family lived. Christophe was, of course, horrified and cut all ties with Hans that night. He wrote to me, many times, telling me that our child was alive, but I never got his letters. My husband was... not a nice man. He intercepted all the mail and destroyed it, and eventually Christophe assumed I had moved on with my life. I had a daughter with my husband, and a whole new life in America. Eventually, he gave up."

Tris gave a ragged gasp and I noted the wetness beneath her eyes. My girl had such a huge heart, sharing in Nadia's decades-old pain. "What happened to your child?" she asked softly.

"My son was nearly five when Hans made his confession. It took several months for Christophe to track down the couple who'd been raising him, but he did. Magdalena was the woman's name, and her husband Borys died in a tragic car accident not long after Christophe found them, leaving Magdalena a single mother, struggling to provide." Nadia cleared her throat, shifting in her seat like the next part of her story was uncomfortable.

I already knew where this was heading, though. Magdalena was my grandmother's name.

"Christophe married her, didn't he?" I asked, already knowing in my bones the truth of what'd happened. There was no tragic car accident. Christophe had Borys killed then married Magdalena to reclaim his biological child. Igor. Now so many things about Igor and Christophe's relationship made sense.

Nadia nodded with a sigh. "It was not the course of

action I'd have taken, but at the time I had no clue any of this was going on. For that, I am so sorry, John. I wish I could have known you as a child. As my grandson."

"Oh shit," Tris breathed, her gaze snapping to mine with concern.

I gave her a small smile back, reassuring her that I was *fine* with this information. It really didn't change anything except knowing my grandmother was alive.

"Does Igor know any of this?" I asked, feeling, for the first time in my life, genuinely bad for my deadbeat dad. As a child, his "father" had been killed, then been replaced by a man who probably *never* loved his mother. Yeah, suddenly I could see why Igor was so bitter toward Christophe, and so scathing any time the old man mentioned Nadia. She was the ghost who haunted his mother's marriage.

Nadia grimaced, smoothing her hands over her knees. "He does. He'd known for longer than I even knew, thanks to Magdalena figuring it all out before her death. Unfortunately, he just refuses to see the truth and believes it all to be a hoax. I hope maybe one day he will accept it... before it's too late."

I rubbed at the bridge of my nose, trying to wrap my brain around her downright heartbreaking story. "So... all this came full circle because I returned a missing Fabergé egg to you?"

Her smile was pure sunshine. That egg must have meant a great deal to her. "Yes. It brought Christophe and me back together, and all the truths came out. In a moment of blind hatred and fury, I demanded Hans's head on a silver platter... which I might point out *was* simply a metaphor for reparations until he tried to have Christophe killed. After that... well. You know how it all turned out."

"Yes, we do," I agreed, running my hand over my face. "Thank you for sharing your story with us, Nadia. We do appreciate it."

"Our story, John. Like it or not, this is your history too. When you're ready, Christophe would very much love to make amends." Her gaze was heavy and intense, filled with sadness and regret. It killed me.

Tris cleared her throat, breaking the tension. "I think you will agree that it's maybe too soon, hmm? John spent a lot of time grieving a man who was never dead. That can't be erased with a quick apology."

Nadia nodded. "Yes, you're right. Just try not to take too much time, dears. We don't have a lot of years left." She pursed her lips, like she was debating saying something more but then shook her head. "I should get going. It's a long drive home to Shadow Grove from here. If you're ever in town, please stop by for a cake and coffee. I'd very much love the chance to know you both."

Neither Tris nor I replied, but she didn't seem to expect anything.

We sat there on the verandah, watching the old woman step out of the bar and into the rain. The mythical Nadia. The woman who'd held my grandfather's heart for so many decades. My grandmother.

That was going to take some getting used to.

Tris
epilogue

My toes curled in the expensive high heels I wore, and I dug my fingernails so hard into the back of John's neck I was surely drawing blood. Fuck it, some things were worth shedding a little blood for, and I knew he agreed.

"Yes," I gasped, my stomach muscles contracting with the first wave of orgasm, "Yes, John, *fuck* oh my god don't stop. Yes. *Yesss...*" I moaned loud, not caring if anyone was around to hear as I locked my thighs around his face, practically suffocating him with my cunt.

He gave me what I wanted, pumping his thick fingers inside me as his lush lips made love to my clit better than any vibrator on earth. He'd made it his mission to make me come faster with his mouth than with the Bang Bang Bunny, and he'd had no complaints from me as he practiced.

Time and place was something we were still working on, though. A waitress from the fancy party we were currently attending walked around the corner and caught us, right as I gasped and panted through the height of my climax, but neither one of us paid her any mind. She quickly covered her eyes and disappeared anyway.

"Holy shit," I exclaimed, gasping for air as the orgasm started to ebb. John was on his knees in the dirt, and my back was against the side of the house, my legs draped over his shoulders. The only thing holding me up was his balance and the hand impaling me. Gravity made it all so much rougher, and I was loving it.

"Wanna come again?" he asked in a rough voice, licking me like I was made of candy as he met my gaze. I loved having him on his knees.

I bit my lip, glancing back in the direction of the party. We technically weren't here to play; we were on a job. Then again...

"Yes, fuck, yes. Quick, though." I dropped my legs off his shoulders and turned to face the wall, arching my back.

John didn't waste any time, lifting my voluminous

gown and loosing his pants before stuffing his thick cock inside me with a groan.

"Holy mother of thieves," I gasped, my vision going spotty with that first thrust. "Fuck, that feels good."

"Shhh, Venus baby, I'm already so close," John confessed, gripping my carefully curled hair and messing it right the hell up as he tugged my head back. His hips rocked, his long, thick cock rubbing over my g-spot in the most delicious way as his mouth claimed mine. It required me to flex in an uncomfortable backbend to kiss him fully, but it was so worth it to taste myself all over his mouth, knowing how I'd just had him worshiping my pussy.

He kissed me like he fucked me, rough and fiercely possessive, and in no time at all he had me spiraling into another climax. He joined me as I came, shooting his load deep as he groaned and held me close. My whole body trembled in his arms, and he feathered kisses down my throat as I basked in the sweet afterglow for a moment, my pussy walls holding him tight within.

"Mmmm, keep clenching like that and we can go again, right here right now," he teased, biting my throat with gentle teeth.

I grinned, high as fuck on endorphins. "Don't threaten me with a good time, Professor."

His chuckle was dark and suggestive, but to my

disappointment he withdrew a moment later to tuck his dick back in his pants. Neither one of us had worn underwear, because we fucked in public too often to bother. Underwear just slowed us down and got in the way.

Of course that did mean that when we rejoined the party a few minutes later, I had slick wetness coating my cunt and dripping down my inner thighs. John knew it, too, and he fucking loved it.

"Champagne, Miss?" a waitress offered, handing me a glass with a smirk. Oh, she was definitely the one who'd just caught John and me in the garden.

I accepted the drink, running a hand over my tousled hair in an attempt to smooth it down. I'd worn smudge-proof lipstick, but I was paranoid nonetheless that it was all over my face, so I took my Champagne with me as I headed for the powder room.

John waited outside for me, not comfortable leaving me alone with the particular guests in attendance, and he claimed my hand when I rejoined him.

"You're so fucking gorgeous, Venus," he whispered as he kissed my hair. "Let's finish this job so I can rip that beautiful dress off you and have a real feast."

I shivered with desire. We couldn't get enough of each other these days. It'd been six months since Nelson's funeral, and shocker, the Game Council had pretended my paintings had never entered their possession. So John and Tink—despite her lingering head trauma—had made it their sole focus to restore each and every painting to me.

They'd done an incredible job, too. Tonight would be the last painting, and then we were done. The Game would be done.

Across the main party room, Tink was in full sparkling delight, creating one hell of a distraction as she staged a very dramatic lovers' quarrel with her poor, unsuspecting date of the night—some trust fund baby named Bartholomew the seventh or some shit.

John gave me a sly wink. "That's our cue."

Buzzing with excitement, we slipped away from the guests and took the stairs up to the third floor where our informant had placed the last painting. I kept watch while John picked the lock on the office door, then he gestured for me to enter with him.

"There she is," I murmured aloud, laying my eyes on the cursed Van Gogh painting that had started our whole saga. "*Poppy Flowers*. Maybe we don't want this one back?"

John scoffed. "You're joking, right? We're taking it, and we're hanging it above our bed." He went to work delicately checking the frame and mounting for any kind of alarm system, then extracted the priceless art piece.

I kicked off my heels then climbed onto the desk, using my fingertips to push up the ceiling panel and retrieve the art case Tink had stashed there days ago.

"Here," I murmured, handing it over to John. He popped it open, taking out my forgery and making the switch with gloved hands. He locked the case again, handing it back to me and I put it back in the ceiling once more. Tink was the only one of us small enough to get through the ductwork to retrieve it, which she'd do while we returned to the party.

The whole thing didn't take more than fifteen minutes, and then we stood back to admire the forgery displayed on the wall of one of the Game Council's offices.

"Do you think he'll notice?" I asked, tipping my head to the side to inspect my own work.

John chuckled. "Not a chance. You're the best for a reason, baby girl." He peeled his gloves off, then cupped my face to kiss me. "Let's get back to the party and give Tink her signal."

I hummed my agreement, linking my hand into his as we left the office and locked it up behind ourselves. The party was still going when we returned to the ground floor, and Tink caught my eye as soon as we slipped into the crowd. She was sobbing into a linen handkerchief, really selling her scorned woman act, but when I winked she dried up the tears quickly.

"You two look like you're up to something," a woman said, jerking my attention from Tink and making me gasp. "You aren't planning to steal anything tonight, are you?"

John's hand caressed my lower back and I leaned against him. "Wouldn't *dream* of it, Carol," he replied with just a little sprinkle of sarcasm. "We just came for the canapes and entertainment."

She narrowed her eyes at us both, casting a glance at our clothing. "You have some mud on your trousers, John."

He glanced down, then brushed his hand over the dirt marks. "Oh yes, I was smelling the roses outside. Lovely flowers."

I nearly laughed out loud and bit my cheek to keep it in. Carol wasn't even slightly fooled, but I suspected she thought we were out there peering through windows for things to steal, not fucking.

"Hmmm," she replied, still suspicious as hell.

A waitress approached, a tray of Champagne flutes in hand, which she offered to us. Carol and John reached for one at the same time, their hands colliding and the glasses falling off the tray in a crash.

"Oh gosh, I am so sorry," John gushed, grabbing the

waitress's cloth from her apron pocket and quickly dabbing at Carol's sleeve where the alcohol had spilled on her. "So clumsy of me. Is this dry clean only?"

Carol whisked her arm out of John's grip, her expression frosted with a double helping of suspicion, bordering on paranoia. "Nice try, *Hermes*," she murmured, shaking her head. Very deliberately, she checked that all her jewelry was still in place. Fair concern, really. She was wearing *a lot* of diamonds, and she touched each one to check nothing had been taken.

I frowned as she checked her rings and took a step forward to get a better look.

"All accounted for?" John asked impishly, handing the cloth back to the waitress, who was on her knees to pick up broken glass.

Carol finished checking her valuables and pursed her lips. "I'm watching you, John Smith. Don't play with me."

"Yes ma'am," he replied, like a fucking *angel*. "Heard, loud and clear. No playing Games with Carol."

She squinted at him a moment longer before giving an exasperated sigh and walking away.

"We should go," John said to me quietly, giving the small of my back a little push toward the exit. "Now."

I didn't question him, hurrying—but not running— to the closest exit from the ritzy party. Once outside, we picked up the pace, and by the time we reached our waiting getaway car we were in a sprint. It was harder than anticipated in high heels, and I nearly fell headfirst into the back of the generic black limo that idled in the driveway.

"Go!" John barked, and the vehicle started moving before the door was even closed.

I grinned, turning to glance out the rear window like I expected to see someone chasing us, but there was no one there. No one knew that we'd just stolen Van Gogh's *Poppy Flowers*... again.

"That was fun," I enthused, shuffling closer to John in the backseat. "I just got the weirdest sense of déjà-vu when we were talking to Carol, though."

"Oh?" he asked, lifting me up and seating me across his lap in a straddle position. My dress skirt got all bunched up, and I knew the evidence of our garden tryst would be all over his suit pants. Too bad. "What about?"

"Her ring," I specified, tapping my right hand. "The three-carat cushion cut in a four-prong claw setting. It looked *so* familiar. Is it weird that I think Nelson might have been working on a replica of that exact ring before he died?"

John's hands pushed my dress up further, his hands gripping my bare hips as his hardness butted against me through his pants. "Hmmm, not that weird. Nelson did a lot of jewelry, didn't he?"

I nodded, a wave of sadness washing over me like it always did when I thought of him. "Yeah, I guess. Maybe it was just similar."

"What did it look like again?" John's hands massaged my rump as I described the ring for him again. Then he gave me a thoughtful look and patted my butt cheek. "It sounds very familiar."

He withdrew one hand from under my dress and reached into the inside pocket of his tuxedo jacket. "Did it look like this?" He presented the three-carat sparkler between his thumb and forefinger and I inhaled sharply.

"You—" I gaped in shock, looking from his gleefully amused expression to the ring and back again. "How? She checked her rings and they were all there!"

His smile softened. "This *is* what Nelson was replicating. The night he died, I took it from his work station for some reason. Then tonight... I made the switch. Carol didn't even notice."

My jaw dropped. "I'm... insanely impressed and incredibly turned on right now, Professor. But... why? Stealing directly off Carol's hand is a hell of a risk."

"Why?" he repeated. "Because I couldn't think of a more perfect ring to give you, Venus, when I ask you to marry me."

My whole world stopped. Just fucking *stopped*.

"So... will you make me the happiest man on this earth? Will you marry me, Tristian Ives?"

I blinked, stunned speechless. Then I crashed my lips against his in a hot and heavy kiss to convey the depth of emotion that I lacked the words to express. "Yes," I whispered against his lips, pure euphoria filling me up inside to the point of astral projection. "Yes, John. I will."

He kissed me back fiercely, slipping the ring onto my finger without even looking. It was heavy, but in a good way.

"I love you, Venus," he told me in a gruff voice.

My heart swelled to bursting. I'd refused to say it back all this time, despite the countless times he'd said it to me. I was making him work for it, but there was no denying it any more.

"I love you, John Smith," I replied, meaning it with every fiber of my being. "More than anything on earth."

His hands slipped back under my dress and I groaned, ready to seal the deal with some good old fashioned car fucking.

"Hey, whoa, guys!" Tink exclaimed from the front passenger seat. "That was cute as *fuck*, don't get me wrong, I got cavities just listening to how sweet you are. But I do *not* need the free porn show. Save it till you're alone, yeah?"

I barked a delirious laugh because I had *totally* forgotten we weren't alone.

"Dude, you stole that off my mom's hand?" Bram asked, glancing in the rearview mirror while he drove us out of town at breakneck speed. "She's gonna kill you if she works it out."

John kissed my throat, not caring about our audience in the least. "Nah, she owes me this one."

Bram scoffed. "I didn't mean the ring, I meant for having the audacity to steal *off her hand*. It's been nice knowing you, John Smith."

My future husband just grinned wickedly. "Worth it."

He was so right. It was all worth it, in the end.

Nelson would have been the first to laugh.

THE END.

also by tate james

Foxfire Burning

#1 The Nine

#2 The Tail Game (TBC)

#3 TBC (TBC)

Undercover Sinners

#1 Altered By Fire

#2 Altered by Lead

#3 Altered by Pain (TBC)

Milton Keynes UK
Ingram Content Group UK Ltd.
UKHW041954300124
436961UK00001B/9